For Mom and Pop

Acknowledgments: Many thanks to my extraordinary editor, Francesca Crispino,
my other pair of eyes, Margery Cuyler, and all the staff at Winslow Press, and to my agent, Gail Hochman.
Special thanks to Sue Alexander, Walter Dean Myers and the SCBWI, early believers, and the Writer's Bloc
in Los Angeles. Also, to my friends and family, especially James Quinn for the freedom to do it,
Tera Liddell, and all the folks in New Jersey, particularly the Black family.

Bauer, Cat.

Harley, like a person / by Cat Bauer.

First Edition

p.   cm.

Summary: Fourteen-year-old Harley, an artistic teenager living with her alcoholic father and angry mother,
suspects that she is adopted and begins a search for her biological parents.

ISBN 1-890817-48-1 (hc.) --ISBN 1-890817-49-x (sc.)

[1. Family problems—Fiction. 2. Alcoholism—Fiction. 3. Adoption—Fiction.
4. Parent and child—Fiction.] I. Title.

PZ7.B32585 Har 2000

[Fic] — dc21

99-046814

Creative Director: Bretton Clark
Cover Photography: Dana Frank
Editor: Francesca Crispino

Printed in Belgium

harley

like a person

cat bauer

WINSLOW PRESS

DELRAY BEACH, FLORIDA   NEW YORK

chapter 1

I'm under the bed. They don't know it. They think I've run away again. And I have. Only this time I'm under the bed.

I can see their shoes as they walk around my room. There are my mother's small fat feet squished into a pair of blue K-Mart specials. My father's cowboy boots stampede across the linoleum floor. In the corner, my tiny sister, Lily, flutters her pink ballet slippers against the metal bed frame. She whispers "row, row, row your boat" over and over.

My mother's sneakers zigzag as she paces. "Where does she *go*? That kid will give me a heart attack!" My father doesn't answer. My father doesn't talk when he's mad. He roars.

My mother shakes my little sister. I crane my neck, straining to see. She grabs Lily's face. She squeezes her cheeks. She is angry at my father, but Lily gets it. Whoever is in the room gets their anger; this is why I'm under the bed. I want to yank my mother's hands away, make her stop. "Where is she?" Her words are hot and Lily gets burned. "Where is Harley?"

My sister knows what's coming. So do I. She starts to tremble. "I...I don't *know*." She speaks the truth. She doesn't know. I feel bad that Lily is being tortured because of me. But although she is only five years old, she is a strong prisoner and does not break.

"Let me handle this, Peppy." My father speaks softly. Not a good sign. Lily is caught in the crossfire; the battle is between the two of them. My father rumbles over to Lily. He removes his belt. It has a big silver buckle in the shape of Texas, even though we live in

1

New Jersey. He never hits people with the belt, only furniture; it is a leather threat. He is a lion tamer and Lily is a kitten. "I'll whip you, girl, if you keep lying like that. I'll give you something to lie about."

Lily wilts. She starts crying. "I'm not lying! I don't know! I don't know where Harley is!" I want to pop out from under the bed and rescue her. Like Superman. Unhand that child!

A pair of black NIKES bounce into the room. My brother, Bean. I hear the tap, tap, tap of Riley's paws right behind him. Riley is a good hunting dog; I hope he doesn't sniff me out.

An apple crunches. "Whatcha doin?" Bean eats apples.

"Get out and mind your own business, Bean." My father pulls in the reins when he talks to my brother.

"You gonna beat the crap outta her? Can I watch?"

"Bean—"

"Come on, Dad. Let's have some action. You go on and on about beating the little runt, but you never do." Bean loves Lily too.

I think about calling out to Bean. A daring rescue. We transform ourselves into shining knights and capture the drunken dragon and his fire-breathing wife. We lock them in the dungeon in the basement and rule the house with peace and kindness. But although Bean is tall, he is not strong.

"Bean. Get out. Now." My father puts on his Commander voice.

It works. Bean's black NIKES hesitate, then shuffle out the door. "I'm goin' over to Earl's."

I hear the drawer of my night table open. I turn my head quickly, silently to the left. My mother stands right next to me. Those sneaky rubber soles have steered her over to my secret drawer. My safe place. My treasures. I try to breathe without making a sound. I could grab her leg and really give her a heart attack, I think. A monster from under the bed. I start to giggle. I force my mind to think of something else.

My mother is rooting through my drawer. She makes noises like a curious raccoon. My heart pounds. I know what she will find. "Roger, look at this!" My father's boots turn away from Lily. I can see the tip of the belt dangling at his side. I peek up at my little sister. She is crying softly. I want to pull her under the bed with me and keep her safe.

"That kid is grounded for six months!" My mother's voice is nails on a blackboard.

"Calm down, Peppy. What's the matter?" Clomp. Clomp. Clomp. The cowboy boots join the K-Mart specials.

"Look at these!" I know what she has in her hand. I keep my birth control pills hidden in my night table drawer under a pile of my drawings and my poems. My pills, unopened and waiting. I always thought they were safe there. My pills and my poems.

"Listen to this." Papers rustle. My mother reads out loud. "'My House' by Harley Columba. My house is a place of pain/ A sea of shame/ A hurtful chain/ My house is awash in gloom/ A desperate room/ A dying bloom…" I hear a ripping sound. Pieces of white notebook paper sigh on their way to the floor. My poem. I blink away my tears.

"Where did she get them? Where does a fourteen-year-old girl get birth control pills?" My father seems bewildered.

"Well, you're no help—"

"Dammit, don't start! Don't start in on me!" The lion tamer curls the belt in his hand.

My mother won't stop. My mother never stops, she has no brakes. She is a man-eating beast that refuses to jump through the fiery hoop. "What are you going to do? Oh, ho, ho. Just try it." I hear a scuffling sound and a shout. My easel in the corner crashes to the floor. I watch my oil painting of Strawberry Fields skid along the linoleum and stop inches away from my fingers. I want to cry.

I close my eyes and soar up to the quiet, peaceful place. Up, up, up I go. Their voices grow dim and hazy. The three-ring circus begins, but I can barely hear it. It's safe up here, all flowers and rainbows. I stand in the middle of my painting of Strawberry Fields. In my mind, I paint a crystal blue lake in the center of the meadow. Far away, I hear the crack of the belt as it cuts through the air and strikes the bedpost. I dip my paintbrush into a jar of yellow and sprinkle the meadow with sunshine. The man-eating beast growls; the lion tamer laughs. The lake. Into the lake. I try to dive into the smooth blue water, but it is canvas, not water, and I am falling....

I open one eye. Lily has curled into a ball in the corner. My arm is asleep. I change positions. There is so much racket, no one hears me. I stretch. A dust ball floats under my nose. I have to sneeze. I try to hold it back. I squish my nostrils shut. The sneeze erupts from me. My eardrums have been blown right out of my head. I lie absolutely still. My body pulses against the floor. Thud. Thud. Thud. Like *The Telltale Heart.*

"What was that?" my father asks. "Did you hear something?"

"Harley, is that you?" My mother coughs.

I hold my breath. I am a mannequin. I am not human. I do not move.

"Harley Marie?" My father crosses the room and opens my closet door. He peers inside. I have hidden there before. He shoves my clothes to the side. My favorite red dress tumbles off its hanger into a heap on the floor. I want to snatch it and drag it under the bed with me. Lily, my painting, and my red dress.

I brace myself. They will kill me, I think. They will find me and kill me and that will be the end.

Instead the telephone rings. My father's boots hesitate, then turn and walk out the bedroom door. My mother's K-Mart specials shuffle right behind. "Lily, clean up this mess." She slams the door. I take a deep breath. Saved by the bell.

I count. …eight…nine…ten… I come out from under the bed. Lily does not seem surprised to see me. I walk to the corner and set my easel on its wobbly legs. I wipe a smudge off my painting and place it back on the easel. There is no crystal blue pond in the center of Strawberry Fields, only grass. One edge of the canvas is loose.

I gather the tatters of my poem from the floor. I dig through my night table drawer and pull out some Scotch tape. I sit on the edge of my bed. I tape the jagged edges back together. All the king's horses and all the king's men… I find all the torn pieces except one. There's a hole in the center of my poem.

I hear a tiny sob. I turn and hold my arms out to Lily. She feels damp and trembly. I rock her until she grows quiet. I take her hand. Gently I pull her under the bed, together with my painting and my favorite red dress.

✸✸✸

I am Rapunzel, locked in my tower. Too bad my hair's not long enough to reach the ground. I pass the time gazing out my bedroom window and dreaming of escape. I do this a lot. Every house on my block is exactly the same, only a different color. Willoby Court. Tract homes, built in the fifties. Everyone calls it the new development, even though it's fifty years old.

I am adopted. They tell me I am not, but I know that I am. My parent's eyes are brown. My eyes are blue. It is impossible to get blue eyes out of a brown-eyed couple. Lily's and Bean's eyes are also brown. Plus, I saw my mother's belly full with them, so they are her children, no doubt about it. It is not unusual for people to have a baby after they have gone out and adopted one. When I found the harlequin, I was convinced.

Last week, I was in the storage area inside my bedroom. I am not allowed in there, don't ask me why. In Lenape Lakes, New Jersey, what we call a storage area is sort of like an attic, only it's not above the ceiling, it runs behind the wall. The door is as high as my chest, painted the same color as the bedroom, Peppy pink. You can't stand up inside, you have to squat; it's very long but not too deep. It's where we stash the junk of the House of Columba — old baby clothes, rugs, broken lamps — and me. It is my hideaway, where I go to get some peace.

Bean was in his bedroom playing Nintendo. He's addicted, I swear. Lily was downstairs watching MTV. She's wild for rap and hip hop. Peppy was running the vacuum cleaner. Every Sunday night my mother gets this ancient monster of a Hoover out of the closet and starts sucking up dirt. The Hoover is truly frightening — it has a headlight for eyes and steel jaws for a mouth. She drives it like a maniac, smashing into furniture and banging against the walls.

I left the storage area door open a crack because it latches on the outside. I yanked on the cord of the bare bulb inside, and the long narrow area flooded with light. I'd cleared a small spot in the front where I could sit, and decorated the exposed beams with John Lennon posters. Wild. John Lennon is my hero. I was born on the anniversary of his death at the same moment he died, in the same hospital. No one else I know is into him except my best friend Carla, and that's just because I am. I swear, that girl wishes she were me.

I fluffed up an old pillow spotted with drool stains and snuggled onto a rolled-up carpet with my sketch pad and charcoals. I was listening to my absolute favorite CD, *Imagine*, on my portable. Roger gave us all his old Beatle music when he went Country & Western a few years ago. "Imagine" is a prayer, not a song. It's about a perfect world where everyone lives together in peace. In New York City, there is a big garden called Strawberry Fields in Central Park, built in memory of John Lennon, full of meadows and trees. It's across the street from where he was murdered. At the entrance to the garden is a beautiful mosaic, a circle with the word "Imagine" in the center. I've never been there, but I have a postcard.

Downstairs, I heard the vacuum roar into battle and thought, good, I should be safe.

It was cozy in there among the castoffs. I was sketching a long-haired girl diving into a teardrop when something colorful behind the far edge of the carpet caught my eye. I'd never noticed it before. I wanted to know what it was. I took off my headphones and set down my drawing.

I wriggled over sheets and curtains, jars of mothballs and forgotten clothes. I knocked a stack of old *National Geographics* over. Uh oh. I hoped no one heard that. I stopped and listened hard. Vrrumph! Bump. Vrrumph! Bump. The Hoover drowned out all noise on the face of the earth.

I climbed over a pile of tablecloths, then past a rusted electric train. I remember thinking: maybe if I crawl in deep enough, I will find a secret door, a door that opens to another world, a world of sunflowers and kaleidoscopes, anywhere out of this house.

I squeezed past a wooden stepladder and then I saw it. There, wrapped inside a plastic bag with a big faded bow on top, was what looked like a doll. It was dark back there, so I grabbed the top of the bag and dragged it toward the light. I was careful. The plastic was old and brittle. I sat down on the rolled-up carpet and took off the bow.

I heard my bedroom door open and realized the vacuum had stopped. I was fast. I yanked the cord and switched off the light. Peppy shuffled into my room. She hollered, "Harley! Harley Marie, are you in here?" I froze into a statue, cold and Roman. I watched her through the crack in the door. "Harley?" I held my breath as her rubber soles headed straight for the storage area. In an instant she would fling open the door. Tag, Harley. You're *It*.

Instead she slammed the door. Great. I was locked inside. Now I'd have to wait for Lily to show up.

I heard her go down the hall into Bean's room. Her voice was muffled. "Do you know where your sister is?" I couldn't hear what Bean said. Damn, that was a close one.

I sat for a moment in the darkness. I got a chill, like a ghost had sat down next to me. I shivered and tugged the cord to the bulb, and the shadows were softened by the light.

My hands were shaking as I opened the plastic and took the doll out of the bag. Oooo. I smiled. It was a clown. Not a circus clown, more like the joker on a deck of cards. He had a soft body, but a porcelain face and hands. He wore a mask and a costume of diamond-shaped patches, like a colorful quilt. Underneath the mask, his eyes were two glowing embers. They were made of glass;

they almost seemed real. It was crazy, but I thought I knew this clown. It was like looking into the eyes of an old friend. In one hand he held a wooden baton. Dangling from the collar around his neck was an old-fashioned greeting card attached to a faded ribbon. I squinted and tried to read the handwriting. On the outside of the card was a balloon with the words, "Happy Birthday Two Year Old!"

I flipped open the card. It was so old, the edges were yellow. The handwriting was a scribble. The words slanted in every direction. I strained to read: "A...har...harlequin for...my Harleykins. Papa loves you for...forever and a day."

The words were a jolt. I almost dropped the clown. I read the card again and again. A tear fell from my eye and splashed a tiny pond onto the crooked handwriting. "Papa loves you forever and a day."

It was not the handwriting of my father, Roger Columba.

chapter 2

It is dinnertime and Bean is late. The steaks are getting cold. I wait for my parents to bring up the birth control pills, but they say nothing. We sit in denial at the family room table, pretending everything is normal. Lily kicks the table leg and hums. I yawn. I am exhausted.

"Get your elbows off the table, Harley."

"Can't we eat, Dad?" I am whining. "I'm about to die from starvation."

"We will eat when your brother gets home." Roger sits there, calm on the outside, but his brown eyes are boiling. He wears his uniform to the table. He owns a gas station in the next town over, and smells like oil changes and tune-ups. "We will wait until he arrives."

"But, Dad—"

"We'll wait, I said. You're lucky you're getting supper." The Commander has spoken. No one dares pick up their fork. We sit in silence except for the tap, tap, tap of Lily's feet and her hushed, "merrily, merrily, merrily, merrily…"

"Lily, knock it off!" Roger's voice is a sledge hammer. Lily stops singing and starts crying. "Oh, for crissake."

"We're doing genealogy in history and I'm going to need my birth certificate," I lie, all perky, as if I'm changing the subject. My mother and father glance at each other. Peppy sighs. I have asked this before.

"I told you, Harley, we lost it in the move," says my mother, eyeing her steak like a hungry brown-eyed lion.

"But you only moved up the street."

"Don't argue," says Roger.

"I'm not arguing! I need it. Lily has hers. Bean has his. I'm the only one without a birth certificate." There is no way these two psychos could possibly be my parents.

"You were born in New York City on the anniversary of John Lennon's death," Peppy says. I've heard this story many times before, but I never get sick of hearing it. I am hoping for a slip-up, for the day they finally reveal that my real parents were two avant-garde film students who didn't want to interrupt their careers.

"What were you doing in New York City?" These people never go anywhere. They're lucky if they make it out the front door.

Roger glares at me. "We were at a tribute for John Lennon. You know all this, Harley Marie."

People think that I am named after the motorcycle, but I am actually named after my mother's family, Harley. I hate my middle name, Marie, but Roger revels in it because it was his mother's name. Columba is not Italian, it is Irish, but because of Christopher Columbus, people get confused.

I stare down at my steak. It is withered and looks like a piece of leather. Gross. I am not letting Peppy off the hook this time. "You went into labor at the concert and they rushed you to the hospital but you got trapped by a bunch of old Lennon freaks crying in the street." It's a tug of war to get information out of these people, I swear.

"Yes, Harley." My mother glances at her watch. "Roger, let's eat."

"No, Peppy. Dinner is a family affair and the entire family is not here." My mother's name is Patricia, but everyone calls her Peppy. I don't know why—she seems so slow.

"Maybe our souls crossed. Don't you think? Me, born on the

anniversary of his death? At the same time he died, in the same hospital? While you were at a memorial for him?"

"I'm hungry, Daddy," says Lily. "Can we say grace?"

"Harley, please." My mother slices into her steak. "I'm starting, Roger."

"Did you really try to run over a hippie with your car?"

"Of course not. It was an accident. We only broke his toe." Peppy's steak knife scrapes the bottom of her plate. She bites. Chews. Roger scowls, but does not pick up his fork. All I can hear is the chomp, chomp, chomp of the steak as it's pulverized by Peppy's teeth.

"He could have sued you."

"Harley, enough." Roger takes a big swig of his drink. His fingernails are rimmed with grease.

I don't know why we keep up this dinner farce. No one else I know has to sit with their parents every night like they're eating the Last Supper. I have this twisted knot that feels like a rock in my belly. My mother swallows. Gulp. Like anyone can eat under these circumstances.

Dinner at the Reardons is what I want. The Reardons are what my real parents must be like. Betty Reardon used to be my best friend before Carla. There is singing and piano playing, huge bowls of pasta and carrots and watermelon; none of the food matches. People run in and out. Someone wrote "BOO RADLEY IS OUT!" on a blackboard in their dining room. Wild. Mrs. Reardon asked me my opinion on *To Kill a Mockingbird* because she knew Betty and I had to read it for English. I spoke for fifteen minutes, and the whole family listened to me, asking questions, agreeing and disagreeing. I felt brilliant.

Peppy reads romance novels with her brown eyes and Roger

reads *Popular Mechanics* with his brown eyes. Bean and Lily do not read at all.

Now I pretend I sit at my real parents' dinner table and we are having a stimulating conversation. I dab my napkin at my lips. I turn to Peppy and ask, "Mother, have you read *The Catcher in the Rye*? What do you think Salinger was saying about phonies?"

Peppy is not interested. "If you'd get your nose out of those books, Harley, and put down that paintbrush, maybe you'd have time to help out around here." The rock in my belly grows into a boulder.

The front door slams and Bean rushes in. He plops down at the table. Bean folds his limbs like a daddy longlegs, collapsing them into a pile of twigs under the table.

"Sorry."

"Where were you?" Roger whacks him on the shoulder.

"Ouch! Nowhere."

"Damn right, you're nowhere. You're grounded."

"Aw, Dad. I was just hanging with Earl. I said I was sorry."

My father picks up his knife and slices into his steak. He bites. Chews.

"This steak is tough."

My mother shrugs. "It's sirloin, Roger."

My father glares around the table. "Well, eat!"

✳✳✳

My mother washes the dishes and I dry. This is my chore. I get nothing for it, not even a quarter. I am the only person I know who does not get an allowance. If I want money, I have to beg for it or steal it from my church envelope on Sundays if I can't get a baby-sitting job.

"Let them drip, Harley," Peppy says.

"I *am*!" I buff my favorite spoon. We do the dishes in silence, like a jail sentence. That's okay, I love to dry the silverware. The teaspoons are the girls; the tablespoons are the big sisters. The forks are the mothers and the knives are the fathers. There is one real sterling silver teaspoon mixed in with the others and she is the princess. Her boyfriend is the sharpest steak knife.

Peppy drains the water out of the sink. "Did you do your homework?"

"Of course." I put on my snob voice, as if the question insults me.

"Watch that mouth of yours."

I ignore Peppy. I rub and rub the silver princess until she is sparkling. At night, the silver princess sneaks out of the silverware drawer and spends the evening in the potholder drawer with the sharpest steak knife. The steak knife's father is long, sharp and steely and only brought out for major jobs. The steak knife has no mother.

"Harley, what are you doing to that spoon?"

I jump. "Nothing!" Peppy's got a voice like an alarm clock. I watch her scrub the sink with cleanser. She is a big fan of Comet and uses it to clean everything, so the whole house is covered with a grimy lime residue. I wait until she heads into the family room, then I sneak the silver princess into the potholder drawer, together with the steak knife.

The phone rings. I toss the dish towel over my shoulder and answer it. "Hello?"

"Harley?"

"Granny!"

"There's a wonderful sky here tonight. So many stars!"

Granny Harley is my salvation. She bought me my easel and most of my paints. She looks like that plastic maple syrup bottle, Mrs. Butterworth, all plump and friendly—not like Grandpa, who wears suits and ties, even at home, and talks to everyone as if they are his employees. My grandparents used to live in Lenape; I have summer memories of Granny holding my hand. Then Grandpa became vice president of the company, and they moved down South. Sometimes I can understand why Peppy is the way she is, having him for a father. He plays tricks on children.

Once, when I was as old as Lily, Grandpa told me he was a magician and put a penny in a paper bag. He waved his hand over the bag, and *presto,* inside was a nickel. Then a dime, then a quarter, all the way up to a silver dollar. He told me I could keep the silver dollar or see what happened next. Well, I wanted to *know.* I put the silver dollar back in the bag, he waved his hand, and out came a penny. He gave it to me and said, here, this is what you get.

"We're coming up in a week or so, honey," says Granny. "Your grandfather wants to visit his sister."

"Great!" My brain works fast. This is the one person who holds the key to the Columba skeleton closet. "Granny…" I stretch the telephone cord to the family room, tiptoe over and peek in. Peppy and Roger are watching the news. I lower my voice. "Granny… I have to ask you something."

"What, honey?" I hear her smile. "Do you need some paint? They're having a big special in that shop I told you—"

"No, no, Granny." I watch a spider tumble off the wall and into the Comet-covered sink. It tries to crawl up the gritty porcelain, then slips back down. Gently, I pick it up by one of its tiny legs and set it on top of the counter. I watch it scamper away. I take a breath.

I want to ask, *why*? Why are they so angry? "Granny, I found this doll up in the storage area, this old clown—"

"Harley, who are you talking to?"

I spin around. "Geez!" Peppy-the-Silent-Snoop has crept up behind me. "God, Mom, you scared me!" I swear, we need to put a cat bell on Peppy, she is so sneaky. "I'm talking to Granny Harley."

Peppy sighs, like the last thing she wants to do is chat with her mother. Granny keeps Peppy on her toes. She puts her hand out for the telephone. "Well, let me talk to her."

"At least let me say good-bye." Peppy is so rude, I swear. She is a bulldozer plowing through my life. "Mom wants to talk to you, Granny."

On the other end, Granny gets the picture. "Is she standing right there?"

"Yes."

"We'll talk...." Granny pauses. "We'll talk when I come up, okay, honey?"

What can I say? I swear, I have absolutely no privacy in this house. Peppy has her arms crossed and this look on her face like I am some jerk in a phone booth who won't give up the line. "Okay, Granny."

"I love you, honey." Granny hugs me through the phone.

"I love you, too." I toss the phone to Peppy and run out of the kitchen. "There's such a thing as privacy, you know."

✱✱✱

I am standing at my easel, repairing the damage to Strawberry Fields. I am listening to *Imagine*, of course. I keep my postcard of the Imagine mosaic clipped to the top of the canvas for inspiration;

harley
like a person

17

it reminds me I am going there someday. I dab fluffy white clouds over the meadow. Maybe if I paint myself onto a park bench…

Lenape Lakes is only forty-five minutes outside of New York City, if there's no traffic, although it may as well be four zillion light years away since no one from here ever goes there. I swear, they should build a white picket fence around this whole town. Lenape Lakes is famous because George Washington slept everywhere, and there were Revolutionary War battles in the hills behind our house. All the towns around here are named after Indian tribes. Lenape is a breeding ground for warriors.

Lily is on my bed, playing Barbie. She has pulled off Barbie's head and stuck pins into the earlobes for earrings. She makes an announcement, one she invented herself, in her squeaky voice: "And now, ladies and gentlemen, ALL the girls and NO boys, starring…Barbie!" No one but Lily knows what this means.

From the basement, my father's voice booms over the intercom: "HARLEY, BRING ME DOWN A DRINK!" Roger has set up intercoms all over the house, like the voice of God. This way he can spy on Lily and me and Bean. He can listen to us, but we can't listen to him, we can only answer when he calls.

"Get it yourself," I mutter. I ignore him. I shade the white clouds with a hint of gray. I resist the temptation to make it rain.

Lily sticks a pin into Barbie's eyeball and squeaks, "Harley, bring me down a drink!" Lily's got a voice like Mickey Mouse.

Roger is in his shop down in the basement. This is what he calls it. I call it a submarine. He spends most of his time down there, locked away from the rest of us, fixing broken appliances. He'll make himself a big glass of vodka and say to my mother, "Peppy, I'm going down to the shop."

I used to sit beside him as he worked. I had my own stool. I would command the submarine while he fussed and bandaged the broken gadgets. One day I went down there and Bean was sitting on my stool and I never went down again.

The intercom crackles: "HARLEY MARIE, DID YOU HEAR ME?" I crank up the volume on the stereo. I plunge my brush into the jar of gray paint and slab on a thundercloud. I grab another brush and dip it into the white. Now lightning bolts shoot across the canvas.

Lily says, "Daddy wants you, Harley." She unties Barbie's pony tail and reveals a bald spot.

"I hear him."

Once more, Roger's voice blasts over the intercom, this time with a nasty edge: "HARLEY MARIE, NOW!"

I slam down my paintbrush and stomp down the stairs into the family room. This is where we are all supposed to be a family and watch television together. This is where we eat supper so we don't mess up the dining room. This is where we hang out so we don't trash the living room, which Peppy has draped in slipcovers. This is where Roger Columba keeps his booze.

I splash some vodka into a glass and deliberately leave out the ice cubes because I know he wants them. I carry the drink down into the command station. Roger looks up from the toaster oven he's working on. "What took you so long?"

"I have homework, you know." I am all superior, like I am shooting to go to Harvard. "I have a lot of studying to do."

"Where's my ice?"

"I forgot it. Sorry."

Roger looks like he wants to slug me, but instead he pours the new drink into the old glass where there are still a few slivers of ice floating in water. He hands me back the glass. "Thanks."

"Don't mention it." Next to him, my old stool is cluttered with pieces of a broken radio. For a moment, I wish I could brush the broken pieces to the floor and sit once again beside my father in the submarine.

Roger glances up from the toaster oven and stares at me. "Do you want something?" He is cranky with vodka. His dark brown eyes are rimmed with red. Those bloodshot eyes nudge me toward the door.

Now I remember why I don't come down here anymore. This man is not my real father. This man is an impostor. I open the submarine hatch. "No." My voice matches the ice in the glass. "I don't want a thing."

I close the door just a little too hard behind me.

chapter 3

"Harley Marie, get over here."

"What, Ma?"

"What do you have on?"

"Clothes."

"Don't be smart. Put on a decent outfit."

"This *is* a decent outfit." Usually I refuse to wear name brands, but I got this sweater at the Salvation Army shop for almost nothing. I swear, no one in Lenape has a clue.

"You look like a delinquent."

"If I get changed now, I'll be late for school."

I am wearing black. My mother hates it when I wear black; she is a gray kind of person. But this battle is an old one, and she gives up without a struggle. "Oh, all right."

"See ya." I peck her on the cheek.

"Eat some breakfast."

"I'm not hungry." I walk out the door and head up the block past the rows of houses that are all the same. I cut through the back of the Anderson's yard and over to the corner to wait for Carla to show up.

Mrs. Woods, the crossing guard, walks me across the street with her stop-sign-on-a-stick. I'm too old for it, but she is kind, so I allow her to cross me. "How was your weekend, Harley?" she asks. "Same old thing," I tell her. "Jetted to Monte Carlo, stopped off in London to catch a show." Mrs. Woods titters. "Always joking, you."

Carla is a speck in the distance. She gets closer and I see she is wearing black, too. She irritates me with that. Whatever I do, she does. Everyone says we look like sisters. We even have the same blue eyes. If she paints her fingernails gold, it will push me over the edge. I painted mine last night and it looks wild. We meet and walk together awhile in silence.

"Did you do your history?" she asks me.

"Last night. Do you need to copy?"

"Naw. I don't care."

I have not told Carla about finding the harlequin. I am very superstitious and don't want to jinx it. If you leak certain things out into the universe, you never know what might happen. I keep tight control over my secrets.

But I have spilled one secret to Carla, which is my crush on Johnny Bruno. He is older than me, but we share one class and that is band. Johnny is the only reason I go, hoping for a glance from those dark brown eyes. Band is full of rejects from the football team except for Johnny. He plays the drums and I play the clarinet. Band is at the end of the day, and I have to suffer through six classes to get there.

Carla and I walk over the footbridge. Lenape Lakes has lots of lakes but these days they are all polluted from the chemical plant where Roger and Grandpa used to work.

"Johnny said hi to me yesterday," I tell Carla.

"Oh, yeah?"

"I think he likes me." If Peppy had bothered to check, she would have seen that my pack of birth control pills has never been opened. I've never had a real boyfriend. Not yet. Just a few sad attempts by some bottom feeders at parties. If I do not get a decent kiss soon, I'm going to die, but I refuse to settle for less.

Carla and I got the pills over at the clinic because her old boyfriend, Vic, wanted her to do it with him, and she was thinking about it. I thought I should get some too, just in case. We went there on a Saturday. The place was dark and gray, and the nurse was bored. She talked to us for about an hour and handed us a bunch of brochures with titles like, *Playing It Safe*, and *Sex: Are You Ready?* She examined me with a smooth, cold piece of metal that slid between my legs. I gazed at the dusty mobile of old war planes that floated above my head. She opened a cabinet and took out the pills. "I'll give you a three month supply, but you should also use a condom." Yeah, right.

"I thought Johnny was still going out with Prudence Clarke."

I pick up a pebble and throw it in the river. Carla knows exactly how to get to me. "I think they broke up," I say. "They must have." Prudence Clarke is the same age as Johnny. She can sing. She was the star of *Annie Get Your Gun*, and so was Johnny. I hate Prudence Clarke. I mean, what kind of name is *Prudence*? It sounds like dried fruit.

Carla and I walk up the hill to Lenape Avenue, the main road. "You wanna go uptown after school?" Carla asks me.

"I can't. I'm grounded."

"You're always grounded. They should just chain you to the wall."

"Don't give them any ideas."

"Look!" Carla points to a small white box on the asphalt up ahead. "Cigarettes!"

I run over and pick up the box. Marlboro Lights in a hard pack. I flip open the lid. Three are missing.

"What should we do?" I ask her. "Should we smoke them?"

Carla stares at the white pack like it is from outer space. I shake out a cigarette. I hand it to her. She takes it and holds it between her fingers like a baton. "I don't know."

The cigarettes are the apple and I am Eve. "Oh, hell, let's." We divide the pack in two. I keep the box. I put them in my backpack. Cigarettes. Wicked.

✳✳✳

We do not have assigned seats in history, but if you're a girl, do not sit in the first row because Mr. Werner looks up your skirt. All the cool people sit on the right side of the room; all the kiss-asses sit on the left. I sit on the right. I am smart without trying. I am always on the honor roll, which means instead of going to study hall, I can go wherever I want, as long as I stay on campus. This is a good benefit.

My father went to Lenape High, and he had Mr. Werner, too. So did my mother. My parents have known each other since they were twelve years old. My father carved his name on his desk: "ROGER COLUMBA." I sit in his desk today. Wild. I try to imagine my father as old as I am, but it is too strange. I have to get out of this town.

If I don't look at the clock, Johnny will say hi to me in the hall. I write, Johnny, Johnny, Johnny over and over in my notebook and then disguise it with flowers. If I wait at my locker just before the bell to the next class rings, sometimes Johnny passes by on his way to English. This is risky because if I am late, I will get detention. I have French next and Ms. Auberjois is a bitch. Johnny doesn't have to worry because he reads the morning announcements over the P.A. system and he can come and go as he pleases. God, I love that boy.

✳✳✳

Mr. Donovan is my Honors English teacher. I adore Honors English. You have to be invited to get in. You have to be smart.

Mr. Donovan is cute and most people like him. He's not that old for a teacher. He's got strawberry hair and always needs a shave. If he knew how to dress, he would be perfect. He wears a bow tie and loafers. Nancy Peterman has a crush on him, but he's married.

Today we are doing *Romeo and Juliet.* I imagine I am Juliet and Johnny is Romeo. We lust for each other. We die for each other. It is so tragic, it is romantic.

"Who believes Romeo was in love with Juliet?" My hand shoots up. "You do, Miss Columba?" Mr. Donovan always calls everyone "Miss" or "Mister." It's sort of elegant, in an old-fashioned way. "How long have they known each other? A few hours? How can that be love?"

"It's love at first sight," I say. "They just *know.*"

"Ah, a romantic. They love each other so much that they kill themselves."

"Because they can't live without each other."

"I don't know, Miss Columba. Real love, mature love takes years to develop, not a couple of days."

"It's Shakespeare, it's not real time!" I am such a loudmouth in this class, I swear. I take a breath. "The few hours they spend together cannot be taken literally. A play is allowed a certain amount of poetic license."

"My, my! Very convincing, Miss Columba." Mr. Donovan sounds impressed. I am impressed myself.

✳✳✳

I always eat lunch with Carla. We never eat in the school

cafeteria because the food sucks. Some people bring sandwiches from home, which is what my mother wants me to do because it's cheaper. I would rather die. Only losers eat in the cafeteria.

We go to Angelo's Pizza or to the Deli where everybody hangs out. I use my baby-sitting money, and I order something like soup. Carla gets five dollars a day for lunch. Her mother is sympathetic. No one knows where her father is. Rumor has it he disappeared from Lenape right before she was born and now he's a wild artist living in New York City. I am fascinated that Carla has this renegade dad, but she refuses to talk about him.

Sometimes Johnny Bruno eats at the Deli with his friends, which is another reason I like to go. To get to the Deli you have to walk down the steps on the side of the high school and cut through the Pond Hole. I guess the Pond Hole used to be filled with water, but now it's the town parking lot.

There's a bunch of elite who hang out on the Pond Hole steps and smoke. It's intimidating to walk through them, so a lot of people go all the way around and down this sloping driveway that the cars use. It's dangerous, and nearly every week someone almost gets nailed by a housewife in a minivan, but for punks and rah-rahs it's still safer than walking through the front line.

I walk right down the middle of the steps. I am not really part of that group, but I am not *not* part of it. I am independent. Carla would give anything to be standing there, smoking, with that crowd. She embarrasses me the way she walks so slowly and looks around, hoping to be asked. Not too many freshman girls hang out on the steps, however. Only two that I know of: Debbie Nagle and Lisa Kowalksi. They are wild.

I meet Carla by the gym. Together we walk toward the

steps. There is a new guy there with long blond hair, smoking. He is adorable, in a tall, distracted kind of way. I don't usually like blonds, girls or guys, but this boy looks like a Nordic god.

Carla and I start down the steps. The blond guy smiles at me. His gray eyes look right into mine. "Hi." His voice is shy, but firm.

"Hi," I say back to him, and I get a tingle. This is a surprise. I am behaving like Romeo when he saw Juliet, falling in love all over the place.

Carla and I continue down the steps. A couple of people nod at us. We nod and smile, being very cool. We cross the Pond Hole.

"Did you see that *guy*!" Carla is all gushy. "He must be new. I wonder who he is."

I don't say anything. I am confused, thinking about the blond guy.

✱✱✱

Guess who is at the Deli. Prudence Clarke. Guess who is sitting next to her. Johnny Bruno. There are two other people in their booth, Gail and Reed. They are Johnny and Prudence's best friends. They are a pack. Prudence has blond hair, which is another reason I don't like blonds. She always wears black glasses; I still haven't figured out what fashion statement she's trying to make. Johnny and Prudence are laughing, and she is hanging all over him. Give me a break.

"What a skank." Carla sniffs and pulls me over to the counter. If I concentrate, I can watch them out of the corner of my eye so it's not too obvious. They certainly look all lovey-dovey. My stomach is a fist.

"What are you getting? I'm getting a burger." Carla pulls a

compact out of her purse and powders her nose, right there at the counter. It's not even shiny or anything, it's a nervous habit she has.

"I'm not hungry. I'll just have a cup of soup." There is no minimum at the counter. Old Man Ferguson gives me a dirty look anyway when he takes our order. Old Man Ferguson has a bald head and gnarly fingers. He hates kids, but he has to serve us because we are all his business. If we didn't come, he'd be putting up a "FOR LEASE" sign like most of the stores around here. I swear, Lenape Lakes is turning into a ghost town. I think I am the only one who realizes this.

I get up and go to the restroom. On the way over, I glance at Johnny. When I pass, he looks up at me and says, "Hi!" like he's really glad to see me. I feel my face turn red. I say hi back, but it comes out like a whisper. Prudence Clarke punches Johnny in the side and giggles. I almost run to the rest room.

There are two wooden stalls. I always go in the left one. Every girl in town has carved something into the doors so they look like Indian cave paintings. I see my initials, "H.C.," with a bolt of lightning underneath. If I die tomorrow, I will have something left behind as long as the Deli is standing. I think about adding an "& J.B.," but everyone would know it is me.

When I come out, Prudence Clarke is standing next to the booth, putting on her white snow-bunny jacket. She is blocking the aisle, and I have to stand there, waiting. I'm sure she sees me and is going slow on purpose. Finally she steps aside and I pass. I feel a foot in front of my ankle and then I am in slow motion, falling into the sawdust on the floor. She tripped me! Prudence Clarke tripped me! I land smack on my hands and knees. Everybody in the Deli starts clapping and whistling and saying stuff like, "Have a nice fall, see you in the spring." I am so humiliated, my face is a beet.

"Are you okay?" Prudence acts all innocent. She does not offer me a hand. I stand up and brush the sawdust off my clothes. "Fine." I do not dare look at Johnny. I limp over to Carla at the counter, who scoops me under her wing like a mother duck. "She tripped me on purpose," I inform Carla. "That bitch."

"Come here." Carla turns me around and plucks the sawdust off my sweater. I watch the back of Prudence Clarke's snow-bunny jacket as she waltzes out of the Deli on Johnny's arm. I make a silent vow: Prudence Clarke must die.

✳✳✳

I think I am getting a C in algebra because I hate it so much. I can't grasp it. I used to try, but now I don't care anymore. Mr. Petranski has an I'd Rather Be Fishing bumper sticker on his Honda in the teacher's parking lot, and I'd rather he were fishing, too. He is the hairiest person I've ever seen, an ape in man's clothes. I sketch a big monkey in a suit and tie in the corner of my notebook. He drones on and on about if a equals b, and c equals d, then what does q equal? I mean, what use do I have for this brain drain? At least I'm not failing like everybody else. Maybe I can do something for extra credit and get a B. I have never gotten a C in my life. Roger is going to kill me. He loves math and science. Einstein is his hero.

✳✳✳

Finally, study hall. I approach Miss Wrigley, the librarian. She's only at Lenape High on Mondays because we have to share her with two other schools since they keep cutting her budget. She looks sort of like Mary Poppins, complete with carpetbag and rosy cheeks. She's like a bloodhound when it comes to hunting for books. Nothing is impossible for her; she's always pulling exactly what you want out of her bag. Last week I asked her for the New York City telephone book.

Sure enough, before I even open my mouth, Miss Wrigley lugs this gigantic book over and drops it on the counter with a thud. "Is this what you were looking for, Harley?"

I've never seen such a huge telephone book: you could cram about five Lenapes into one New York City. I feel a little guilty that I made her drag it around half of New Jersey, but this is important. "Thanks, Miss Wrigley. You saved my life," I say, and Miss Wrigley's cheeks get even rosier.

I carry the phone book over to an empty table and start at the beginning. Community Service Numbers. Amazingly, there is a category called Birth Certificates. I write down the phone number. I have been saving my quarters for this very day since I do not want to make this call from home.

There is a pay phone right outside the library door in the hallway of the school. I am all jittery, but I force myself to dial the number. I plop in the quarters. My hands are shaking. I am so nervous that I drop a quarter on the floor. I pick it up and jam it into the slot. Clink.

It rings. A recording clicks on from the Department of Health, Vital Records. Good, I don't have to deal with a human. "If you are requesting a birth certificate…" I scribble down the information. I throw in more quarters and listen again, then hang up. I take a breath and sway against the pay phone.

chapter 4

I am in heaven, and that is art class. I only have it twice a week. Miss Posey is the teacher, but she looks like one of the students, all dimples and bangs. I heard she was having an affair with a senior boy.

Today we are working in charcoal, sketching portraits of famous people. I have chosen John Lennon, surprise, surprise. I love doing portraits. They are easy for me; faces pour from the charcoal right onto the paper. Miss Posey comes over to check my work.

"Wow, Harley. Great." Miss Posey seems to like what I am doing. Even though John Lennon is smiling, I add a crack to one of his lenses to symbolize his murder. It is difficult to concentrate with her gazing over my shoulder, but I carry on. "I love what you've done to his glasses, Harley. It gives me the chills." I grin. I adore Miss Posey.

"You know what, Harley? I'm gonna put on *Imagine* while you're working." Miss Posey has an old record player she lugged here from home because the school is too cheap to give the art department a cassette player, let alone a CD. She brought in a whole bunch of her own albums and plays them all the time.

"Anybody care if we hear a little John Lennon?" hollers Miss Posey.

"Who's he?" I swear, Bobby Brown is such a jock.

Miss Posey rolls her eyes. "Uh, duh. Who's he? Are you kidding, Bobby? Ever hear of The Beatles?" She places the needle on the turntable, all scratchy and hissy, and the music starts. It gets stuck on the word, "hell," and everybody laughs. "Hell…hell…

hell…" Miss Posey rips the needle off the album, blows off some dust and plops it down in the middle of the song. Now it jams on the word, "dreamer…"

✳✳✳

I am in band. I can feel Johnny sitting behind me. This is my dream that I dare not tell anyone for fear of jinxing it: Johnny Bruno asks me to the Spring Ball. I twist the pieces of my clarinet together. I get to sit in the first chair, and the entire band tunes up from me. If I cared, it would be something. Carla is in band, too. She plays the flute, but she is a third chair. The flute makes me dizzy.

Mr. Michaels thinks he is Leonard Bernstein or something the way he conducts with his face all scrunched up and his arms all berserk. I mean, *really,* it's only a high school marching band. I peek over my shoulder and steal a look at Johnny. He sees me watching him and winks. The "Stars and Stripes Forever" is a glorious song. I have these cool clarinety slurs and frills to play. *Fortissimo*!

✳✳✳

The phone rings and it is Carla. "Did you smoke a cigarette yet?"

"No. Did you?"

"Not yet."

"Harley, who is it?" Peppy hollers from the kitchen.

"It's for me, Ma."

"Who is it?"

"None of your business," I mutter. "It's CARLA!" I yell. "Can you believe this woman?" I say to Carla.

32

"What is her problem?" Carla giggles.

"Harley, come help set the table!" Peppy's voice could shatter glass, I swear.

"Oh, for God's sake. Carla, I've gotta go."

"Call me later," she says. "Send me a *smoke* signal."

"HARLEY MARIE!"

"Talk to you later." I hang up the phone. "COMING!!!"

✳✳✳

"Would you like a drink, Rog?" my father asks himself. "AB-SO-LUTE-LY!" Roger sits in his Barcalounger, staring at *Wheel of Fortune*. I am alone in the kitchen, drying the dishes. I hear him get out of the chair, then the glub, glub, glub of the vodka as it trickles into the glass.

"Harley?" Roger's voice is already slurry.

I want to ignore him, but he knows I'm in here. "Yeah, Dad?"

"Get me a coupla ice cubes, will ya?"

I sigh and throw open the freezer and grab a tray of ice. I don't want to get the ice, but more than that, I don't want to argue about it. There are only two cubes left. Carla has an ice cube maker, and boy, we sure could use one in this house. I crack out the cubes, fill up the tray and shove it deep in the freezer.

Roger is back in the Barcalounger with his feet up. I drop the ice cubes into his drink. I am a slave and he is the plantation master.

Roger smiles at me. He reaches for my hand. He squeezes it. "You're a good girl, Harley."

I toss him a grin and try to leave. He won't let go of my hand. Not this game again. I tug. "Come on, Dad." He squeezes hard.

"Come on, Dad. Let go!" I try to yank my hand away. Roger laughs. He rolls my knuckles. It hurts. "Dad, let go! You're hurting me!" I tug as hard as I can. He lets go and I fly backwards. I storm out of the room. He laughs again and punches the remote.

✷✷✷

I am upstairs in the bathroom. I lock the door. I climb on the edge of the tub and open the window. I pull my backpack out of the hamper. I take out the pack of Marlboro Lights.

I stare at my face in the mirror and my blue eyes blink back at me. I don't feel pretty, but I hope I am. Carla is allowed to wear make-up, but I am not. I wear it anyway. I sneaked some lipstick out of my mother's drawer and now I spread it across my lips.

I shake a cigarette out of the pack and put it between my red lips. I light it with shaky hands. I puff. Cough. Smoke pours out between my teeth and sails up towards the window.

I know I'm supposed to inhale, but I cannot fathom doing it. This takes practice. I pose with the cigarette between my fingers. Now the white filter has red lips on its tip. I toss my hair into a lion's mane. "Sure, Johnny. I'd *love* to go to the ball with you," I say to the mirror.

I take another puff and breathe in at the same time. The smoke fills my lungs. The bathroom starts spinning. A thousand tiny needles explode over my face, hot then cold. Coughs erupt from my body. The smoke bursts out of my mouth. I am nauseous.

I throw the cigarette into the toilet bowl and flush. I think I'm going to throw up. I hang onto the edge of the sink. I fumble through the medicine cabinet and pull out a can of air freshener. I spray the room. The droplets mingle with the smoke in the air and

I am in a toxic shower. I hack and retch and yank open the bathroom door. I run to my room and throw myself on my bed, spread-eagle on my back. I am so sick I want to die.

✳✳✳

"Admit it, we made a mistake…"

"Shut up! Just shut…"

The voices are below me, raging. I hear the tap, tap, tap of Riley's paws as he walks across the linoleum floor. "Here, boy," I call softly. Riley trots over to the foot of my bed. I pat my pillow. "Up, Riley, up." Riley hesitates, confused. My parents won't allow him on the bed. "It's okay, boy," I tell him. "I need you tonight." Riley seems to understand, and jumps up next to my feet.

"No more, Roger, I can't…" The voices grow uglier. I have to make them stop. I cannot take one more night of this. I lean over and push my bedroom door shut. I bury my face in my pillow. I press it tight against my ears. *"Goddamn it, Peppy…"* The voices start to fade away. I feel myself float up, up, up. I breathe and breathe until the world gets bright and quiet and I am far away, inside Strawberry Fields, painting trees and butterflies.

My brush flows with every color I imagine. I paint the grass green. I paint yellow daisies and pink tulips. I paint smiling parents walking their babies in polka dot strollers. I paint fluffy white clouds….

Far below, back on earth, there is a shout, then something made of glass shatters. Paint, Harley, paint.

The clouds turn gray. It starts to drizzle. There is a flash of lightning, then a rumble of thunder. Now the rain pours down, and my colors start to smear. I struggle to paint against the rain but my paintbrush melts into a puddle of color and I am dissolving....

Riley barks. I open my eyes and blink into the darkness. A tiny figure stands next to my bed. "God, Lily, you scared me!" I switch on my lamp.

Downstairs the voices still snarl. I hear a door slam, then a shout. "*You call this a life?*" I swear, one of these days they're going to kill each other.

Lily looks like she's been crying for hours. "Sorry, Harley." Poor kid. I brush the hair off her face. I lift up my covers. "Climb into my tent, Pocahontas."

Lily tumbles in next to me. Riley raises his head and yawns. Lily's body is quivering. "You wanna see something cool?" I ask her. Lily nods her tiny head. She's got a head like a cantaloupe. "You have to promise not to tell anybody." She nods again, very solemnly. "I promise."

"Okay. Close your eyes." Lately I've been sleeping with my harlequin. I know it's stupid, but he makes me feel safe. I pull him out from under the covers. "Okay, open!"

Lily turns around, and I hand her the doll. She smiles. "Ooo, it's a clown." She cradles the harlequin like a baby. "Where'd you get him?"

"A long time ago, when I was younger than you, my real daddy gave him to me for protection. It's a magic clown. He watches over me with his baton so no one can hurt me. See, it says, 'Papa loves you, forever and a day.' Nice, huh?" I click off my lamp. I wrap Lily and the harlequin together in my arms. She weighs as much as a cobweb.

Lily kisses the harlequin. "Will he protect me, too?"

"Protect you from what?" Lily and I jump. Roger looms in the doorway. His victory downstairs was not enough to satisfy him. He has tasted blood and come upstairs to conquer the rest of the house. I feel thunder enter the room. I close my eyes and pray he is a nightmare. "Down, Riley," says the thunder. The voice is real, not a dream. Riley doesn't move. Lily starts whimpering. "DOWN, Riley!" I feel Riley jump off the bottom of my bed. His footsteps patter down the hallway. He collapses in front of Bean's door.

"Get in your own bed, Lily." Now Roger stands over my bed, swaying. Lily cries harder and pushes her body tight against mine. "I don't want this daddy, I want my real daddy."

Roger grabs her by the arm and yanks her out of my bed. "When I say get in your own bed, I mean it."

Lily is sobbing now. "Stop, Daddy, you're hurting me."

Roger tosses Lily in her bed like she is dirty laundry going in a hamper. He stands in the middle of the room, fists clenched, breathing, breathing. He is a thunderstorm turning into a hurricane. "Keep that goddamn dog off the bed." As suddenly as he appeared, he is gone.

I tremble from the aftershock. I take a breath and listen, sniff the air. The storm has passed, for now. I wrap my harlequin in my arms and listen to Lily weep.

harley
like a person

chapter 5

"Do you know where to get a certified check or money order?" Me and Carla are on a picnic at German Lake, which is at the top of Federal Hill. The air is still chilly, but we have a couple of Cokes, and this is the place to be. Riley is with us, and he dashes back and forth across the edge of the water, barking at nothing. They say Federal Hill is haunted. At night there are flickering lights and moans from Revolutionary War soldiers who were executed for their mutiny against George Washington. I have never actually seen the ghosts, but I have been told.

"Can you get them at a bank?" Carla burps.

"Gross." I sip my soda. "I guess maybe a bank."

I am filling out the paperwork to get my birth certificate. Carla looks over my shoulder.

"Now, that's stupid, Harley."

"What?"

"It makes no sense. How can your name be Harley Columba and your father's name be unknown? Your last name is Columba, Roger's last name is Columba. You've either got to put down 'Roger Columba' or put your last name unknown." Carla touches a pimple on her chin. This is the first time I have seen a blemish on her face.

"If my last name is unknown, then how are they going to find my birth certificate?"

"Face it, Harley. You're not adopted."

I do not want to get into it. A person knows. I am sorry I broke down and told Carla about my adoption project. She is uninformed, but she does have a point. My real last name can't possibly be "Columba." They probably altered the birth certificate.

"This is something that has to be done, Carla. This is something you should be interested in yourself."

"Meaning?"

"Meaning, you should try to find your dad."

"My father is a mad bohemian living in squalor in Greenwich Village. I have no interest in seeing that man." She says this as if it is her mother talking.

"He's gorgeous." I've seen pictures.

"*Was* gorgeous. Now he's an old pothead." Carla flips her hair. She wears lipstick and eyeshadow for this trek in the woods. We both have the same color hair, long and brown. Mine is curly and hers is straight. I stare at her. She is turning pretty.

"My mother says your father was a cad," I inform Carla.

"How would she know?"

"Rumor has it."

Carla grabs the paper. "Harley, just get rid of the 'Unknowns' and put down 'Columba' or forget the whole thing."

"If he were my father, I'd certainly track him down."

"Well, he's not your father. If he wants to see me, he knows where I am."

I can tell she is getting annoyed. I will appease her. I erase the "Unknowns." Under mother's maiden name I put "Patricia Harley." Under father's name I put "Roger Columba."

Carla examines the paper. "Erase the 'Reason Needed: Adoption,' too."

"They say you need to give a reason."

"Put down 'Passport.'"

Actually, that is a very good idea. Carla excels at practical matters. I erase "Adoption" and write "Passport." I grin. "Now all I need is the cashier's check and fifteen bucks."

✳✳✳

I am in church, surrounded by androids in suits and dresses. The androids kneel, stand, and recite long passages. Church is a bore except for one thing: Johnny Bruno is Catholic.

Peppy drags me and Bean and Lily here. Roger refuses to come, and that's one thing I like about the guy. "Lemmings," he calls them. Lemmings are rodents that commit mass suicide. Millions of them follow the leader into the water and drown. That is what church reminds me of. Once, I asked God to make a zit go away by the end of the service and it did not happen.

It is time for Communion. This is my favorite part because Johnny Bruno sings in the choir. They shuffle up to the altar first so they can get back to the choir loft in time to sing.

I can see the back of Johnny's head. He holds out his hand. The priest hands Johnny a thin wafer that he puts in his mouth. That wafer is the Body of Christ. If you chew it, you are biting Jesus. On the way back to your seat, you're supposed to cast your eyes down and look very solemn and pray in ecstacy.

Johnny keeps his eyes wide open and heads back down the aisle. I pray quickly to God. When Johnny passes by me, I gaze right into those beautiful baby browns. He winks. "Hi," he whispers.

"Hi," I whisper back. Finally a miracle!

"Ssshh!" Peppy pokes me in the shoulder. "Show some respect."

✳✳✳

I have never bought a cashier's check or money order before. I

harley
like a person

41

am in the bank, standing behind this red velvet rope on a line that never moves. This is my first time here alone without my mother. It seems to me that the tellers go slow on purpose. Every customer is all hushed and dressed properly as if they were doing Serious Business. I try to act like I know what I am doing, but I am so nervous, I do not have a clue.

Finally it is my turn. I step up to the next open window and stare right into the big horsey face of Mrs. Liechtenstein, our gossipy neighbor who lives down the street. Too late, I remember that she works here.

"Harley *Columba*, all grown *up* and in the *bank*!" Mrs. Liechtenstein is one of those people who talks to you like you just crawled out of a cradle, emphasizing everything to be sure you *get* it. I feel my face turn hot and red, and I want to run right out the door. "What can I *do* for you today?"

Telling Mrs. Liechtenstein anything is like splashing it across a billboard. I think I should tell her it is a mistake, I was just visiting, anything to get out of here. "I need a cashier's check or money order for fifteen dollars," I mumble.

"Do you know the *difference* between the two, sweetie?" Her lipstick is all soaked into the wrinkles around her mouth so she's got these tiny red crevices surrounding her lips. I shake my head no.

"A money order costs *two* dollars and *you* fill it in, and a cashier's check costs *three* dollars and *we* fill it in."

I didn't know they cost anything. I have exactly fifteen dollars. This is the worst.

"I—I don't have—I didn't know—I have exactly fifteen." My face is flashing like an ambulance bulb and I can hear the siren screaming inside: "Emergency! Emergency! Retreat! Retreat!"

All I can see is Mrs. Liechtenstein's huge red wrinkly mouth moving and words coming at me through a tunnel. *"I'll* loan you the money, Harley. You can pay me back."

Mrs. Liechtenstein leaves the window, and I stand there gripping the edge of the counter. I do not want to owe Mrs. Liechtenstein anything, but I don't know how to stop this. She is back in a minute, waving a paper at me like she has just won the lottery.

"Okey dokey, honey. Now just tell me *who* you want it made out to. Write it down *exactly* the way you want it typed." She passes me a pen and a scrap of paper. Oh my God. She wants me to do this now, right here, in front of her. I move in a dream. I pick up the pen. I write: New York Department of Health: Vital Records. I hand Mrs. Liechtenstein the paper. Things have gotten beyond my control. Soon the entire town of Lenape Lakes will know I am adopted.

"Vital *Records?* Isn't that for *birth* certificates?" Mrs. Liechtenstein can barely contain herself.

"I…I, uh, I'm applying for a passport."

"A *passport!* How *thrilling!* Are you going overseas?"

My mouth is no longer connected to my brain. I hear myself say, "New York City. I'm going to New York City."

"New York *City!* Why, you don't need a *passport* to go to New York City, honey."

Breathe, Harley, breathe. "New York City, then on to Liverpool."

"*Liverpool!*" Mrs. Liechtenstein's mouth turns into a wrinkly red exclamation point. "My, *my!* In *England?* Why Liverpool?"

"To see where John Lennon was born. You know. The Beatle?"

"How *fascinating!*" Behind me in line, a man in a suit clears his throat. Mrs. Liechtenstein gets the hint. She turns to her typewriter. "This will be ready in a jiffy!"

I watch Mrs. Liechtenstein type the words, fast, like a machine gun. She hands me the cashier's check with a flourish. It looks impressive and official. "Now, sweetie, don't *forget*, you owe me three dollars!"

I grab the check and practically leap over the red velvet rope. Behind me, Mrs. Liechtenstein calls, "Tell your mother I said *hello*!"

✶✶✶

I am walking past the fence of the grammar school when I see my mother's gray minivan parked up ahead. Strange. My mother never picks us up from school anymore, not since she started answering phones over at the Jaspers' real estate office. Then I think: she is spying on me, making sure I am truly, totally grounded. Then I think: it is not her. It is another gray minivan mother.

I get closer and I see yes, it is her. Bean and Lily are already in there. I put my hand on the front handle and tug the door open. I look at my mother's face. It is the face of a stranger. I am scared. I climb up into the passenger seat. I stare straight ahead and wait.

"Your grandmother is dead."

"No." I wait for her to tell me she's playing a horrible joke. "No."

"Yes, Harley. Last night."

I feel the scream, all red and raw, rip out of my throat, louder, louder, filling the minivan until I think the doors will blow out. I don't realize the sound is coming from me until Lily and Bean start crying. This is a deep, bloody wound, metal jaws to the belly, ripping, ripping—not a clean, even slice, but a ragged chunk of flesh torn from my soul.

And then I am numb.

My father's mother died before I can remember, so this is my first real death. Relatives arrive at our house from all over the East Coast because Granny and Grandpa moved down South and we are centrally located. My mother's younger brother, Uncle Fitz, and Grandpa Harley fly up with Granny's body because this is where she wanted to be buried. "If we hadn't moved down South, she would be alive today," says Uncle Fitz. "Bunch of hicks."

I haven't seen Uncle Fitz for about ten years. He never came up with my grandparents. He is seven years younger than Peppy, and she treats him politely, like an acquaintance, not like a brother.

There's no place to put all the relatives so I sleep on the family room sofa and listen to Grandpa and my parents and Uncle Fitz sit around the table and cry and talk and drink and cry. I've hidden my harlequin back deep inside the storage area so some nosy great-aunt who's sleeping in my bed won't find it.

All I can think is: two more days. Granny would have been here in two more days. I can't talk. I can only weep. Every sentence begins with a "why?" but no one can give me a reason.

It is past midnight when the voices wake me up. I hear a grown man crying. For a second I don't know where I am; then I remember Granny is dead and I am sleeping on the sofa. I open my eyes into two tiny slits. My eyelashes make it seem as if I'm looking through a forest of black trees. I can see across the family room to the table where three men sit. It is my father, my grandfather, Uncle Fitz and a bottle of vodka. They are swaying. My grandfather is crying. It is a frightening sound.

"…a piss-poor excuse for a son-in-law. A *gas station*." Grandpa spits out the words. "You had a good job at the chemical plant. Look at how you live now." My grandfather gestures at the room like he is visiting a slum. "You did my daughter some favor, marrying her."

"I'm...*not*..." Roger slurs his words, but there is no disguising the hurt in his voice. "I *try*. I work hard to take care of the kids, *all* the kids, not just—"

"Ssshh!" Uncle Fitz interrupts. He points to me lying on the sofa. I watch Uncle Fitz stand up. He grips the table for support. "I think it's time we all went to bed." He clicks off the light and the men turn into three wobbly shadows. "Come on."

Grandpa lifts his hand to protest, then drops it to his side as if he is exhausted. They stagger out of the room, leaving behind a table of empty glasses and half-eaten sandwiches. I wait until they are gone to turn over on my side and wrap the covers over my head. The whole world's gone crazy, I think. I will wake up tomorrow and this will all be a dream.

✳✳✳

We are at the funeral home looking at my dead granny in a coffin. I cannot believe this is a human tradition. It is so morbid, I swear. They put all this orange makeup on her face and pink lipstick and rouge and straightened out her hair. She *always* put curls in her hair, and it upsets me that they would do this to her when she is dead.

There was a big discussion about whether me and Lily and Bean would go to the funeral at all. First it was none of us until I started crying; then it was only me, and Bean started in; now even Lily is here wearing a dark navy dress because they don't make black dresses for five year olds, at least not in New Jersey.

Granny had lots of friends, people who are strangers to me.

Relatives I've never seen before know me because I am the oldest. Everyone calls me over: "This is little Harley? Why, she's all grown up!" Everyone is kissing and hugging and reading the cards on the flowers to see who ordered the biggest arrangement. People are clumped together in groups, chatting, like there isn't a dead body lying in the middle of the room.

I wait until the crowd around the coffin clears away. Then I approach. I pretend I am the only one in the room and that Granny is sleeping. I kneel down and whisper: "Granny, please come back. Don't leave me down here all alone." Tears stream out of my eyes but I make no sound. Granny is a hollow shell; whatever was inside her is now gone. The pain inside me is so big I can feel it in my blood, pumping through my whole body. I keep my head down so no one can see me weep. This is a new, horrible feeling; this feeling must be grief. I cannot take it. I slip away from the casket and dash down the hall to the ladies room.

Some old bag who I think is my great aunt Betsy on my father's side is in there talking to someone inside a stall. The voice behind the stall is saying, "…I don't know, she doesn't look anything like him…" As soon as Great Aunt Betsy sees me she says, "Harley!" real loud, like a warning to change the subject. The voice behind the stall says, "Harley Columba, is that you, dear?" I grab a paper towel and blow my nose. "Yeah." I am very suspicious. I get this feeling they were talking about me.

The toilet flushes. I do not want to stand around and chit chat with Great Aunt Betsy and some voice behind the stall, so I throw some water on my face and go back to the room where dead Granny is. An old priest with white hair is preaching up front, and everybody is sitting down. I slide into the seats next to Bean and

Lily. Peppy is already there, sitting between Roger and Uncle Fitz. Next comes Grandpa, who stares straight ahead, showing nothing. I see that my mother's eyes are wet. I realize for the first time: her mother is dead.

The priest talks about Granny, but it's obvious he never met her before in his life. He calls her Susan and her name is Suzanne. He says, "I know Susan would be happy to see all her friends and loved ones gathered in her memory." Every time the priest calls Granny "Susan," Bean snorts and punches me in the ribs.

In the row behind us, Aunt Joan's stomach growls so loud you can hear it across the whole room. The priest drones on and on like he doesn't hear it, even though we all know he does. It growls again and Bean giggles. He punches me and I pinch him back. It growls again and the priest keeps talking and we keep trying not to giggle which makes us laugh even harder until we are shaking like a bunch of spastics.

Then the priest says, "Let us bow our heads and have a moment of silent prayer for our beloved Susan." For a second, the entire room is quiet. Then Aunt Joan's stomach growls *real* loud, like a starving lion. Bean and I burst out laughing. I can't control myself. I put my hands over my face and pretend I am crying. I peek through my fingers and see that other people are trying not to laugh too. I am all bent over and laughing so hard my stomach hurts. More people join in until the entire room is snorting and spitting, trying not to laugh. The old priest looks like he is going to have a fit with all these Harleys and Columbas roaring in the middle of a funeral. My father tries to put on a stern face, but even he can't keep his smile down, and his eyes look like they're going to pop right out of his head. He leaves his seat and grabs the three of us and yanks us out of there, which is just as well because I'm laughing so hard I pee in my pants.

On the way out, I take one last peek at Granny. Now she looks like she's got a smile on her face. And then, I swear to God, I see her give me a wink, and I know everything's going to be all right.

harley
like a person

chapter 6

There are people walking through the house, cooking. Neighbors bring plates of lasagna and chicken. People talk to me and I think I answer them. I see through my eyes and words come out of my mouth, but in between my voice and my mind is a vacuum.

It's Saturday and I have to get away from this house full of strangers. After seeing this bunch, I am even more convinced I am adopted. In my head I try to figure out how we are all related, but I really need a piece of paper to do it properly. I slip out the front door and up the block, drifting past the rows of houses that are all the same.

I walk over the footbridge and up toward the firehouse. We never have any fires in Lenape, so it is more like a clubhouse for the volunteer men to drink beer and play poker. Mr. Hughes calls out to me, "Sorry to hear about your grandmother!" and I say thanks.

My feet don't touch the ground these days. Part of me has floated off the earth with Granny. I don't know where I am going, and I wind up at the church.

I have never been here on a Saturday before. I pull open the heavy wooden door and enter the vestibule. I hear voices talking normally, not in the quiet church hush. I will just light a candle and leave.

I walk into the main part of the church. The voices are louder here and there is banging. I dab some holy water on my forehead. I close my eyes and say a prayer for Granny. When I open them, I look right into the dark brown eyes of Johnny Bruno.

"Hi!" he says. "Come to help with the new organ?"

I want to reach out and touch him and make sure he is real, but I do not. To open my eyes and have Johnny Bruno standing in front of me should surprise me, but it doesn't. It is a gift from Granny, I think. To Johnny I say, "Sure!"

Johnny leads me upstairs to the balcony where the choir sits. A bunch of men and older boys and girls are wrestling with the organ, trying to shove it into its new spot. Johnny and I grab an edge and start pushing. We giggle and yank. "Heave ho!" yells a guy who looks like the usher on Sunday but now wears jeans, not a suit and tie. We get the organ in there and everybody shouts and claps. I didn't know you were allowed to make this much noise in church.

Johnny moves closer. We are almost touching. Now it hits me: I am actually standing here next to Johnny Bruno. We chat about nothing, about everything, and the words just flow. I think I must inform Mr. Donovan: I, Juliet, would definitely kill myself for my Romeo, Johnny. After a long while I tell Johnny I have to get going. I have to get back to the relatives.

Then Johnny does something amazing. We are leaning against the balcony railing. He brushes the hair back from my face and bends over and kisses me, sweetly, on the lips. I am stunned. This is not happening to me, I think. This is happening to Romeo and Juliet and I've got my balconies confused.

Johnny takes my hand. He tugs me down the stairs to the front of the church. He opens the door for me. He holds it as I float through. I look at him. His eyes are shiny, like he is excited too. He gazes at me for a long moment. He grins.

"Well, good-bye." I am almost crying, I am so happy.

"Good-bye." He kisses me again. This time I know I am not dreaming.

"No, go on!" says Carla.

"I swear."

"On the lips?"

"Softly, gently, right on the lips."

"With tongue?"

"Carla! It wasn't that kind of kiss."

I have been sitting on this information for days now, afraid to tell anyone, even Carla. If you give all your secrets to one person, they have a lot of future ammunition. Sometimes Carla has a mouth that won't quit, and I don't want to jinx it. But some things are so big they burst right out of you, there's just no holding them back.

"Where?"

"In the balcony of the church."

"Oooh! How scandalous!"

We are walking in the graveyard of the old Dutch Reformed Church. We like to hang out in haunted places. This church is much older than the Catholic church because the Dutch were here first. There are tombstones from the 1700s. Soldiers from every war are planted under the ground, all the way back to the Revolutionary War.

It is dusk. No one at home will notice I am gone because of the left-over relatives. They have forgotten I am grounded, another good perk that Granny has provided. God, how I miss her.

"Johnny was waiting by my locker after English today."

Carla's eyes grow big. "Wow! I do not believe it. I do not believe that Johnny Bruno actually likes you back."

harley
like a person

"Thanks a lot, Carla." This is the attitude I am talking about. I am not going to let her jinx me, not this time, not when the hole in my heart left by my grandmother is softly being mended by Johnny Bruno.

"Don't be so touchy, Harley. I just meant that it seems so astounding. I'm jealous! I never had a boy like me back that I liked. Except Vic, but he doesn't count 'cause I don't even like him really, he's just convenient. You are so lucky."

She seems sincere and I am sorry I doubted her. "Do you mean it?" My eyes start to fill with tears. My emotions are all mixed up. I try to blink the tears away, but instead I start to cry, I can't help it.

"What, Harley? What's the matter?" Carla looks scared.

"I–miss–my–granny–is–all." I want to stop crying, but I can't. Instead I cry harder. The next thing I know, I am sobbing and choking and I think I will never be able to stop. "It's not fair! It's not fair!"

"Oh, Harley." Carla stands there like she doesn't know what to do. Then, gently, she reaches over and takes me in her arms. I have never hugged a girl before and her breasts feel funny against mine. I relax into her, heaving and weeping. We stand there for a long time in the graveyard, wrapped in each other's arms. She pats my back awkwardly like I am a baby and says, "It's okay." Finally my tears stop and I wipe my nose on my sleeve.

"Sorry."

Carla brushes the hair off of my face. "Don't be silly. I wish I had a grandmother to cry about." Carla's eyes are kind as she looks into mine. For a wild moment, I almost feel like kissing *her*. Then the feeling passes, and I turn away.

"We'd better get going."

Carla giggles, all nervous, and I wonder if she was feeling

the same thing. "Yeah. These gravestones are giving me the creeps."

We walk together toward the rusted wrought-iron gate, shadows touching. It's crazy, but I can almost feel Granny walking beside us too.

✱✱✱

Miss Posey corners me after art class. "Harley, can I talk to you?" I just got done with a plaster-of-Paris Jesus-on-the-cross. Well, it didn't start out that way, it started out as a hang glider, but things didn't work out. Maybe I've broken some First Amendment rule between church and state.

"Yes?"

"Listen, I want to ask you a favor." Miss Posey has on tight jeans and clunky shoes. She looks like she's twelve. "The drama department needs someone to paint a portrait for a play they're doing. *Anastasia*. I know you're going through a rough time, but sometimes… Well, I remember when my dad died. Just getting behind an easel helps. Can you handle it?"

"Me?" My voice squeaks like Lily's. A senior usually does the artwork for the drama department plays, never a freshman.

"Harley, I can teach you the technical stuff, but, kiddo, you've got a real gift. In fact, you're the best artist in the whole district. If you've got the time…"

The best artist in the whole district. I am so honored that Miss Posey would ask me to do this, I can't say no. And she's right. Whenever I am painting, the whole world can collapse around me, and I will remain standing. I think this is another gift from Granny. I realize Miss Posey has stopped talking and is waiting for my answer. "I…I would love to."

"Great. They don't have a big budget, but it should be a hoot. I think they need it in a month or two. And I'll always be here to help you. Okay?"

I nod. "Okay."

"Good." Miss Posey scribbles something on a slip of paper. "The director's name is Mr. Roman. They'll start rehearsing in a week or so. I'll let you know." She hands me the paper like she is handing me a ticket out of here. She grins.

I smile. I take the paper. "Thanks."

✳✳✳

Now that the relatives have gone and taken their chatter with them, the house settles back into its normal state, sparks smoldering beneath our sentences. One wrong word, and the whole thing will ignite. I go to the dining room table where the mail is stacked every day before Roger files it away. Peppy is in the kitchen; Roger is in his Barcalounger. I am very discreet. I flip through the pile. No birth certificate.

"Whatcha doin'?"

I jump. Bean stands next to me, crunching on an apple.

"Geez, Bean! Mind your own business, will ya?"

"Expecting a love letter from Johnny?" His voice is sing-songy. I hit him on the head with a magazine.

"Shut up!"

"Earl's sister says it's all over school." Bean's grin is wicked. "Harley and Johnny sitting in a tree…"

"Grow up, will you? You're a real jerk."

Bean makes kissing noises with his lips. I pound his back. He runs around the room, kissing the air. I chase after him. Peppy yells from the kitchen: "Knock it off in there!"

***

"Miss Posey told me I was the best artist in the entire district," I inform the earthlings at the dinner table.

"That's nice." Since it is Friday, we are having fish. This is an archaic Catholic custom that, for some unknown reason, Peppy has decided to carry on in the House of Columba. It's not even a real Catholic rule anymore, except in this place. Lily whispers, "fish, wish, fish, dish, fish, kish," over and over and will not shut up.

"I'm not hungry," says Bean.

"Eat," says Roger. "If I have to eat it, so do the rest of you."

"They want to me to do the art for the drama club play." I try again. "Isn't that great?"

"What's wrong with fish?" My mother puts down her fork. "You think it's easy cooking dinner for five people every single night of the week?"

"Fish sucks." Bean reaches for a bottle of ketchup and squirts it all over his filet.

"Watch your mouth," says my father on automatic.

I nibble a limp green bean. "Miss Posey said I've got a real gift."

"What about hamburgers, Peppy? We all like hamburgers." Roger reaches for the bowl of French fries. Everyone is eating everything except the fish.

"This isn't a restaurant." My mother's lips get tight. "I do not enjoy working all day long and coming home and listening to all of you complain."

"So, don't make fish." Roger takes a swig of vodka. I watch my mother's eyes follow the glass as he tips it to his lips, but she says nothing. "Why make it when no one likes it?"

harley
like a person

"I like it, Mommy," says Lily.

"Usually they ask a senior to do the art for the plays." I gnaw on a soggy French fry. "I'm the first freshman."

"You're supposed to have fish on Fridays." Peppy squeezes her lemon and drips it, hard, all over her filet until not a drop of juice is left.

"What are they gonna do, Ma, throw us out of heaven?" Bean has mixed mounds of French fries and beans all over his plate so the fish looks like it's been eaten. "May I please be excused?"

"No," says Peppy. "Sit there and finish that fish."

"Aw, come on!" Bean squirms. "I told Earl I'd be over."

"Go ahead," says my father.

Bean jumps up from the table. "Thanks, Dad!" Peppy's lips get tighter and whiter, but again she says nothing.

No one but Lily finishes their fish.

✳✳✳

It's hard to sleep when you're in love. All I think about is Johnny, Johnny, Johnny. I cradle my harlequin in my arms and practice kissing his porcelain lips, pretending he is Johnny. I become an angel on earth. I fetch ice with a smile and vacuum the floor. My mother and father say, "It's nice to have our daughter back." This annoys me, but I am so happy I forgive them. I let them think it is the death of my grandmother that has transformed me, not the love of Johnny Bruno.

School is over for the day. I head to my locker. Guess who is standing there. Johnny Bruno.

"Wanna walk home?" His eyes are brown like Peppy's, but in a warm way.

"Sure!" I get my French book, since Ms. Auberjois likes to ruin every evening for us. Johnny takes it out of my hand.

"Allow me." I am thrilled. I've read about guys doing things like this. Then I worry: Have I written any "Johnny and Harley" stuff on the cover? If so, I hope it is properly in code.

We walk down the hall. He steps ahead of me, pushes open the heavy fire door and holds it open as I waltz through.

Tattletale Betty Jo Clemings is on the other side of the door. She runs with this pack of goddesses who think they are God's gift to Lenape High. She has an enormous jaw that always gets stuck open like the hinge is jammed. I heard it got stuck open for hours at the freshman car wash and a doctor had to be called. Now when she sees me walk by with Johnny Bruno, her jaw drops straight down and I smile sweetly at her as we pass and hope she never gets it closed.

Carla is standing outside the gym door, waiting for me. She sees me with Johnny, and I see confusion on her face. I don't know what to do. We walk up to her.

"Hi!" says Carla.

"Hi!" I say. "You know Johnny, right? You know Carla."

"Hi!" says Johnny.

No one says anything. Then I say, "Johnny is walking me home."

Something new flashes across Carla's face, something I've never seen before. "Oh, okay," she says, turning away. "I have to run uptown anyway." She flips her hair. She heads down the steps toward the Pond Hole and does not look back.

For a second I feel bad, but I am too happy to let it bother me. Carla knows how important this is. Besides, she has done the same to me with Vic, and she doesn't even really like him.

Johnny walks me down the street and over the footbridge. Sometimes his jacket brushes my arm and gives me a tingle. I must make brilliant conversation, I think, but no words come out. I wait for him to charm me with his wit. He says nothing. We walk together in silence, but underneath there is a whole conversation going on.

We stop at the top of Hill Court. Mrs. Woods is signaling to a pickup truck with her stop-sign-on-a-stick like she is guiding in an aircraft carrier. Here is where Johnny and I must part; I live in one direction and he lives in the other, closer to Carla's house. Mrs. Woods has her back to us, but keeps turning around, casual-like, pretending she isn't spying. She waves the pickup truck forward.

Johnny hands me back my French book. There is a big "J.B. & H.C." in the upper right-hand corner, but it is in the shape of a flower. I don't think he notices. He leans over and kisses me. This is different from the church kiss, which was soft and sweet. This kiss is a little sloppy. I wish I had a tissue.

"See you tomorrow," he says.

"See you tomorrow," I say back. God, I am so unoriginal.

He grins and heads off in the opposite direction. I walk over to Mrs. Woods. She holds up her stop-sign-on-a-stick and crosses me, even though no cars are coming. I turn around and look back at Johnny. He is watching me. He waves. I wave back to him and fly all the way home.

chapter 7

I want to paint clouds on my bedroom ceiling. Of course, Peppy won't let me. Carla is over, and we sneak inside my storage area, which I have transformed into Harley's Happy Hideaway. Peppy doesn't know this, or she would rip it all down. In addition to my John Lennon posters, I put up wooden beads and tacked on East Indian scarves like a veil you must whisk aside to enter. Red, orange, green, blue. I know Carla will steal this idea next. She practically *lives* in her storage area, and Ronnie lets her.

Peppy is ironing in the family room, so we should be safe.

"Johnny's walked me home three days in a row," I inform Carla. She is filing her nails, which, of course, are now gold.

"Did he kiss you every time?"

"Yeah, but just a little one cause we didn't want to give Mrs. Woods a thrill. She spies."

"Maybe he'll ask you to the Spring Ball." Carla looks at me sideways. The Spring Ball is the biggest bash of the season. It is almost better than the prom, because all grades can go, not just seniors. The Spring Ball is in April, when the buds start to bloom and the frost disappears. It is the dream of every girl in town to get asked to the Spring Ball. I think my dream is about to come true.

"It's a month and a half away," I tell her. "I don't dare think about it. If we talk about it, it'll get a jinx."

When I unrolled a rug I found my mother's yearbook stuffed into a corner. Now we flip through it. It is depressing. No one wants to do anything with their life. Under the girls' pictures it says things like: "her outstanding skills will assure her a secretarial position," "should make an excellent beautician," "hopes to become a dental assistant."

The boys are not much more ambitious: "should make a fine electrician," "plans to venture into carpentry after graduation," "has hopes of being a car mechanic." We know lots of people in the yearbook because they are the parents of our friends. Lenape Lakes, land of opportunity.

I flip to Patricia Harley. Peppy was really pretty when she was young, all smiles and hopes. There is a cute quotation under my mother's picture: "Catch your dreams before they slip away." Then it says: "Peppy…loves to laugh…dislikes phony people…hobbies are swimming and listening to music…college is in her path."

"Did your Mom go to college?" asks Carla.

"I guess she took a wrong turn," I giggle. "No one in this family ever goes to college." I toss the yearbook at Carla. "Take a look, Carla. Here is your destiny. No one ever leaves Lenape Lakes, and if they do, they always come back."

Carla flips through the book. I am sad. I don't think my mother caught her dreams; I don't think she even got a nibble. Lenape Lakes is a sneaky little town. If you don't escape, it wraps you in its claws and the next thing you know you're living on Lenape Road with a husband, three kids and a dog. One thing I vow: That will never happen to me.

Carla stops turning the pages. She grabs me. "Look!"

She points to the picture of Roger Columba. My father has written a message to Peppy around his picture. "Pep. Knowing you has meant a great deal to me. I love you more than anyone I've ever known. Through a stupid move on my part, I lost you, and I'll regret it forever. Don't forget the good times and good fights we had. Take care and be good. Love, forever. Roger."

"They broke up!" Carla is excited.

"They broke up." I can't believe it. "All this time they told me they were together since eighth grade."

"Are you going to ask them?" Carla wants the dirt. So do I. I read the rest of my father's picture. "Cast your fate to the wind." He certainly accomplished that. "The Commander…a valuable member of our basketball team…loves to laugh…hobbies include hunting and fishing…hopes for a career in aerospace engineering." Aerospace engineering! Well, owning a gas station is close. So, Roger's been the Commander from way back. Probably because he's so good at giving orders.

I flip back and forth between their two pictures. They are young with big grins. It says they both "love to laugh," but I can't remember the last time I saw either of them smile.

"Let's look up your mother," I say to Carla.

"She's not there. She was two years behind."

"What about your dad? Wasn't your dad in their class?"

"I think so…."

"Look him up! Look him up!"

"Geez, take it easy, Harley. What is this obsession with my father?" Carla flips through the book to the S's.

"I thought your name was 'Van Owen.'"

"That's my mother's name. My father's name was 'Shanahan.'" She stops at the same gorgeous picture I've seen before. Her father has long hair and a devilish grin. "There he is."

I take the book. "Sean Shanahan. Your father was a hunk." I pronounce his first name "See-an." "What kind of name is See-an?"

"Sean." Carla pronounces it "Shawn." "He was an Irish rogue."

I read the saying underneath his picture: "'Weathered faces lined in pain are soothed beneath the artist's loving hand.' Oooh. How romantic." Next to the picture is chicken scrawl handwriting. "Oh, wow. Look. He wrote something to my mother. I can barely make it out…."

Carla takes the book from me. She examines the handwriting. "It says: 'Peppy. Well, playtime's fi…fi—' I can't read this. *'Finally* over. Time to start the game of life. We had some wild times together, didn't we, kid? You own a piece of my heart. I won't say good-bye cause I'll still be around. Make your life beautiful, babe. Love always, Sean.'"

I am shocked. So is Carla. "Sounds like they knew each other."

"*Really* well," I say. "Do you think they slept together?"

"Don't be ridiculous, Harley."

"Well, I'm going to ask her."

"I'm sure she'll be thrilled to tell you." Carla is sarcastic, but I let it pass. She is very sensitive when it comes to her father.

"Eeet's not easy getting information from zee enemy." I put on my spy voice and make her smile. "But ve have vays of making zem talk."

✶✶✶

"Harley, get down here." Peppy's voice crackles over the intercom. What now? I ignore her. *S'il vous plaît*! I am doing French.

"HARLEY MARIE, NOW!"

I slam shut my French book. No wonder I'm getting a B. A person cannot concentrate with all the racket in this house.

I stomp down the stairs. I stomp into the kitchen. My mother is whipping potatoes in the mixer. I stand there. She keeps buzzing the mixer as if I'm not standing there like some kind of moron.

"WHAT?" I have to shout to be heard over the whir.

Peppy scoops the potatoes off the edge of the bowl as it spins around. "You come when I call you. What were you doing, *painting*?" Peppy says this like it's a dirty word. "God forbid you should come down here and help me with dinner."

Her words are needles, and they sting. "As a matter of fact, I was doing my homework," I enlighten her. "What, did you just call me down here to yell at me?"

"Watch your mouth." Peppy turns off the mixer. She wipes her hands on her apron. She puts her hands on her hips and faces me. "I saw Mrs. Liechtenstein in the Acme today."

"So?" I swear, it is impossible to keep a secret in this town.

"So, she tells me you owe her three dollars."

"Yeah, so, I'll pay her back."

"I already gave her the money."

This really ticks me off. Peppy is always meddling in my affairs. This is *my* project. *Mine*.

"Why do you always have to stick your nose in my business?" I holler. "Why can't you let me have something of my own?"

"I don't like to owe people money."

"You don't owe her any money, I do. I said I'd pay her back. I didn't even *want* to borrow the money. She made me." It isn't worth explaining things to Peppy because she never listens anyway.

"What were you doing in the bank?"

"Something personal."

"What?"

"I don't want to say."

"Listen to me, Harley. You have to stop this nonsense. You are not adopted. You are not adopted." She turns back to the potatoes. "Sometimes I wish you were."

So there it is. Even Peppy looks shocked at her words. She spins around and tries to touch me. "I'm sorry, Harley. I didn't mean that."

"YES, YOU DID!" I run out of the kitchen. I pound up the stairs and slam the door to my bedroom. Lily is on the floor playing. She looks at me and starts crying. She always cries when I cry. I get blamed for *that*, too.

I turn on the stereo and crank it up: John Lennon singing "Mother." His mother was killed when he was a little older than me; his father left when he was a small boy. At the end he just screams the words, which is what I feel like doing right now. I stand in front of my easel, pick up my paintbrush and plunge it into some angry orange paint.

✳✳✳

"We're playing a couple of tunes at Midtown Lanes in Wynokie tomorrow night, if you wanna go."

Johnny is walking me home and my heart is pounding. It is crazy to get affected like this. He's just a guy. I say, "In a bowling alley?"

"It sounds weird, I know, but they've got this separate lounge. They let us play there even though we're underage."

Wynokie is the next town over, not within walking distance. "I don't know. It's kind of far…."

"If you can get there, I'll get someone to take you home." Johnny puts his arm around my shoulders. We walk in the same rhythm. "I have to set up the mikes, so I'll be there already."

I guess this sort of qualifies as getting asked out on a date. I'm not sure, since I've never been on one before. Meeting Johnny at a bowling alley is not the same as being asked to go to the movies and having pizza at Tony's, but it's close.

"I'll see if I can get a ride," I say.

"I hope so." Johnny squeezes me and gives me a kiss. "It's just me and Reed and a drum machine, but it should be good."

✳✳✳

I do listen to other music besides John Lennon, like Patti Smith, Blondie, Talking Heads, Smashing Pumpkins; sometimes I even get in the mood for show tunes and Mozart. But I think Johnny and Reed play folk music like Bob Dylan in the sixties, which is not high on my list. But I am dying to see Johnny in action, so I call Carla.

"I don't wanna sit in some bowling alley with a bunch of butt cracks and watch you drool all over Johnny."

"Come *on*," I beg. "There'll be lots of people there, lots of guys. And Johnny'll be busy playing. I'll only be able to talk to him on his breaks."

"You know, Harley, you're really pushing it. I'm feeling like I'm only here if you want something from me."

"Oh, please. What about when you first met Vic? You were worse. And you didn't even like him."

Carla knows I got her. She laughs. "Yeah, you're right." She pauses, then: "All right, I'll go."

✳✳✳

I wash and dry all the dishes, then approach the door to my parent's bedroom. "I'm going bowling with Carla tonight, okay, Ma?"

"Bowling? You want to go bowling?" My mother is not in the family room because my father is watching the news over and over again on different channels. Peppy camps out in the bedroom, ordering junk from the shopping channel.

"Yeah, it's good exercise." I can't tell her about Johnny because then she'd never let me go. I swear, I always get tortured if I want to go somewhere. You want to go to the movies? Do three piles of dishes, dust and sweep the kitchen. You want to go to the mall? That's one car wash, two loads of laundry and clean the bathroom. Peppy stares at the television set and does not answer me. "Well, Ma?"

A real ugly hair comb with white silk flowers has come up for sale. Peppy opens her pocketbook and takes out her credit card. She reaches for the phone. "Ask your father."

I sigh and walk into the family room and stand next to Roger in his Barcalounger. The winning lottery numbers are on the screen and he checks his ticket. "Mom said I could go bowling with Carla, okay?"

My father does not look up. "Not on a school night."

I knew he would be like this. Roger is very predictable, and I am ready. "Please, Dad. I've done all my homework and washed and dried the dishes *and* put them all away."

"No, Harley. Not on a school night."

"WHY?"

"Because I said so." My father crumples his numbers into a ball and throws it across the room. He punches the remote. Flash! Flash! Flash! The channels fly by.

"That is not a good reason!" He does this just to be a cretin. The doorbell rings. It is Carla, I am sure. I stomp to the front door and throw it open. I am almost in tears. "My father won't let me go," I tell Carla. "Can you believe it?"

"Why?"

"'Because he says so.'" I do my whiny Roger impersonation. "What a jerk."

I see Carla's mother get out of the car. She's wearing deep red lipstick and tight jeans. She is one of those moms that everybody says to Carla: "That's your *mother*? She looks like your *sister*!" Carla's mom is cool; you can talk to her; she's pretty understanding. Her name is Veronica, but she lets us call her "Ronnie," not all formal like "Mrs. Van Owen."

"Hello, Ronnie," I sniffle. "I'm sorry you came for nothing."

"I will talk to your father," she declares and marches into the house, straight into the family room, the two of us right behind her. My father is startled when he sees her. He pushes down the feet of the Barcalounger and stands up. He is flustered and I feel vindicated.

"Roger, I'll drive the girls and pick them up." Ronnie smiles like she's flirting, and my father goes for it.

"I don't know, Ronnie. On a school night?"

My mother emerges from the bedroom. "Hello, Veronica," she says with an edge. Peppy has problems with other females, I've noticed. She particularly hates Ronnie. She calls her, "that woman."

"All right," says my father. "But be home by 10:00."

"I don't know Roger...." I can almost hear Peppy sharpening her claws.

"I'll take good care of her, Peppy." Ronnie winks at me.

"Harley can take care of herself, Veronica." Peppy looks like she wants to grab Ronnie by the waist of her tight jeans and toss her out the door.

It is a mother tug-of-war and I am in the middle; their eyes yank me back and forth. I move fast. I give Roger a quick kiss on the cheek. "Thanks, Dad!" He looks surprised. It's like an espionage plot trying to get out of here, I swear. As I dash out the door, I hear my mother lower her voice: "That *woman*..."

✶✶✶

The parking lot is jammed with pickup trucks and old Volkswagens. Men with beer bellies and bowling balls weave their way through folkies dressed in jeans and flannel. People hang outside, smoking and talking. Ronnie drops us at the back of the lot so we will not be seen being driven by a parent; she is very understanding that way. "I'll be back at 9:45," she says. "No smoking."

We go inside. It's bright and noisy. A big sign says: KIWANIS CLUB VS. AMERICAN LEGION! There are nine lanes and they're all packed. Bald men wearing baseball caps slam balls against the pins. Women with blue eyeshadow drink beer from cans, hooting and clapping. Carla and I stand there and blink.

"Oh, wow," I say.

"Come on," says Carla. "The lounge is over here."

We make our way past the teased hair and Wal-Mart shirts and into the back. The lounge is another world, dark and tiny, jammed with granny skirts and flannel. I am glad Carla is here because I know no one. Everybody is older than us.

Up front, squeezed into a corner on a little platform, are Johnny and Reed, sitting on stools, strumming guitars and singing.

It's sort of hard to hear them, though, with the Kiwanis yelling in the other room. I try to catch Johnny's eye. He sees me, I'm sure. I smile and wave. It seems that he is looking right at me, but he doesn't nod or anything. Strange.

"There's a table in the back," says Carla. We squish through the crowd and sit on two plastic chairs. There is a half-eaten bowl of peanuts on the table. A wrinkled lady with stiff platinum hair piled on top of her head swaggers over holding a tray. She's wearing short shorts and has a bad case of varicose veins. "Coke only, girls, without I.D."

I have a few dollars from babysitting. I will treat Carla to a soda. It's the least I can do. "Two, please."

Johnny and Reed sound good, I guess, if you like folk music. They write their own songs. To tell the truth, the music is a little boring. People are not really listening, they are talking and laughing and coughing. Every so often a roar comes from the other room when someone gets a strike. Carla yawns and looks at her watch.

Finally Johnny speaks into the mike. "We're going to take a short break. We'll be back in a few." Johnny and Reed pull their guitars over their heads like they are taking off tee-shirts. Now is my chance.

"I'm going to say hi," I tell Carla.

"I'll stay here." She takes a sip of her Coke and flips back her hair. If there are any single boys around, Carla is definitely a target.

I push my way through the crowd to the front. Johnny is not on the little platform. I look around the room. And then I see him: sitting at a table next to Prudence Clarke, laughing.

My face goes numb. I am such a fool. I want to get out of here.

I want to get out of here right *now*. Instead, I stand staring at them, this awful totem pole with a twisted look on my face. I feel someone grab me by the elbow. I turn. It's Reed.

"Are you okay?"

I know my cheeks are red, but it is dark inside the lounge, so hopefully he can't tell. I open my mouth to speak, but nothing comes out, I am so stunned. Then I think: Well, who the hell does Johnny think he is, inviting me to come and then sitting with Prudence? I will not retreat. This is war.

"Reed!" I force a smile and kiss him on the cheek. "I was just coming over to say hi to you and Johnny."

Reed grins back. "For a second there, you looked like you were going to be sick."

"Too many peanuts." I link my arm through his. I fight the urge to crawl back to my table and hide under the chair. I flip my hair like I have seen Carla do a million times. I point to Johnny and Prudence. "Want to walk over with me?"

If Reed is surprised, he doesn't show it. He walks me to where Johnny and Prudence sit, deep in conversation.

"Look who I found, Johnny," says Reed, pulling a chair out for me to sit in. Reed seems to be enjoying the situation.

Johnny is flustered. "Prudence, you know Harley, right?"

Prudence is not wearing her thick black glasses and looks very pretty and blonde. She seems annoyed. "Actually, we've never been formally introduced."

I will not let her get away with this. "Now, Prudence, that's not true," I scold. "We met at the senior show. After the last performance."

Prudence actually looks down her nose. "Oh, really? There were so many people there that night, I must have forgotten." She smiles, all teeth. "Sorry."

Well, I know how to handle this chick. "You were *so* wonderful in that show, Prudence. You really are an incredible singer." I put on my most sincere phony voice. It works.

Prudence is thrown. She stammers. "Why…why, *thank* you, Harley. That's sweet of you to say."

I stand up. "So…nice to see you all, but I've got to get back to my friend." I smile at Johnny. "You guys sound *great*."

Johnny stands up next to me. "Hey, thanks for coming."

I wink at him. "No problem." And then, I don't know what comes over me, but as I turn to leave, I knock my arm against Prudence's soda. The can spills over and Coke splatters all over Prudence's tight white sweater. She jumps up and shrieks.

"Ow! Oh, my God! My new sweater!"

"Oh, I am *so* sorry, Prudence!" I watch the dark stain spread into the shape of Mexico across Prudence's chest and I feel avenged. "I am such a *klutz*! But if you put water on it right away, it won't stain." I grab a napkin and dab at Prudence's sweater. She rips it from my hand.

"Give me that! I can't believe it. I just bought this yesterday!" Prudence wails and screams like the Wicked Witch after Dorothy threw a bucket of water on her.

Reed laughs. "Oh, relax, Prudence. It's soda, not battery acid."

I decide to make a quick exit. "I'm sorry, Prudence. I'm *really* sorry about your sweater." I leave Prudence glowering and dabbing water on her stupid white sweater. I squeeze through the crowd, back to my table. Carla is surrounded by three older guys.

"Everybody make room for Harley!" giggles Carla. One of the

guys offers me his chair. I collapse into it. That little performance took up a lot of energy. Carla turns to me. "You look pale, girl."

"I'll tell you later."

Carla introduces me to the guys. "Harley, this is Duane and Bobby and uh, uh, now don't tell me." She giggles, playing the dumb girl. I swear, sometimes I think I don't even know her. The guys just grin and eat it up. "Wait…I know: TROY!"

The boy called Troy is gorgeous. "Would you girls like to go for a ride?"

I look at Carla. She shakes her head a tiny bit. "We would *love* to," she says. "But not tonight. We've got to get home by ten."

"What happens then?" asks Troy. "You turn into a pumpkin?"

Carla giggles again. "Worse. Asparagus." She sure can charm them.

"Well, you've still got five minutes." Troy glances at his watch.

"Five minutes!" I say. "What time is it?"

"Five to ten."

"Oh, no!" I jump up.

"My mother is going to kill me!" Carla moans. "She's waiting outside."

We grab our jackets and push toward the door. Troy chases after us. "Give me your phone number," he says to Carla, and she does. "I'll call you." He smiles at her and I am jealous.

Back on the platform, Johnny and Reed step up to the mike. Johnny says, "I'd like to introduce a good friend and a fantastic singer, Prudence Clarke." The crowd applauds. In the other room, the bowling pins crash.

chapter 8

The phone rings and it is Carla. "Guess what, Harley?"

I am in my pajamas. "Why are you calling so late, Carla?" I keep my voice low. I'm sure Peppy is listening in the family room.

"Troy asked me to go to the movies."

"Great." I am not thrilled with this bit of news. Now Carla's going to have a boyfriend and I'm not.

"You don't sound too happy for me."

"I'm ecstatic. I'm just tired."

"Oh, Harley, don't be upset about Johnny. He's just using you to get back at Prudence. He's not worth it."

Using me? Could she be right? She means well, I know, but I'm not in the mood for any advice. "Look, Carla, I've gotta go."

✳✳✳

I am sketching a caricature of Johnny with a dagger in his heart. I am contemplating whether I should add some dripping blood when Miss Posey comes over to me. "What's up, Harley?"

I sigh. "Nothing."

"Hey, are you in a bad mood, or what?" Miss Posey is all decked out in a tiny skirt and jacket. I wonder if she has a class with her favorite senior boy later in the day.

"I'm sorry. This guy I like is being a jerk."

"What a drag. Listen, I was talking with Bud Roman, the director of the play. He's ready to see you."

"Really? When?" With all this Johnny distraction, I'd almost forgotten about the drama club play. Well, I am not going to let some stupid *guy* interfere with what's important.

"They're rehearsing after school in the auditorium. Stop by and tell him I sent you."

"Okay."

Miss Posey picks up my Johnny caricature and examines it. "You know, Harley, maybe you should add a little blood...."

✶✶✶

I wait for Carla by the gym. She doesn't show. This is the third time she's left me hanging. All I hear about is Troy, Troy, Troy. I am getting really fed up. At least she could inform me that she's going home with Mr. Wonderful instead of me.

I walk over to the auditorium. I haul open the enormous doors and enter through the back. It is dark, except for the lights on the stage. There are a few people up there, all older than me, huddled in a pack, discussing motivation and emotion. Their voices echo. Actors. They are gods on Mount Olympus.

Usually the only time I'm in the auditorium is for home room when they take attendance. It looks different now, like a Greek temple. I get this urge to genuflect, but I restrain myself. I'm not sure what I should do, so I tiptoe up the aisle and sit in the front row. The wooden seat squeaks when I flip it down.

On stage, an older man with a goatee stops talking and looks at me. He is wearing a shirt and tie, but he's got sneakers on his feet. His eyes are black and wild and he has a booming voice. "Can I help you?"

"I...I'm Harley Columba. Miss Posey sent me over to paint a portrait?" I am stammering; I'm a little nervous.

"Oh, hi. Yeah. I'm Bud Roman. I'm the director." He turns to the people on stage. "Take a break, all."

Bud Roman jumps off the stage. He talks like he is spitting out thunderbolts. "What I need is a life-size portrait. Of a princess. See, this girl shows up claiming she's Anastasia—but we don't know whether to believe her, because, well, you know, she's supposed to be dead—so I want this full-size portrait of a princess, but I want her features to be fuzzy, so she doesn't look like anybody—maybe even leave the face blank. Have fun with it." He tosses me a small booklet. "Here's a copy of the play—come back in a week or so and show me what you've got. What was your name again?"

I am exhausted just listening to him. "Harley...Harley Columba."

"Harley. Like the motorcycle, eh?"

"No, Harley, like a person."

Bud Roman grins. "Okay, Harley like a person. See you next week. I like to keep the rehearsals closed until the actors get on their feet."

Bud Roman jumps back on stage and claps his hands. "People!" He is Zeus and the other gods obey. "Okay, people. Let's get to work."

I pick up the play, a small, blue paperback book full of mysteries and promises. I walk out of the auditorium and back onto the earth.

✱✱✱

Peppy and Roger are still at work, and I am stuck watching Bean and Lily because my parents are too cheap to hire a babysitter. Of course, they don't pay me. I'm supposed to do it *because they said so*. Peppy even wants me to get the supper ready, but this I refuse to do. I have homework and I hate to cook. I say, if you can't afford to have three kids, then don't have them. But you shouldn't turn your oldest daughter into a mother before her time.

Bean goes wandering. I don't care as long as he's home before my mother. It is Lily who is the pain. I don't really think I should have to plan different ways to amuse a five-year-old child. Most of the time I just toss her in front of the television. She does a great Celine Dion impersonation, throwing out her arms and pounding her heart.

I settle into Roger's Barcalounger and push the feet up. Ah. I am Goldilocks and he is Papa Bear. I can just hear Roger when he gets home: "Someone's been sitting in my chair!"

I open my copy of *Anastasia* and turn to the first page. I'm just planning to skim it, but I end up reading the whole thing. I love it. It's about a girl who claims she is a long lost princess who was supposed to have been murdered during the Russian Revolution. Nobody believes her and she's got to prove it. They think she wants to claim the royal fortune, but she just wants to find her family.

I have all sorts of ideas. I hop out of the chair to get my sketchbook when I remember to check the mail.

I walk to the front porch and open the door. Getting the mail is one of my favorite things, like little gifts on your doorstep every day. It is one good benefit of babysitting, otherwise Peppy and Roger have first grab at it. Today there is an envelope addressed to Harley Marie Columba from New York City.

My birth certificate has arrived.

I toss the rest of the mail on the dining room table and head into the family room where Lily is singing at the top of her lungs, falling on her knees and pounding her chest with her fist. I sink into my father's Barcalounger. I stare at the envelope, then rip it open. Inside is an official-looking piece of paper with a raised seal from the Department of Health, The City of New York.

I force my eyes to the page. "Borough: Manhattan. Sex: female. Mother: Patricia Ann Harley, homemaker. Father: Roger Joseph Columba, proprietor, service station…"

So. This confirms it. Those two creatures really are my parents. At least I was really born in New York City and not Lenape Boring Lakes.

I read the words over and over. Something bothers me. I touch the bumps of the raised City of New York seal. They match the goosebumps on my arms.

I have a new memory, one I've never had before…. I am Lily's age, five years old. My mother is enrolling me in kindergarten. I sit in front of a lady with black hair. I am drawing the lady with my crayons. The lady asks for my birth certificate. My mother is saying, I'm sorry, I've misplaced it, how stupid of me, and the lady is telling her it's impossible for your daughter to go to school. I am worried because all my friends are going to school and now I will be the only one home in the neighborhood. I start to cry and my mother tells me to be a big girl, not a baby and I say I am not a baby, I am a big girl and I want to go to school. Before we leave I give the lady the drawing as a present so she will let me go to school.

✳✳✳

Johnny waits by my locker like nothing has happened. "Thanks for coming the other night."

"Yeah." I open my locker and stick my head in so he can't see my red face. "It was fun."

"We're playing at a coffeehouse next Tuesday if you wanna go."

I grab my French book off the top shelf. Who does this guy think he is? Maybe he is just trying to drum up an audience for his band. I turn around and look him in the eye. "You know, Johnny, you ask me to come hear you play and then you ignore me all night. What's that about?"

"What?" He looks off down the hallway at nothing. "I didn't ignore you. I was busy playing."

"You know what I mean."

Johnny puts his arm around me and kisses me, even though we're not supposed to show signs of affection in the hallway. "Don't be upset, Harley."

Upset? I am fuming. I want to push him away and tell him to drop dead, but he kisses me again and looks at me with those brown puppy dog eyes. I hear myself say, "It's just… I just would have liked to have spent more time with you." I swear, I am so lame.

"Next time." Johnny brushes hair off my cheek. "I promise."

✳✳✳

We are in Carla's kitchen doing beauty parlor. Ronnie helps us. She's a beautician with her own hair salon. We have steam rollers, make-up, manicures, pedicures, facials, the works. Ronnie is wrapping rollers around my hair. She's got these long fake fingernails decorated with stripes and tiny rhinestones and I am afraid she's going to impale me. Bruce Springsteen is blasting and she dances as she twists my hair. She's a real Jersey girl.

Carla talks about her date with Troy. "Then we go see that vampire movie." She is painting her nails blood red.

"You were late getting home," says her mother.

"Did he kiss you?" You can ask questions like that in front of Ronnie.

"He kissed me like a gentlemen. His lips were soft. He's a great kisser."

"Where was this? In the car?"

"No," says Ronnie. "On the front porch for fifteen minutes. I was watching."

"Mom!"

"Me and all the neighbors. It was better than what was on TV." Ronnie is cracking up.

Carla scowls, but we know she is proud of her front porch kiss. We are all laughing, but underneath I am so jealous—of her date, of her kiss, of her mother, of her life—everything.

"So, Ronnie... Do you ever hear from Sean Shanahan?" I ask.

Ronnie drops her comb. "*What* did you say?"

Carla is shocked. "HARLEY!"

Ronnie picks up the comb and starts rolling my hair again, but now I can feel her hands shaking. "What makes you ask, Harley?"

"Me and Carla found my mother's yearbook and he wrote her a note."

"Oh?" Ronnie sounds *very* interested. "What did it say?"

"Harley, just drop it, will you?" Carla knifes me with her eyes. I don't care. I want to know.

"It said something about the wild times they had together."

Ronnie sprays my hair with a puff of water. I can see her face in the mirror. She looks upset. "I think you should ask your mother about that, Harley." Her voice cracks. "I haven't seen Carla's father in fourteen years."

✴✴✴

The last place on earth I want to be is at my father's gas station, but that is where I am. If anybody I know drives by, I will die. My mother has taken Lily and Bean to the dentist and dropped me here because she wants to use me later as a slave at the supermarket.

I hide out in the waiting room which consists of one metal chair and an ashtray. Out in the garage, my father is fixing a flat tire, whistling "Home on the Range" off-key. He's driving me nuts.

I sketch a series of princesses with blank faces. Hmmm... Maybe I should do two portraits—*after* Anastasia is accepted by her grandmother, a new portrait could appear onstage with her features filled in. Yes. I know I'm onto something. I can't wait to show Bud Roman. I am absolutely in love with this project.

My father pokes his head in. "You okay?" The creases in his forehead are lined with grease. He looks tired. "You want to help me out? Wash windshields or something?"

Oh, right. I can just see me lurching around in public with a paper towel and a spray bottle. "Uh, I don't think so."

He stands there like he doesn't know what to do with me. He reaches into his pocket and offers me a handful of oily coins. "Here. Get yourself a Coke or something. I've got to finish a tune-up."

I don't really want a Coke, but I think he's trying to be nice. I take the coins. "Thanks, Dad." He heads back into the garage, his cowboy boots clomping against the cement floor. When I was little, I used to love to put the coins in the machine and watch the soda appear in the slot. This is what he remembers, and I wonder if he realizes that I am now a grown woman.

I slip out the front of the gas station and go over to the soda machine, one eye on the pumps. The only person there is a gray minivan-mother, filling 'er up. As I drop the quarters into the slot and listen to them clank, it hits me: Roger did not own this service station when I was born. He was a foreman in the chemical plant that polluted all the lakes back when Grandpa Harley was the vice president of the company. He did not buy the gas station until I was five years old. I am sure of this. I am *positive*. That birth certificate is a lie.

chapter 9

Me and Carla walk down the hall to homeroom where they take attendance and say the Pledge of Allegiance. The auditorium in the daylight no longer looks Olympian; now it looks all drab and brown. Lenape High is so small the entire school fits in the auditorium, freshman through seniors. A lot of people don't say the Pledge of Allegiance, they just stand up and slouch. Roger told me you used to *have* to say it, but then the Supreme Court changed the rules. I stopped saying it in sixth grade because it was no longer fashionable.

Johnny is never in homeroom because he reads the morning announcements over the P.A. system. Boring Lenape stuff like if there's a spaghetti dinner at the firehouse, or who received the Daughters of the American Revolution award.

Carla is just sunbeams and rainbows and all she talks about is Troy, Troy, Troy.

"One more month 'til the Spring Ball," says Carla. "Guess who asked me to go."

"Oh, well, let's see," I say. "Vic?"

"Actually, he did ask me too, but I said no." Carla is making me sick with these gloats. "It's Troy."

"What a surprise." I would like to be happy for her, but I am too envious. Carla is getting out of hand. She is rubbing it in deep.

"Do you think Johnny is going to ask you?"

"Come on, Carla. How the hell should I know?"

"Testy, testy."

"I really don't want to talk about it." I am sorry to be so mean, but half the school already has a date for the Spring Ball, and I am the cheese, standing alone.

"My mom is buying me a new dress and everything." Carla gets in another dig. I think she is punishing me for asking her mother about Sean Shanahan.

"Shut up." There are tears in my eyes. I blink and turn my head away. My emotions just ooze all over the place, I swear. It's so embarrassing.

"There's still time, Harley." Carla's voice turns kind. She knows when she's gone too far. "There's still time for Johnny to ask you."

At that moment over the P.A. system Johnny's voice booms: "AND REMEMBER KIDS, THERE'S STILL TIME TO BUY YOUR TICKETS FOR THE SPRING BALL! DON'T MISS OUT ON A SPECTACULAR EVENING OF FUN AND ROMANCE! ASK THAT SPECIAL SOMEONE TODAY!"

Oh, please, God, let him ask me, I pray. I will clean my room and wash and dry the dishes and get straight A's and be a sweet darling angel if he just asks me to the Spring Ball.

✳✳✳

I am in Bud Roman's office, underneath the stage. I had no idea that these rooms were down here. It's a secret world where the actors rush through an underground passage to change costumes between scenes and put on makeup. There is a girl's dressing room, a boy's dressing room, a storage room for scenery and costumes, and Bud Roman's tiny office.

Yellow legal pads are scattered everywhere. Broadway show posters cover the walls. Stuffing spills out of the arms of the sofa that Bud Roman sits on. He is flipping through my sketches. I am holding my breath.

"Well, Motorcyle Mama, I like where you're heading. First act, blank face, second act, fuzzy face, third act, complete face. Problem is getting the supplies." Bud Roman is chewing on a pencil like he's smoking a cigarette. "You wanna use oil and canvas, but it's *so* expensive you'll eat up the entire budget for the play."

I realize that I have no idea how much the supplies cost because Granny always got them for me. I don't want him to think I'm totally out of it. "Maybe I can use acrylic and poster board or something?" I suggest.

"Yeah, but even that's pricey, when we're talking life-size…" He shakes his head. "If these idiot politicians had their way, there wouldn't *be* art classes or theater, just target practice." He tosses my sketches onto my lap. "Don't get me started."

I must look concerned because he jumps up and claps his hands like he's ready to get down to business. "Don't worry, Motorcyle Mama. I'll talk to Emma—uh, Miss Posey. We'll figure something out."

✳✳✳

Johnny is not waiting for me at my locker and Carla is not waiting for me at the gym. Fine. I don't care. I don't care about anybody or anything except the Drama Club play.

I walk down the steps to the Pond Hole. I am going nowhere in particular, maybe uptown. That cute blond guy is standing there, smoking. I smile at him and keep walking.

"Hey, slow down," he calls to me. I stop. "Come over here, beautiful." Beautiful! No one has ever said that to me before. I shuffle over to him. He really does have these incredible gray eyes.

"What's your name?"

"Harley," I say. "Harley Columba. What's yours?"

"Evan Lennon."

My jaw drops further than Tattletale Betty Jo Clemings', I'm sure. "Lennon? That's so wild. I was born at a John Lennon concert. Well, not at *his* concert, but a memorial concert for him."

"Yeah?" Evan grins. "What are you, named after the motorcycle?"

I giggle. "No, my grandmother." Then I'm serious. "But she just died."

Evan inhales his cigarette. "That's sad." He offers me a smoke. "Want one?"

My first public cigarette. I am not sure, but I say, "Sure." My hands shake a little as I hold it to my mouth. Evan lights it for me. I take a tiny puff and pray I don't cough.

"Are you new?" I ask.

"No. Used." Evan smiles, and in that moment he does look wise and weary, like he's all grown up. Then the moment is past and he is young and gorgeous and blond. I've never been this close to a blond boy before. I wish I could touch his hair. "I'm from Wynokie," he says. "My folks got divorced and divided me in half. My dad just moved to Lenape and dragged me with him. So here I am. Weekdays, anyway."

"*That's* sad. Not the you being here part, the part about your parents getting divorced." I can't stop staring at his gray eyes. I wonder if everyone just stares at him when he talks, hypnotized by the color.

"Yeah. It was savage." Evan throws down his cigarette and grounds it out with his boot. "You want a ride home?"

I'm impressed. "You have a car?" I'm nervous. I've never been alone in a boy's car before. But I stroll along beside him down into the Pond Hole like I do this every day. I hope no one sees me with this cigarette, but it is still too long to put out. If my parents find out I'm smoking, they'll kill me. Plus, I don't know if I want to get a smoking reputation. Then again, maybe I do. Maybe I'm just wild.

Hardly any of the high school kids have a car in Lenape. The town is so small you can get around the whole thing in less than an hour on a bicycle, though nobody would be caught dead riding one. Just a few senior guys have some old clunkers they work on. Certainly no one has a car like the one we stop in front of.

It's blue. It's gleaming. It's a space ship. It is the coolest car I've ever seen.

"Wow," I say. "What is it?"

"A Camaro. My dad got it for my birthday."

He opens the passenger door for me. I certainly am being squired around by polite boys. I toss the cigarette to the ground and scoot onto the white leather seat. The car smells like hours of Turtle Wax. I cannot believe I am doing this.

Evan slides in behind the wheel. He turns the key. The engine kicks over with a deep, quiet roar, like it's itching to go fast. I hope no one is home at my house. My parents will have a fit if they see me pull up in this car.

Evan eases out of the Pond Hole, all casual and confident with one hand on the wheel. "Where to?"

"Willoby Court."

The blue Camaro thunders through town and everyone turns and looks at us. Evan's hair is golden silk fluttering out the window. My stomach trembles; it is so exciting to be riding next to a guy who is driving. I wish we could cruise past Johnny's house and give him a look, but that would be too crass.

Evan swings the Camaro down Willoby Court. We rumble right up in front of my house. My mother's car is not in the driveway. Thank you, God. I see Mrs. Perez across the street pull her curtains back. Get a good look, you old biddy.

I turn to Evan. "Thanks a lot."

His gray eyes are so deep, they look like they can see all the way into outer space. "You're welcome," he says. "Anytime."

I hop out of the car and close the door. It is heavy, not tinny like the door on my father's pickup truck. The Camaro roars off down the street. I watch Mrs. Perez shake her head and drop the curtain as I waltz into the house.

✶✶✶

"Please, Carla. If you guys go with me, then it won't be so obvious." It is Tuesday night. I *have* to go to the coffeehouse.

"Me and Troy are going to the movies."

"You can go to the movies any time. The coffeehouse is only tonight."

"Come on, Harley. The way Johnny treated you last time… he totally ignored you."

"I'm begging you on my hands and knees." If I have to, I will go there alone, I swear.

"Let me ask Troy."

"Thank you from the bottom of my heart." I hang up.

I lay out my outfit. See-through black blouse over a tight black tee and tight black pants. Very nice. The phone rings. I answer it.

"Okay," says Carla. "Troy will drive. Meet us over my house at seven-thirty."

"I love you."

"You owe me."

Now the hard part. I walk downstairs to the Barcalounger. The ice cubes are tiny white islands floating in Roger's drink. He sips. The islands clink against each other. Wind chimes in a glass. "You need anything, Dad?" I approach with caution.

"What do you want, Harley?"

"I want to go to the coffeehouse over in Wynokie."

"A coffeehouse? What's a coffeehouse?"

"A place to hang out and drink coffee."

"No."

"WHY?"

He punches the remote, but slowly, like it's a great effort. Ever since Granny's funeral, he seems tired all the time. "Since when do you drink coffee? I know what you're up to."

"I drink a *lot* of coffee." This is not true, but how can he know it? Does he know about Johnny? No, it is impossible. I have been very discreet. "Please, Dad?"

"Your mother says you didn't clean up your room."

"I *did*! I spent *hours*. It's never clean according to her." Peppy is not home tonight; my fate lies in Roger's hands.

"The answer is no."

"Come on, Dad—"

"Keep asking, and you'll be grounded for the rest of the week."

"But why?"

"*Because I said so.*"

I feel the fuse ignite inside my stomach. The war has gone on too long. The conditions are too unfair. The fireball burns bigger and brighter until the words explode out of my mouth. "I HATE THIS HOUSE! I HATE THIS HOUSE, AND I HATE EVERYBODY IN IT!" I cry and run out of the family room. I stomp up the stairs. I slam my door. I open it and slam it again. Harder. I open it and slam it a third time as hard as I can. WHAM! It feels good. I throw myself on the bed and wail.

I hear my father's cowboy boots pound up the steps. My door bursts open. He grabs my legs and flips me over. He is a dragon standing over me, breathing fire. He roars. "YOU ARE GROUNDED FOR A MONTH, YOUNG LADY. YOU COME STRAIGHT HOME FROM SCHOOL FOR A MONTH."

I turn back on my belly. I sob. I kick my feet. "I don't care," I cry. "I don't CARE!"

"LOOK AT ME, HARLEY MARIE," the dragon thunders.

"No."

"TURN OVER AND LOOK AT ME WHEN I'M TALKING TO YOU!"

"NO."

Roger yanks me backwards off the bed. My hair rips through his claws. He spins me around and forces me to look at him. Flames shoot out of his mouth. "WHEN I TELL YOU TO LOOK AT ME, YOU LOOK AT ME, DO YOU UNDERSTAND?"

My mouth is frozen shut and I cannot answer. The dragon roars. "ANSWER ME!"

I open my mouth, but nothing comes out. The dragon's claw rises high above his head and sweeps down toward my face. I try to duck, but the claw knocks me on the side of the head, and the world turns black and starry. I feel myself falling, falling onto the bed, falling into the quiet darkness.

Far way, I hear Roger's cowboy boots leave my room. He closes my door. I listen for his footsteps to go downstairs. I sniffle. Breathe. Breathe. Breathe. I get up. I look at the clock. Six-thirty. One hour. I go in the bathroom and put water on my face. I look in the mirror. I open the cabinet and dig way in the back for my little plastic makeup bag. Zip. I fumble with Peppy's lipstick and eye shadow and blush. I make up my face with war paint.

I go back into my room. I take off my clothes and put on my coffeehouse outfit. I walk over to the window. I pop off the screen. I slide open the glass. I put a stool under the window. I step up. I put one leg over the ledge, then the other. I push myself out the window and onto the roof of the garage. I slide the window shut behind me. I shimmy down the roof and hop onto the picnic table below. I jump off. My feet touch the ground. I am free.

chapter 10

Troy has a beat-up old station wagon. The three of us sit in the front seat. How cozy. Carla twines around Troy worse than a snake. I worry that she is going to put her foot on the gas by mistake and kill all of us.

I don't tell them I am an escapee because I don't want them to get weird and not go or something.

"Ya got enough room over there, Harley?" Troy seems to be a polite boy in addition to being gorgeous. Carla is practically sitting on his lap, so I have all the room in the world.

"Yeah."

The coffeehouse turns out to be this little hole-in-the-wall in the center of Wynokie. I guess it's a step up from the bowling alley. We push our way through the crowd. I search for signs of Prudence Clarke, but the room appears to be diva-free. There is a table right up front.

"Let's sit there," says Troy.

"No way!"

"Harley, if we're going to do this, let's do it right. Johnny can't ignore you if you're sitting in front of his face." It's easy for Carla to talk when she has Troy the Magnificent dangling from her arm.

They pull me over to the table and push me down. A thin, wispy waitress comes by for our order. I try not to look at Johnny and Reed, but they are standing there singing only five feet away. Finally I sneak a peek. Johnny looks right at me and smiles and mouths the words, "Hi!"

"Hi!" I mouth back. Good. He knows I'm alive.

The wispy girl comes back with three coffees. She sets two mugs in front of Troy and Carla. She turns to me. "Johnny in the band says to tell you this is on him." She places the steaming mug in front of me. I am amazed. I look up at Johnny. He is grinning. "Thank you," I mouth. He winks. I wrap my fingers around the mug and feel the heat soak into my hands. I put the edge against my lips and sip. Mmmm. Molten java.

"Well, what do you know," says Carla, who has watched the transaction with an impressed look on her face. "The boy has some class after all."

I am too happy to be smug. I sit there and beam and sip. Johnny and Reed finish their song. The room applauds.

"Thanks," Johnny says as he steps up to the mike. "And now we'd like to do one more tune before our break. This one goes out to Harley." My mouth falls open. Johnny nods at Reed. He strums a chord and Johnny joins in. They harmonize about a guy who wants this girl to run away with him. I am riveted. I can't believe Johnny is singing me a song. I look at Carla. Her eyes are enormous, like she can't believe it either.

Then it's over and the room is clapping. Johnny and Reed set down their guitars. Johnny strolls over to our table and sits next to me. He throws his arm around me and gives me a long, soggy kiss. He pulls back and looks into my eyes.

"Did you like the song?"

"Loved it," I whisper.

Reed pulls up a chair. "Hey, you two, knock it off."

I giggle. "Reed, Johnny, do you know Troy? You know Carla, right, Reed? Carla's my best friend."

"And I'm her father," says a voice like whiskey and ice behind me. Oh my God. Oh my GOD. Roger, the Fire-Breathing Dragon, is making his first public appearance.

"Dad, what are you doing here?" My face gets red and my breath is quick. Breathe. Breathe. Breathe. I look at Carla. She is in shock.

"No, Harley Marie. What are *you* doing here?" Roger's voice is quiet, but it roars.

Johnny and Reed scramble up from the table like a cartoon in fast motion. "Well, we'd better get back to work. Nice to meet you, Mr. Columba," says Johnny with a grin, pretending everything is normal. I am dying.

"Who the hell are you?" I swear, Roger is all charm.

"I'm a friend of your daughter's, and we're just hanging out, singing some tunes." Johnny is not thrown. "We know each other from church." Good pitch, Johnny, but Roger isn't swinging.

"Harley does not have permission to be here. Get your jacket, young lady, and let's go." My father grabs my arm.

"Oh, come on, Mr. Columba," Carla tries. "Me and Troy will take her home."

"Harley is going nowhere with you, Carla," Roger the dragon snarls. "And if your mother cared about you, she wouldn't let you run around town like a tramp. She should learn from her own mistakes. You can tell her I said so."

"*What—*" This is the first time Carla has felt the full force of a Roger attack, and she is speechless.

My father yanks me away from the table. "I'll call you," I tell Carla.

"Oh, no you won't," growls Roger. "You are grounded to eternity."

✱   ✱

It is hell being inside this house full time. I have no privileges: no phone, no dessert, no television. As if I care. People talk to me, but I do not answer them. I walk about the house in silence. I go to school, come home and shut myself in my room. I listen to dead John Lennon and dead Kurt Cobain and dead Janis Joplin because I want to hear the music of people with tragic endings. I stand at my easel and paint a screaming girl diving off a cliff. I paint like dead Vincent Van Gogh, thick, gobby, furious strokes. Red, orange, purple, black. Maybe I should cut off a chunk of my ear.

I write a poem: "Escape," by Harley Columba.

I hide away
here, alone,
separate from the rest of you.
In my heart
a candle is still burning,
a tiny light still burning.
You cannot put out my fire.

I am drained. All I want to do is sleep. I carry my harlequin clown into bed with me. "Papa loves you, forever and a day." I take his hand with the wooden baton and jab it into my pillow. I pretend my pillow is Roger. I close my eyes and drift to the place right before sleep….

I am in a dark theater. I am the only one in the audience. I wait for the show to begin. The curtain rises. My harlequin, now as big as a man, comes on stage. He waves his wooden baton. He shouts, "*En garde!*"

Another man in a black cape leaps out of the wings. He

charges the harlequin with a lance. He spears the harlequin in the heart. I scream, "No!" and jump onstage. The harlequin lies on his back, dying. I try to pull the mask off his face, but it does not budge. I turn, crying for help, to the man in the cape, but he has disappeared. I take the wooden baton from the harlequin's hand and raise it above my head. Now there is an audience, and they applaud.

✷✷✷

I am about to go into Honors English when I see Johnny and Reed walking down the hall. I run up to them. "Hey," I say.

Johnny doesn't stop. "What's up?" he says like he really doesn't want to know.

"Hey, Harley," says Reed. "You still grounded for eternity?"

My face gets red. "My father is a jerk."

Johnny walks faster. I stumble along next to him. He talks without looking at me. "You're…you're a good kid, Harley, but…"

Kid. The way he says it makes me feel five years old. He tosses Reed one of those guy looks.

Reed pats me on the head like an older brother. He grins down at me. "You hang in there, kid." He slaps Johnny on the back. Together they haul off down the hall. I am numb. I stand there eating their dust. I think this kid has just been dumped.

✷✷✷

No one is home. My mother and father are at work. My brother is over at Earl's. My sister is at work with my mother. I am a leper. I am in solitary confinement. I inhale the stillness. It smells good.

There is a scream in my belly that does not go away. I can't remember what my body feels like without it. It is part of me now, like another organ. My liver, my heart, and my scream.

I go to my father's liquor cabinet. Once before, Carla and I each drank three of Ronnie's beers from the refrigerator and threw up. Now I uncork the decanter of vodka. I pick up a glass and pour in the clear liquid. Glub, glub, glub. I take a sip. Fire. It tastes like fire. I drink the firewater. It burns down my throat and washes into my belly. It splashes over my scream and douses it with a hiss. The scream is still there but it feels cooler now, less red and raw. I take another sip of vodka. And another. I take three big gulps and empty the glass. I extinguish my scream.

I pour water into the decanter so the level of the liquid is the same as before I started. I rinse out my glass. Inside, I can no longer feel my scream. It is not peace, but it is something.

I wobble into my parent's bedroom. The curtains are drawn and it is dark and cool. The room spins. I lean against the wall and take a breath.

I open the door to their closet. I reach up to the top shelf and feel for a key. It is there, next to a pile of winter sweaters. I push their clothes on the hangers aside and pull out a steel safety box where they keep their important papers. I insert the key into the box. If Peppy has my original birth certificate, she would stash it here. I turn the key and the lid pops open.

Roger is in charge of the box, so it is neat and orderly with clear printing on the file labels. I flip to the file marked "Certificates." I rifle through the papers and stop. My birth certificate *is* in here. It's exactly the same as the one that came in the mail, only it's the original, not a copy. Why would Peppy tell me she lost it when they moved?

I glance at Peppy and Roger's marriage certificate. The words on the second line stop me. "Bride's Occupation: Secretary. Groom's Occupation: Factory foreman." Wait a second. *Factory foreman.* So I'm not crazy. How come my birth certificate says he owns a service station? It makes no sense.

"Harley Marie, what are you doing?" I jump. My mother stands behind me.

I drop the marriage certificate. "You scared me!"

"What are you doing in my bedroom?" Peppy is fuming.

"Nothing." I swear, my mother is a stealth bomber.

"I don't want you snooping around my room, Harley Marie!"

"Why not? You're always snooping around mine. It's the only way to get information around this house." The room is spinning. I think I might be really drunk.

"Watch your mouth, young lady." Peppy's lips are white. "Are you looking for something?"

"You know I am." The liquor makes me daring. "Why did you tell me you lost my birth certificate when it's right here?"

Peppy looks away from me. She bends down and picks the marriage certificate up off the floor. She places it back in the file and closes the box. "Not this again, Harley."

"How old was I when Dad bought the gas station?"

"Why do you want to know? Is there something wrong with you? You look funny." Peppy is staring at me like I just crawled out of a hole.

"You told me you lost it because you didn't want me to see it said he owned a service station, right? Because he was a foreman when I was born, right?" I have to watch it. I'm starting to slur my words.

Peppy moves close to me and sniffs. "What is that smell?"

I must have vodka breath. I try to talk without opening my mouth. "Well, *wasn't* he a foreman?"

Peppy turns away from me. She locks the box and pushes it back into the closet. She doesn't put the key back on the shelf. "Harley, I lost your birth certificate when we moved. You needed it for kindergarten. When I sent away to get a copy, your father owned the gas station, he wasn't a factory foreman anymore. It's that simple."

"Then why didn't you just tell me that? Why did you lie about it?"

My mother grabs me by the arm. "I'm getting a little tired of your attitude, Harley Marie. Go to your room. Get up there and don't come down for dinner. And if I find out that you've been drinking, you will never leave this house."

I yank my arm out of her grip. I look her in the eye. Her face is a blur. "I am so sick of all these secrets," I inform her. "I am so sick of all these lies." I wobble out of the bedroom and grip the banister as I head up the stairs.

chapter 11

I do not want to go into the band room. I do not want to see Johnny. It is too hard to concentrate knowing he is in the back of the room behind the drums. I do not want to play my solo. I am sick of it. I am tired of being surrounded by mutant band members. I heard even Nancy Sidebottom, this total freak who plays the tuba, is going to the Spring Ball. Everyone but me. I open the door and walk in.

Everybody's already got their instruments and they're in the middle of tuning up without me. Marsha Miller, who plays first clarinet, second chair, has got her cheeks all puffed out and is blowing with this smug look on her face, like she is some kind of conquering hero. Good. I don't care. Mr. Michaels taps his baton and raises his arms. Everyone stops playing. They all look at me. "Columba, you're late." Mr. Michaels is dressed in a black suit and tie as if he is a grand maestro, about to open at Carnegie Hall.

"So shoot me." The words spill out of my mouth before I have a chance to stop them.

"*What* did you say?"

I don't know what's come over me. "Sorry."

Mr. Michaels sets down his baton. "I'll do better than shoot you, Columba. I'll demote you. You're now second chair and Miller is first."

His words sting my face. The rest of the band shifts and titters. I want to burst into tears. But there is no way I am going to stand in the middle of the band room bawling my eyes out with Johnny watching. Instead I raise my chin, defiant. "Fine," I say. "I quit."

Mr. Michaels' face turns purple and for a moment, I think he is going to explode. When he finally speaks, his voice quakes. "Get your clarinet and get out."

I march into the back room where the instruments are stashed. I know I am acting crazy, but I can't seem to stop myself. I pick up my clarinet case. I head back through the practice room, ignoring the whispers and the finger pointing. I sneak a peek at Carla. Carla shrugs and rolls her eyes. I want to look at Johnny, but I don't. I head out the door and listen to the tap of Mr. Michaels' baton behind me. The band bursts into Beethoven's Fifth. Da da da DUMMmmm…

∗   ∗

"Harley Marie, get down here!" My father is not using the intercom, he just bellows from the bottom of the steps. I open my bedroom door and walk halfway down the stairs.

He stands in the alcove waving a piece of paper. My report card has arrived.

"C in Algebra. C in French. Incomplete in Band. C in World History. C in Science. C in Physical Education, for chrissake. The only subject you got a B in is English. Not one A."

"I got an A in art," I correct him.

"Art doesn't count."

I say nothing. I just stand there.

"You got all two's in effort and conduct. You are an A student. What is wrong with you?"

I say nothing.

"Answer me!" Roger's face twists into a gargoyle. I gaze at it, amazed by the transformation. "ANSWER ME, HARLEY MARIE!"

"I don't know," I mumble.

"I don't know," Roger whines, mimicking me. He sounds like a thirty-four year old baby.

"Grow up." I think this in my head, but somehow the words come out of my mouth.

"Did you say something?"

"Nothing." My skin itches. I squirm. "Can I go now?"

"Go ahead." He is disgusted. I turn and walk up the steps. Far away I hear his voice. "I don't know what we're going to do with you. I just don't know."

✳   ✳

"Can you stay a minute, Harley?" Mr. Donovan is discreet and asks me after most other people have left. "What's your next class? I'll give you a pass."

I am completely thrown. Mr. Donovan has never asked me to stay after Honors English. Never. "Uh…French," I stammer. "No, wait…lunch. I have lunch."

"This'll only take a second. Sit down, Harley. Don't look so scared." Today Mr. Donovan's bow tie is bright blue with little gold stars.

I plop down in the closest desk. I hit my knee. "Ouch!"

"You okay?" Mr. Donovan's eyes are concerned. I nod. "Good." He paces. "I'll come right out and say it. Is something wrong? Your grades are slipping. You're not paying attention. You don't participate in class like you used to. You were one of my top students. Now you're not even doing average work."

I wish everyone would get off my back, I really do. I fidget and gaze out the window.

"Harley, are you doing drugs?"

"NO!" I am so surprised, the words burst out of me. "Did you think it was that? It's not that."

"What, then?" Mr. Donovan is trying hard, he is, but I have been trained to state only my name, rank and serial number. I can't look at him. I say nothing. I cannot tell a stranger as nice as Mr. Donovan about the horrors of the House of Columba.

"Harley, listen to me. I saw you smoking a cigarette the other day. I saw you get into an older boy's car. I was crossing the Pond Hole just when you were getting in."

So that's it. He thinks I'm a druggie because of Evan. "I don't smoke," I say. "It was my first one."

"I see," he says and turns away. What I see is Mr. Donovan doesn't believe me. Fine. He is a grownup and not to be trusted. For a second he almost had me fooled.

I offer him a crumb. "I'm adopted," I hear myself say. Mr. Donovan's face gets all surprised. Then he tries to act like he hears this news every day.

"That… that must have been a shock for you. To find out."

"Yeah."

"When did your parents tell you?"

"They haven't told me anything, but I have plenty of evidence."

"I see." Mr. Donovan gives me that doubtful "I see" again.

"I've always known I was adopted." I want him to believe me. I want *anyone* to believe me. "Ever since I was little."

"All kids feel that way at one time or another." Mr. Donovan puts his hand on my shoulder. It feels weird having a teacher touch me. "Harley, you are a smart young lady and I'm going to give you some advice." Oh, no. Mr. Donovan is morphing into a geek right in front of my eyes. "Get a job, Harley. Be independent. Earn some money. People like you need to be on their own."

Right. I'm not even old enough to flip burgers at McDonalds. "Doing what?"

"I'll talk to Mrs. Sousa. You know her, right? She's a guidance counselor."

"You mean a shrink?"

Mr. Donovan laughs. "No, she just steers you in the right direction. Like careers, college, jobs. Things like that. Okay?"

I am suspicious. "Okay."

***

Instead of study hall, I am in Mrs. Sousa's office. She is two thousand years old, all bent over with gray hair and knobby fingers. The only guidance she looks like she can give is where to buy a cemetery plot.

"Now, honey, what are your goals?" She sniffs and her upper lip brushes against a big wart on the tip of her nose.

I sigh a Peppy sigh, long and deep. "My goal is to be an artist."

"An artist!" she cackles. "My, my! A lofty pursuit, but impractical." Mrs. Sousa's eyelashes are white like spider webs. Her teeth are kernels of corn. Every sentence that comes out of her mouth sounds like it's from some how-to-be-a-good-guidance-counselor textbook. "Even though you're a freshman, you must think about your future. You should be taking computer classes. That's where the jobs are."

I am amazed. "You mean I should study computers whether I like them or not? Just to get a job? Is that what you're saying?"

"I'm saying that you must prepare for college."

harley
like a person

"I'm not going to college, I'm going to art school in New York." Now that the words are out of my mouth, I realize that, yes, that is *exactly* what I'm going to do. "John Lennon went to art school before he became a Beatle. That's what I want to do."

Mrs. Sousa shakes her head as if I am brain dead. "Honey, you must get your head out of the clouds. Only a handful of people succeed in the creative fields." She coughs and blows out a puff of garlic. Eew.

"Well, why can't I be one of the ones who do? I mean, somebody's got to, right?"

Mrs. Sousa waves away the question with her gnarly hand. "My job is to give practical advice, not encourage pipe dreams."

I am getting a little impatient with this woman. This is such a waste of time. I squirm in my chair. "Look, Mr. Donovan said you could help me get a job. I need money. My parents don't give me an allowance."

Mrs. Sousa brightens. "That, I can do. In fact, a woman phoned this morning, Mrs. Tuttle, asking for a girl to help her with housework after school, once a week. Are you interested?"

Housework never really interested me, but I need the money. The dragons will let me out of the dungeon to go to work, I'm sure. With my own money, I could get to New York City, no problem. I wouldn't have to beg from Peppy and Roger anymore. I would be an independent woman. "I'll take it."

chapter 12

My new employer, Mrs. Tuttle, lives across town on Washington Hill, the ritziest section of Lenape Lakes. Two marble lions guard the entrance, an invisible line that separates the folks on the hill from the rest of the serfs of Lenape. A polished brass plaque reads: "Washington Hill Estates." Enter at your own risk.

I step across the line. A blue jay swoops down and screams, Intruder! Intruder! Maybe I should have worn a dress.

Old oak trees line both sides of the street. Their roots poke through the sidewalk, cracking it into raised chunks. No tract homes up here; these houses are historic. Everyone's really into brass plaques over the door, engraved with words like "Warwick House" or "Built 1697." I walk past a stone house that says it was the headquarters for the Continental Army and that George Washington slept there. I think that's where this snoot named Lucy Stowe lives. I wonder if ol' George sleeps in her bedroom, haunting her. I see an acorn still in its shell on the sidewalk and put it in my pocket. I will plant a piece of Washington Hill in my own backyard.

I walk up to number 401 and stop. Mrs. Tuttle's house is a three-story white wooden manor, with a porch that circles the entire house. A wicker swing sways in the breeze. Whoa. I've always dreamed of living in a house like this. Well, now I get to clean it.

I ring the bell. I hear high heels click to the door. A silver-haired woman opens it, her skin the same color as the porcelain face of my harlequin. She looks like a grandmother you don't really hug.

She smiles. "Hello! Come in. You must be Harley Columba. I'm

Eliza Tuttle." She has a sing-songy voice, gentle and creaky, like a rocking chair. She offers me her hand.

I reach out and shake it. "I'm very pleased to meet you," I say, all formal and polite. I stand up straight, put my shoulders back and walk into the house.

It's a museum. Oriental rugs cover the hardwood floors. Oil paintings decorate the walls. Plants and trees and bushes bloom from every corner like some mad gardener has been on the loose.

I check out this huge painting of a woman holding a bunch of drooping red roses. "Nice."

"Do you like it?" Mrs. Tuttle blows a puff of dust off the corner of the gold frame.

"Yes, very much. I love the use of contrasting colors." I speak as if I'm this informed art critic.

"Oh? Do you paint?"

"Yes, yes I do. Right now I'm painting a portrait for the school play." I swear, I don't know what's come over me. I'm talking like some prep school geek. It must be the vibe of the neighborhood. "But I'm probably going to have to use acrylics 'cause we've got no budget. It's difficult to get the flesh colors right."

"Oh, don't get my dander up," says Mrs. Tuttle. "Taxes, taxes, and not a penny for the arts." She gazes up at the woman with the drooping roses. "I used to dabble myself, you know." I notice the signature on the painting. It says, "Eliza Tuttle."

"You painted this?" I am impressed.

Mrs. Tuttle sighs, all wistful. "A long time ago. When the boys were in diapers and the light was right for painting." She flicks on a lamp. "When *did* the light change in here…."

"Well, you should keep it up. It's fun." Listen to me, giving this rich lady a pep talk.

"Oh, honey, I've tried. I can't seem to capture the feeling."

On the coffee table I see this huge book called *New York City*. "Ooo, have you been to New York?"

"We used to go all the time, before my husband died." Mrs. Tuttle brushes her fingertips across the cover of the book, as if she is caressing a cheek. "Have you?"

"I was born there, but I've never been back. I plan to visit soon. That's why I took this job."

"Any special reason?"

To find my real parents, I want to say. "No," I fib. "Just to see the sights. The Metropolitan Museum. You know."

"Well, it's just a bus ride away." When she says that, I realize she's right. New York City is just a bus ride away, not four zillion light years. I can go there. By myself.

Mrs. Tuttle gets me started dusting. She tells me she has a regular housekeeper, but she needs me for extra jobs. She turns on some classical music. Flutes and violins skip through the air. Happy Mozart music. For a moment, it makes me wish I still played the clarinet.

I polish the wood and realize how nice the furniture is compared to the junk at the House of Columba. She has a whole wall of figurines from other lands like Europe and Asia. I pick up each piece and pretend I'm in that country. A beer stein. Poof! I'm in Germany. A carved wooden lady with a basket on her head. Poof! I'm in Africa. It's fun. Civilized.

I buff the coffee table. The *New York City* book lies there, tempting me. I lift the cover and sneak a peek. I open to a dark castle called the Dakota, surrounded by a wrought-iron fence and gargoyles. I try not to gasp, but out comes a soft "oh!" I know the Dakota is the building where John Lennon lived and died. *Here*, I think. *Here is where he took his last breath*. I am so lost in the photograph that I don't hear Mrs. Tuttle come into the room.

"Tea time!"

"Ah!" I jump. "You scared me." I shut the book with a bang.

"Sorry. Come sit down, Harley. Take a break." I follow Mrs. Tuttle into the kitchen. "Oh, it's good to have a young woman in the house!"

On the table, she has laid out two cups of tea and cookies, which, she informs me, are biscuits, like tea in London. I pull out a chair as if I live here. I realize that I feel at home. Comfortable. I sip my tea and munch on a biscuit. Mrs. Tuttle chats about her last trip to Paris, and how the how whole city lights up at night. She talks about foreign countries like they are right next door, not impossible dreams. I listen, enthralled. I wonder if she has hired me to do the housework or just to have someone to talk to.

After tea, I finish dusting and Mrs. Tuttle hands me some cash. "Next week we'll start on the windows. Okay?"

"Sure." Windows don't sound as much fun as dusting, but I think I would pay *her* to visit this house again.

"Would you like to borrow that New York book? I know it's a little heavy…."

Oh, boy, would I! "Oh, I couldn't…."

"You can return it next week. Go on." Mrs. Tuttle picks up the book and hands it to me. It weighs five tons, but I don't care. I put the money in my pocket and the book inside my backpack and head home. I am starting to feel better. I am a working woman.

✻   ✻

On the way home, I swing by the bus stop, which is the old

railroad station. Some businessman converted part of the station into a luncheonette after the trains stopped running through Lenape, but he is not a local, and business is not good. The natives are like that here, circling like a wagon train. They boycott newcomers right out of town.

A red caboose is moored in the parking lot just for show. A long-haired guy with a green duffel bag climbs into an idling bus with a big "New York City" sign lit up across the front. New York City. Just a bus ride away.

Outside the luncheonette is a rack of schedules. I open one up and read. A bus leaves every hour, every half-hour in the morning. I stick three schedules in my backpack and head home on the train tracks, the railroad ties forcing me to walk in a rhythm of their own.

✳✳   ✳

I mosey into art class and Miss Posey is all smiles and hugs. "Close your eyes, Harley!" She grabs me and drags me over to the side of the room. "Okay, open." I blink. "Ta da!" she shouts. There, in the corner, is a large canvas, taller than me. *CANVAS*. Canvas is gold. I stare at it with my mouth open.

"You are so lucky, Harley. Someone just donated this to the art department. Even me, the old pro—I've never worked with a canvas this large." Miss Posey is bouncing on her toes, she is so excited.

"I…never expected canvas." I am in awe. I walk over and touch the edges of the coarse cloth. Pure. White. *Big*. I wonder if I can actually do this. "I love it." My voice is a whisper.

"They donated a bunch of oils, too." Miss Posey hands me a box full of tubes of paint. "You'll do the first two portraits in acrylic, the final one in canvas and oil. You can work during art class, study hall, lunch, after school, whenever. Set up a schedule with Lena, the girl who's playing Anastasia. I'm giving you a permanent pass so you can finish the portraits in time for opening night."

I am still in shock, so I barely hear her. *Canvas.*

"I'm also giving you your own key to the art room."

This part I hear. "My own key?" I look at her. In her hand is a big brass key dangling from a red shoelace.

Miss Posey grins. "Yeah. Just like having your own studio." She hands me the key. "Come in anytime you want, even if there's a class. You'll have your own little corner."

I turn the heavy key over and over in my hand, stroking the smooth polished brass. This is too good to be true. I am so happy, I give Miss Posey a hug. She laughs. "Thank you," I say. "Thank you, thank you, thank you!"

✱✱✱

I am walking down the hall when I see Johnny come out of his chemistry class with his arm around Prudence Clarke. She is giggling. Oh, no. No, *no*! Just when I let my guard down, life clobbers me on the head.

The happy couple does not see me. I turn around and duck into the girls' room. Debbie Nagle and Linda Kowalski are in there sneaking a cigarette. They are ready to jump when I open the door. Then they see it's me and relax. They sit on alert next to an open stall in case a teacher drops in. I lean against the sink and take a deep breath.

"Hey, Harley. You look like you seen a ghost," says Linda.

"Just that bitch, Prudence Clarke." I run the cold water and splash my face.

"OOOoooh. That bitch can sit on it," sniffs Debbie. "She thinks she's so hot."

"I heard she's going to the Spring Ball with Johnny Bruno," says Linda.

I turn off the water and stare at her. "Where did you hear that?"

"I was in the office after morning announcements and she was all, 'you should see my dress, it's black' and crap. She's such a user, she only wanted him back 'cause she can't get a date to the ball." Linda spits into the sink. "Harley, I swear your face is white. You wanna smoke?"

"Sure," I say. Smoking in the girls' room is an automatic suspension, but I am too upset to care. Linda hands me a Marlboro out of the red pack. She lights it with an old Zippo lighter like a pro. I inhale and try not to cough. "Thanks."

"Weren't you going with Johnny Bruno?" asks Debbie.

"Sorta."

"She did you a favor," Linda snorts. "He's gutless, going back to that skank. What a puppy."

Gutless? I never thought Johnny was gutless, but maybe he is. Maybe I've just had blinders on my eyes. Whatever he is, it doesn't stop my heart from aching. I must face it, I am still in love with the gutless puppy.

The bell rings. Damn. That means I am late for algebra. I am frantic. We toss our cigarettes into the toilet and flush. I grab my books.

"Looks like another detention," sighs Debbie.

"What do you care?" Linda brushes her hair. "We're already on permanent detention anyway."

"I've got to run. I've got Petranski next." My fingers smell like cigarettes. I don't have time to wash my hands. Mr. Petranski is famous for giving out detentions, and I have never had a detention in my life. I fly down the empty hall and stop in front of my classroom. The door is closed so I can't slip in the back and hope Mr. Petranski doesn't notice. I take a deep breath and walk in. The entire class turns around to see which unlucky Christian will get eaten by the lion. Mr. Petranski stops writing on the blackboard and puts his hands on his hips.

"Nice of you to join us, Harley." The back of Mr. Petranski's shirt sticks out of his pants and I see tuffs of hair poking through the crack.

"Sorry," I mumble and slide into my seat.

"Why are you late?" Mr. Petranski is right next to me. His breath smells like stale coffee.

Because this class is such a bore, I want to say, and so are you. "I don't know." I examine the top of my desk.

"How original. 'I don't know.' I'm getting tired of your attitude, Harley." Mr. Petranski scribbles something on a slip of paper and hands it to me like a traffic cop handing out a ticket. "Have your parents sign this. You can join your fellow delinquents in Room 103 after school tomorrow."

My fellow delinquents. I take the paper and stick it into my backpack. There is no way I can ask Peppy or Roger to sign my detention slip. None. Life is slipping through my fingers, and I can't get a grip.

✳✳   ✳

I am lying on my bed. I reach for Mrs. Tuttle's *New York City* book at the bottom of my night table. It's not there. Hmmm. I think Peppy has been snooping again. Then I look across to Lily's side of the room. There, underneath her headless Barbie and a box of crayons, is the book. That little jerk. I swear, I don't have a moment of privacy living in this house. I jump up and carry the book over to my bed.

I flip to the picture of the Empire State Building and gasp. Lily has scribbled all over the picture with a red crayon. Oh, no! Oh, no, no, *no*! I leaf through the pages. She has colored every one. Crayola rainbows stretch across the World Trade Center. Yellow bats and orange witches fly out of the Dakota's steeples. I have *had* it. This is too *much*. I slam the book. I open my bedroom door and yell down the stairs.

"LILY! LILY GET UP HERE RIGHT THIS SECOND!"

I stand there waiting for the little monster. What am I going to tell Mrs. Tuttle? She's going to fire me, I'm sure. This time I have been pushed over the edge.

"LILY!" I roar.

Lily's tiny face appears at the bottom of the stairs. "What?" she squeaks. She looks scared.

I run down, grab her arm and pull her up the stairs. I yank her into the bedroom. I jam the book in front of her face. "What do you call this?"

Lily starts crying. "I was just playing."

"Playing? What makes you think you can touch things that aren't yours? Do you understand that I'm going to lose my job because of you? What's the matter with you?" I shake her, I'm so angry.

Lily is sobbing now. "Harley, stop. You're hurting my arm!" She twists and turns, trying to get out of my grip.

"What were you *thinking*? Do you know you've ruined my *life*?"

"Harley, please!" Tears are streaming down her cheeks.

"Why did you *do* it? WHY? *WHY*?"

"I just want to be an artist like you!"

Her words stop me cold. I look down at my fist clenching her tiny arm. I see the fear in her face. She is looking at me the same way she looks at Roger. What is happening to me? The thunder of Roger has invaded my body; my hands are not my own. All the rage drains out of me, and I loosen my grip.

"Oh, Lily." I sweep her up into my arms. I press her body against mine and smooth back her hair. "Lily, I'm sorry. I'm so sorry. I didn't mean to hurt you." I cradle and rock her. She wraps her arms around my neck. I kiss her cheek. "Please forgive me, Lily. I don't know what's the matter with me. I'm so, so sorry...."

chapter 13

It is 3:00. I head for Room 103. Ms. Minelli is the dean, and I hear she revels in detention. She doesn't know me; I am not a regular like some of these people. Detention is in the same room for the whole school—we are all lumped together in one handy prison cell.

The bell rings. I sit down. Ms. Minelli's hair is dyed carrot-red and she's got age spots all over her face and hands. She takes attendance. I glance around the room. Most of the guys have spikey hair and look bored. Most of the girls are all gothic and dark. Everyone looks like they have a disease. This is a world where rah-rahs fear to tread.

"Harley Columba," calls Ms. Minelli.

"Here."

"Do you have your slip?"

"Uuhh, no. I forgot it."

"You *forgot* it?" Ms. Minelli brightens at the prospect of fresh meat. "Do you know what happens when you forget your slip, young lady?" I shake my head no. "DOUBLE DETENTION!" She sounds absolutely delighted. "You get to keep me company for forty minutes instead of twenty." Great. My mind races, trying to think up a forty-minute lie to offer Peppy and Roger.

She continues running down the list. Bobby Frankel. Maria Hernandez. Evan Lennon. "Evan Lennon? Is Evan Lennon here?" Ms. Minelli's eyes roam over the room. No answer. My heart flips. Evan, Evan, where are you? I could really use a buddy right now. As if God were actually listening to me this time, Evan flies into the room. "Sorry!" he says and collapses into the seat right next to mine.

"Thank you for gracing us with your presence, Mr. Lennon." Ms. Minelli is Moses on the Mount with her attendance book.

"Always a pleasure, Ms. Minelli." Evan smiles at her, and, I swear, the old bag almost swoons.

"Double detention for you today, young man. Five minutes late to detention earns double detention. Ten minutes late earns triple, so keep that in mind." Ms. Minelli is running this detention room like a military base. "You can stay with me and Miss Columba here after the others leave."

Evan sees me for the first time and gives me that gorgeous smile. God, he is so cute. "Sounds good," he says, still looking at me.

Twenty minutes seems like forever when you're sitting in a classroom doing nothing. The clock on the wall has an enormous second hand that goes tick…tick…tick…as if keeping the time was a huge effort. We are not allowed to do our homework because that would be a benefit. Hands folded, we sit like we are praying, although I think that's about the last thing on this group's mind. I sneak a look at Evan. His eyes are far away.

Finally, one minute and counting. Everybody shifts in their seats and watches the clock on the wall. The second hand struggles to the top. Ms. Minelli coordinates her watch. Three…two…one. "That's all folks," she snickers. Everyone bolts out the door. When the dust settles, only me and Evan are alone with Minelli the Hun.

"So, are you two looking forward to the Spring Ball?" I look up, startled. I swear, the old bag is actually trying to make conversation. Nice gesture, bad topic. "The only time I go to a dance is if I'm playing in the band," says Evan.

"Oh! You're a musician! What instrument?" Ms. Minelli sounds almost interested.

"I'm a drummer." Evan raps on the desktop. "We play original stuff. Rock. Rap. Reggae. You know." This is news to me. I must have a thing for musicians.

"What about you, Harley?" Ms. Minelli is smiling at me.

"I—I…don't…no. I'm not going," I stammer.

"Well, if not this time, next year." I swear, Ms. Minelli is a Jeckyl and Hyde.

Ms. Minelli picks up her pile of papers. "I'm going to let you two go early since I've got an appointment. Harley, this is your first time, so you're getting off easy. I don't want to see you in here again, okay?" She winks at me.

"Okay." I am astonished at her transformation.

"And you, Evan. What am I going to do with you? Hang in there, kiddo. Only one more year and you can go out and become a big rock star. Now, scat, the two of you!"

Evan and I get up and walk out the door. The hall is empty. It's a little spooky, like a ghost school without students. I turn to Evan and notice he has a sort of lightning bolt tattooed on his neck. "I heard Ms. Minelli was mean, but she seems kinda nice."

"She's okay," says Evan. "You, uh, want a ride home?"

Boy, do I. But if I show up in front of my house in Evan's super-blue space vehicle, I will definitely get murdered. "Um, I'd love one, but I can't today."

Evan looks disappointed. He is so sensitive, every thought is a newsreel flashing across his face. I feel bad. "Okay," he says. "See you around." He turns and walks down the hall. I watch his blond hair sway along the back of his jacket. His jeans are tight. His butt is cute. He pushes open the heavy fire door. It slams behind him. Wham. And then I see myself running after him down the empty hallway as fast as I can. "Evan! Evan, wait!"

✸✸✸

We are up on Lover's Peak, this cul de sac at the top of Crescent Hill overlooking a chunk of Lenape. It is so late, I'm sure the fire-breathing dragons will rip my arms off, but being with Evan is the first good thing that's happened to me in a long time. He is so easy, the words tumble out of my mouth. We talk and laugh and give up our secrets. I tell him about my wicked parents and Granny Harley dying. I don't tell him that I'm adopted because everybody I tell thinks I'm crazy and I don't want to blow it with Evan.

He talks about his parents splitting up. His father has been married four times, always to blonds. Evan calls his father "Q.C." because his real name is Quentin Charles. He builds entire neighborhoods and names them all after himself: Quentin Court, Quentin Road.

"I call my father Roger, but never to his face. My father is a total drunk," I confess.

"Oh, yeah? Mine, too." Evan shakes his head. "I think the only reason my dad bought me this car was so he wouldn't have to chauffeur me around."

I run my hands over the Camaro's white leather. "Some people show their love with things." God, I sound corny.

"Yeah. Things are nice, but…" Evan turns to me. "Do you like grass?"

"Grass?"

"You know, pot. Marijuana."

"Oh!" I am thrown. "I've never tried it."

"You want to?"

I hesitate. "I…I never thought about it before." Part of me is tempted, but the thought of arriving home this late to the battlefield all whacked scares me. "Uhh…I better not. I'm already grounded."

"Yeah, you're probably right." Evan zeroes in on me with those eyes. "You wanna go home?"

"I don't want to go. But I'd better go."

Evan reaches over and runs his finger gently down my cheek and stops at my chin. He turns my face toward his. "You are so pretty." I feel my eyes get moist. I am not used to hearing these things. I try to turn away, but he does not let go of my chin. Instead he leans across the stickshift and kisses me sweetly on the lips. His lips feel different from Johnny's. Tender. I almost sob, it is so lovely. He pulls me closer and kisses me again, long and deep. I wrap my arms around his neck, and he presses me close. I lean my head on his shoulder. His body is hard and his arms are strong. He strokes my hair with his fingers. For the first time, I almost feel safe.

harley
like a person

***

Evan drops me off on the corner, and I run home. It is getting dark. I open the front door and brace myself for the firing squad. Instead, the house is silent. Strange. Usually the television set is blasting and Peppy and Roger are slugging it out in the combat zone. I walk upstairs, looking for signs of life. I find Bean, sitting in front of his Nintendo, blowing up the galaxy.

"Where's everybody?" I imagine they are down at the police station, reporting a missing person.

Bean doesn't take his eyes off the screen. "Emergency room. Lily fell on a glass and cut her knee."

"Is she okay?"

"Yeah, she just needs a couple stitches. No big deal." Zap. Zap. Zap. Down goes the evil empire.

"What did they say when I didn't come home?"

"To tell you the truth, I don't think they noticed. Whoa!" The screen bursts into colors. "Cool!" Bean shouts. "I am God!"

"Congratulations."

I have been granted a pardon. Evan brings me luck. Maybe Johnny was only a crush. Maybe Evan is the real thing. I am confused. I don't understand how I can be madly in love with Johnny one day and madly in love with Evan the next.

The phone rings. I am so used to not being allowed to answer it that it rings four times before I remember that me and Bean are the only ones home. I run downstairs. "Hello?"

"Harley, hey. It's Evan. How's it going over there?"

I almost drop the receiver. "Evan? Hi! They're not even home."

"Good." I love the idea of Evan's voice zipping along the telephone wires and into my hand. I caress the receiver.

"I…I wanted to ask you," he says. "Do you think you can go to the movies Friday night? I'll pick you up. We can get something to eat first."

A *date*. Evan is inviting me on a proper date. This is how it's supposed to be, not meeting losers at bowling alleys. "Oh, wow. I would love to." This gives me time to work on Roger and Peppy. No more crawling out windows for this girl. This date is going to be pure.

"Great. I'm cutting school the next couple of days 'cause the band's rehearsing. We can't use the space after six o'clock, so we'll be outta there early. I should pick you up like around seven. Okay?"

"Sounds good." Rehearsing! I swear, I know nothing about him.

"See ya."

I stand with the phone pressed against my ear long after Evan has hung up. I cannot wait to tell Carla. This should put Miss Spring Ball in her place. But first I have to figure out a way to swim across the moat of the House of Columba without being eaten by the sharks.

harley
like a person

chapter 14

"What about Johnny?" Me and Carla stand in line with plastic trays in our hands. We are in the cafeteria for lunch because it is pouring rain. This is the first chance I've had to see her in days; she's been giving me the full snub treatment. She's been running out with Troy for lunch. He drives all the way from the next town and cuts study hall just to eat, or *whatever,* with her. Now I am graced with Miss Spring Ball's presence.

"Johnny is a gutless puppy," I inform her. I examine the blackboard for today's special. Meatball sandwich. Gross.

"What about the Spring Ball? It's only a week away. *Everyone* is going. Is Evan going to take you?"

Here we go. "Maybe I'll go alone."

"That means no." Carla is all smug, like she feels sorry for me.

"Maybe I'd *rather* go alone. In fact, maybe I'd *rather* not go at all!" We move ahead a couple of steps in line. The aroma of the meatballs hits me full in the face. Ugh. Maybe they have a salad.

"Yeah, right." Carla sniffs. "You're dying to go. I can tell."

"It's only a stupid high school dance, Carla, it's not like you're going to the Academy Awards." I have had it with her attitude. It's time to put a stop to this. "I know this is hard to believe, but I am so tired of getting jerked around by everyone. I don't give a damn about the Spring Ball. I really, really could care less."

Carla gets all defensive. "What do you mean 'jerked around?' Who's jerking you around? Are you including me?"

"Take it anyway you want it."

"You know, Harley, you left me hanging when you thought

Johnny *might* walk you home. You can't take a taste of your own medicine."

We are getting loud and everyone in line turns and looks at us. I drop my voice to a hiss. "At least I told you when I couldn't be somewhere. You don't even show up!"

"How can I tell you? You got thrown out of band. I can't call you, you're always grounded. I heard you even got a detention! Now you're going out with a druggie. Harley, you're a mess!"

I want to slug her, but I don't. Instead I grab her hair and yank it. Carla gasps, she is so surprised.

"OUCH! Harley! How dare you!" Carla grabs my arm and pinches me, really hard, digging her nails into my skin.

Everyone in line is watching us now. The boys are cheering and hooting: "Cat fight! Cat fight!" I see Mr. Petranski, who happens to be eating lunch at the teacher's table, approaching. I let go of Carla's hair.

"Girls! Girls! What's going on here?"

"She pulled my hair." Carla nails me right away.

"She asked for it." Right now I think I hate Carla's guts.

"Harley Columba, you just had one detention. Are you looking for another?" Mr. Petranski has meatball breath. I try not to inhale.

"No, sir." I go the obedient route.

"I think both you girls should pay a visit to the dean. Go down to Ms. Minelli's office."

"But—" Carla starts to protest.

"Now." Mr. Petranski waddles back to his table.

"Thanks a lot, Harley." Carla stabs me with her words.

I don't answer her. All I can think of is what Ms. Minelli is going to do when she sees me in her office again.

Ms. Minelli does not seem mad when she looks up from behind her desk. She seems sad.

"Again, Harley?" I am so humiliated, I just nod. Ms. Minelli sighs and puts down her papers.

Carla and I sit on the hard wooden chairs in front of her desk. "I don't remember seeing you in here before," Ms. Minelli says to Carla.

"Harley's trying to drag me down the tubes with her," Carla says, flipping her hair.

"What's your name?"

"Carla Van Owen."

Ms. Minelli peers over her eyeglasses. "Veronica Van Owen's daughter?"

"Yeah."

"Hhhmp." Ms. Minelli snorts like she remembers Carla's mom. "Harley, is your mother from Lenape?" I nod. "What was her name in high school?"

"Patricia Harley." I pray Ms. Minelli doesn't tell our parents about this. Maybe we'll get off with a warning.

"I thought so. Do you know I had your mother in my sociology class? She was an excellent student, that Patricia. Shy, sweet girl."

It's hard to think of loudmouth Peppy being shy. She was probably a kiss-ass who never showed teachers her true ogre self.

"She's not shy anymore," I inform Ms. Minelli. "She's very vocal."

Ms. Minelli pushes her eyeglasses on top of her carrot hair. "In fact…" she pauses. "In fact, if I remember correctly, years ago both

harley
like a person

129

your mothers sat right in front of me, just as you girls are sitting here today." She snorts again. "Very strange!"

"But they weren't friends," I say.

"Neither are we," mutters Carla.

Ms. Minelli tilts her head and scrunches up her face, like she is concentrating. "It was a disagreement over some boy, I believe."

Carla fidgets in her chair. "Well, this disagreement is not over some boy. This disagreement is over Harley ripping my hair out."

"Did not."

"Did too."

"Did NOT."

"DID TOO!"

"Girls, girls. Please!" Ms. Minelli is all dean again. "Now where is your file...." She bends down and starts rummaging through her desk. Carla sticks her tongue out at me, but Ms. Minelli doesn't see her. She is busy opening and closing drawers. "Harley, Mr. Donovan tells me you're quite an artist," she says from under the desk.

Carla snickers. "She's a regular Vincent Van Gock."

I am so surprised that Mr. Donovan has been talking about me, I ignore Carla. What does Mr. Donovan know about art? I wonder if all my teachers have been sitting around the faculty lounge, discussing the trials and tribulations of Harley Columba. Maybe this has something to do with the witchy guidance counselor. "Mr. *Donovan* told you that?"

"Ah, here it is!" Ms. Minelli pulls out a folder with my name on it and tosses it on top of her desk like the FBI secret files. "Apparently he's concerned about you. Your grades are slipping. Is there something wrong?"

"Yeah, there's something wrong with her. She thinks the whole world is here for her convenience." Carla slumps against her chair.

Ms. Minelli frowns. "Carla, I am talking to Harley."

"Ms. Minelli, can't I go, please? I've never been in trouble in my life." Carla is all pleading eyes and smiles.

"You just never get caught," I mutter.

Ms. Minelli peers at Carla over her glasses. "All right. This should probably be a private conversation anyway. But I'll see you in detention tomorrow. Have your mother sign this slip."

Carla drops the angel act and turns into her demon self. "But I didn't *do* anything! I've never had a detention! I'm not going!"

Ms. Minelli doesn't even look at her. "If you keep this up, it'll be double detention. Now get that slip signed and be in Room 103 tomorrow."

Carla grabs the slip off Ms. Minelli's desk and crumples it into a ball. "This is so not fair." She starts to storm out of the room.

"Not so fast. First shake hands with Harley."

Carla makes a face like she'd rather kiss a toad. "You've got to be kidding."

"Shake hands or you can keep me company after school the entire week."

Carla rolls her eyes like this is the worst torture ever. Slowly she extends her hand out to me, all limp and lifeless. I stare at it. This is my best friend's hand gone cold. For a second I want to jump up and hug her and squeeze her and tell her that I'm sorry. Instead I reach up and brush her fingertips with mine.

"Can I go now?" Carla doesn't even look at me.

"Yes." Ms. Minelli shakes her head as Carla struts out the door. "Are you two good friends?"

"We used to be best friends." My words sound sad, even to me. For a second I am afraid I am going to break down and bawl right here in front of Ms. Minelli. I look down and squeeze the tears back into my eyes.

"So, Harley. Is there anything wrong? Problems at home?" Ms. Minelli really tries to be a nice person, I think. I want to tell her that my wicked stepfather has taken over my body and I am no longer in control. But everything I say will end up in that folder, I'm sure. I will be branded for life.

"No, everything's okay," I fib. "Usual stuff, you know."

"Well, I can't let you off with just a warning this time." Oh, no. She *is* going to drag my parents into this fiasco. I am doomed. "Do your parents work?"

I was right. "Yeah."

"What time do they get home?"

"Different times. Sometimes four o'clock, sometimes six o'clock. I have to watch my little sister—she's five—and I'm supposed to keep an eye on my brother...."

Ms. Minelli lets out another sigh, a Peppy sigh, a big long sigh like she's exhausted. "Okay, Harley. This time we'll try something different. Instead of detention, I want you to illustrate the word, 'compassion.'"

"Compassion?"

"Yes. You can write a poem, draw something, I don't care. You have until Monday. Otherwise, it's triple detention. Does that sound fair?"

"I don't think I know what compassion means."

"You will by the time you get done. Okay?"

It actually sounds like fun, sort of. "Sure."

"Any questions?"

"I don't think so." I stand up. "Is that all?"

Ms. Minelli picks up her papers. "Try to stay out of trouble, kiddo."

"I will," I say, and at that moment, I truly mean it.

✳✳✳

I am in the art room. I let myself in with the heavy brass key on the red shoelace. I am alone. I am an artist, and I am alone. Finally I can breathe. I walk over to the dinky record player and put on the *Imagine* album. John Lennon's music fills the room. I imagine my painting on stage, in front of a huge audience.

"Hey, I love John Lennon." I spin around. Lena, who is playing Anastasia, is in the room. "Did I scare you?" I nod. "Sorry. I had some free time, so I thought we could work, if that's okay." She has long brown hair and a perfect nose. She will be easy to paint, I think.

"Sure. I've…uh, never had anyone pose before, so…I don't know…just stand over there." I get my supplies together. I haven't quite finished the first acrylic with no features, but having Lena here in person is too important to pass up. Luckily, I have already prepped the canvas. I pick up my favorite sable brush I brought from home, one that Granny Harley got me. I have a good feeling about this, I don't know why.

"Well, I've never posed for anybody, so it should be interesting." Lena laughs. She has straight, white teeth. I will paint her smiling, I think.

She strikes a pose and I begin. I thin the oil paint with a little turpentine and sketch lightly, directly on the canvas. I have no fear. If I make a mistake, I fix it. I use my paintbrush like a sword, thrust and parry. While I'm working, Lena and I chat like we are old friends, even though she is a senior. The time flies and I cannot believe it when the bell to the next class rings. Neither can Lena. "That was fun!" she says. "Can I see?"

"Sure. It's just the preliminary...." I step back, and she comes around the front. I watch her face.

"Wow! It's incredible! It looks just like me. You're really good, Harley."

I grin. "Thanks." I should be humble, but I know it's good. I wish I could stay in this room forever.

✱✱✱

I have decided to tell Mrs. Tuttle the truth about the *New York City* book. There is nothing else I can do. She will probably fire me. I ring the bell.

Mrs. Tuttle opens the door wearing a painter's smock and a beret. "Harley, hello! You've inspired me! Come see!" Mrs. Tuttle tugs me into the living room where she's set up an easel. On it is the beginnings of a still life with grapes. This is the worst. I blink and try not to cry.

"What's the matter? Don't you like it?"

I hold the *New York City* book out to her. "Mrs. Tuttle, my little sister got hold of your book and colored all the pages. I kept it on my night table where I thought it would be safe, I really did. I will work for you for free for a month to pay for it. I'm sorry. I'm very, very sorry." My voice is quivering and my eyes are wet. Sometimes I think I am nothing but salt water inside.

Mrs. Tuttle sets down her palette and takes the book. She opens it and looks at the Statue of Liberty with long yellow hair holding a torch that burns in orange Crayola. Then she does something amazing. She starts laughing. "Very creative!" She puts her hand on my shoulder. "You must feel terrible, Harley. Don't worry about it. When my boys were small, they cut up my illustrated edition of *Robinson Crusoe* and stuck the pictures on the refrigerator. This book is outdated anyway."

"I'll work for free...."

"Don't be ridiculous. I'm not paying you enough. These things happen. That's life. Now let's get started on the windows."

I can't believe she is acting this way. Peppy would have locked me in the dungeon without bread or water. I wish Mrs. Tuttle was my mother, even if she is old.

Mrs. Tuttle places the *New York City* book back on the coffee table. "Now it's a real conversation piece."

✳✳✳

"Mom, can I talk to you?" Me and Peppy are peeling potatoes. She finally got the hint and stopped with the fish. Tonight we are having ham with boiled potatoes. Oh, yum. Just looking at all that pink meat makes me long for red snapper.

"What now, Harley?" Peppy sighs and tosses another potato in the pot. The lines around her mouth are deep and droopy. She's only two years older than Carla's mother, but she looks ten years older. For a moment I feel sorry for her, thinking about the girl in the yearbook who was supposed to catch her dreams before they slipped away.

"I was just going to say, did you know Carla's father, Sean Shanahan?" I ask nonchalantly, like I'm asking what's for dinner.

Peppy drops her potato peeler. I swear, Sean Shanahan must

have been some guy. All these women drop things just at the mention of his name. "Why on earth do you ask?" Peppy always says "on earth" when she's hysterical but pretending she's not.

"Me and Carla found your old yearbook, and we read the stuff he wrote to you."

"You *what*?" Peppy makes a move like she is going to slap me, then stops her hand a moment before impact. "Don't you ever snoop through things that aren't yours, Harley Marie! Don't you ever!"

I flinch. "Why not? You do."

"I am your mother. Don't you talk to me like that."

"I only asked you a simple question. Why are you getting so nuts?"

Peppy picks up the peeler and starts carving potatoes like a madman. "I'm sorry, Harley, but sometimes you just make me so angry." Slice. Slice. Slice. The skins fly everywhere. "I don't want you spending time with that Carla anymore. Her mother lets her run wild. You're getting too many ideas in your head."

Any other time I would probably storm out of the room, but I want information. "I had a fight with Carla." That should make her happy.

"Over what?"

"Nothing in particular. We're not speaking."

"Best friends change all the time at your age." Peppy seems preoccupied.

"Are you upset because I asked about Carla's father?" I keep going. I can tell I am onto some good dirt.

"Harley, I do not wish to discuss it."

"But, Mom…"

"Harley…"

I push ahead. I am tired of being lied to. "Is that why you broke up with Dad? Because of Sean Shanahan?"

Bulls-eye! Peppy's mouth gets all tight. She puts down her potato peeler. "Harley, there are some things between grownups that aren't meant for children." Her voice is sharper than the knife.

"I'm not a child! You're always treating me like one! Why don't you trust me and be honest with me and maybe I'd act differently! Everything's a secret around here! What's the big deal?"

That stops her. There is a mountain of potato skins beneath her fingers. She pretends to examine the pile of naked potatoes that are spilling out of the pot, checking each one for a fleck of skin. "Oh, Harley. You're just so young. Don't try to grow up so fast."

"I'm as old as you were when you started going out with Dad."

"That's hard to believe...."

"Why did you marry him, anyway?"

Peppy looks up from the potatoes. "What kind of a question is that?" She moves to the sink and turns on the cold water. "He's under a lot of pressure, you know, with money.... You don't know what he's sacrificed for this family. It's not easy trying to raise three children these days." She's trying to convince herself, I think. Then her voice gets soft and for a moment she morphs into a human being. "Do you know what his favorite movie is?"

"*Star Wars*?" We have it on video.

Peppy smiles. "*It's a Wonderful Life.* You know, with Jimmy Stewart? About the man who always wanted to see the world but instead stays home with his wife and children? We watch it at Christmas."

No, I don't know it, but I shake my head yes to urge her on. She opens her mouth to tell me more, then catches herself. She has revealed too much. She searches through the cabinet and takes out the mixer. "Dinner's almost ready, Harley. Now set the table."

✶✶✶

I am upstairs in my room. I dig through the storage area and pull out my mother's yearbook. Then I pull my harlequin out from under my bed. I don't know why I didn't think of this sooner. I try to breathe quietly, but I am almost gasping for air.

I flip open the yearbook to the chicken scrawl around Sean Shanahan's picture. I slide the harlequin card next to the yearbook. My hands tremble. There is only one word in common, and that word is "love." I think it's a match. The "o" is a little different…. I'm not sure…. Yes. It is the same. I am scared. I am relieved. Now I know.

Sean Shanahan is my father.

chapter 15

"Ronnie, is Carla there?" I am home alone. I've just got to tell Carla that Sean Shanahan is my father, too. Carla is my half-sister. I can no longer keep this to myself.

"Hold on, Harley. Carla?"

I hear Carla holler in the distance: "Who is it?" Ronnie covers the mouthpiece. Her words are muffled. Then she says, "I'm sorry, Harley. Carla isn't home."

So that's the way it is. I speak real low so Ronnie will not know how upset I am. "Tell her I need to talk to her, okay? Tell her it's important." I hang up the phone fast.

The hell with Carla. I whip out a piece of paper from the kitchen drawer. I write: "COMPASSION" by Harley Columba. I write in red ink. Blood ink:

> No one cares
> if you're stuck
> no more prayers
> no more luck
> no one shares
> compassion sucks.

Ha, ha, ha. That should get old Minelli-poo.

I go into the family room and get the dictionary off the shelf. I love this dictionary. It used to belong to Granny Harley's mother, my great-grandma Harley. I look up "compassion": "a feeling of deep sympathy for another's suffering, accompanied by a desire to alleviate the pain or remove its cause." Hmmm. Dictionaries are so wordy, I swear.

I run up to my room and get a piece of drawing paper and some charcoal pencils and my calligraphy set. I carry them downstairs to the family room table and spread out. I sketch a girl peering through a huge magnifying glass. Under the glass, I write: "COMPASSION." I pause. I must be a cold-hearted beast. I can't think of one single person I have sympathy for. Except…Granny Harley. I will write it to her.

"COMPASSION," by Harley Columba. Underneath the title, in small letters, I print: "Dedicated to Suzanne Harley." I am getting all misty just thinking about it. I miss my granny. I blink really fast, but still the tears blur my eyes. I write:

> If you could hear me, I would say I love you
> If I could touch you, I would never let you go
> If I could stop your pain, I would ache myself
> If I could, I would do anything for you
> But you are gone and I can't
> And I can't.

A tear drips onto the paper and smears the last word. I breathe on it gently, then retouch it. I could use a little compassion myself. I blow my nose. I pick up the phone and dial. I listen to Evan's phone ring and ring and ring. I know he is rehearsing, but maybe… Evan has his own line, lucky him. I let it ring about twenty times. I love the sound. Then I hang up, wait a moment, and dial again.

This time, after the third ring, someone picks up and this deep voice says, "Hello?" Oh, wow. It must be his father, Q.C. I sit there frozen with the receiver to my ear and say nothing.

"Hello? Hello? Who is this?" Q.C. sounds angry. He waits. I say nothing. "Answer me, if you have any guts."

Whoa. I don't know what's come over me. I cannot talk. I can't even move to hang up the phone. The receiver is glued to my ear.

"You must be a real jerk to call up and not say anything. You must be some kind of loser. Answer me, goddamn it." I say nothing. Finally Q.C. says, all deadly, "Go to hell," and hangs up.

So that's Evan's dad. Boy, I'd like to lock Roger in a room with him and see who comes out alive.

✶✶✶

I see Carla heading down the hall with Nancy Peterman, all laughs and giggles. Brother. Nancy Peterman is such a rah-rah. I run up to them.

"Carla, I've got to talk to you." I am breathless.

Carla gives me a look like she is staring at a sloth. "We have nothing to say to each other, you traitor." She flips her hair and keeps walking. I run along next to her.

"Look, I'm sorry, but I've got to tell you something really, really important."

Carla stops. "Go ahead, Harley. Tell me this really, really important thing." She is all sarcastic, and Nancy Peterman giggles.

"I think I should tell you in private."

"I think not."

I don't want to blab this in front of Nancy Peterman, but this may be the only chance I get. Carla has been avoiding me worse than the plague.

"Let me whisper it."

Carla rolls her eyes and bends over to me like I'm this idiot child. She is getting so tall, I almost have to stand on my tip-toes. I cup my hand around my mouth and whisper. "Sean Shanahan is my father, too. That makes us half-sisters." The words are hot, burning from my mouth to her ear.

Carla straightens up and her blue eyes are wild. "You are so crazy, Harley. You are so out of your mind. You need to see a shrink." She tugs Nancy Peterman away. I have lost her, I think. My heart is a ball of yarn, one end attached to Carla, unraveling down the hall.

✳✳✳

I decide to take Miss Posey up on her offer to use the art room instead of going to study hall. There is only one problem. When I open the door, thirty pairs of upperclassmen eyes turn to look at me. My first instinct is to back out the door and run away. But Miss Posey sees me and motions me inside.

I try to be invisible, but I feel like Gulliver walking through Lilliput as I tiptoe over to my corner and put on my smock. I want to finish the painting for the first act, the princess with no face. I set up my easel so that my back faces all the other students.

I pick up my paintbrush and begin, but all I can think about is thirty pairs of eyes on my back. I dab my brush onto the portrait. I stop. Try again. It's impossible. Then I hear the soft simple chords of a piano begin playing. Miss Posey has put on *Imagine*. I turn to look at her and smile, Thanks.

I relax. Squint. Touch up the hair. Shade the chin. Now the colors start flowing from my paintbrush. When the bell to the next class rings, I am just adding the finishing stroke.

"Hey, that's *really* good, Harley," says a voice behind me. I nearly drop my brush. Johnny Bruno has appeared at my side.

"Tha…thanks." I wipe my hands on my smock. It's funny, but I'm not even glad to see him. In fact, I feel nothing at all. "Are you in this class? I didn't see you when I came in."

"Yeah. But I'm not an artist." He steps back and admires my painting. "Not like you, anyway."

"I'm happy with it." I state this as a fact, not a gloat. I take off my smock and hang it up.

Johnny looks at me as though he is seeing me for the first time. "You know, Harley, I was thinking. Do you want to go with me to the Spring Ball?"

"*What*?" I stare at him as if he has lost his mind. "I thought you were going with Prudence Clarke."

"Well, that's what she thinks, but it's not what I want."

I rinse my brush off in some turpentine. I push my easel into the corner. Then I look him straight in the eye. I say: "Johnny, I wouldn't go across the street with you, let alone to the Spring Ball." I watch his mouth drop open as I walk out the door.

✳✳✳

Six o'clock on Friday night. One hour to Evan. I am in black. I look great. There is only one problem. I have no plan of escape. I decide to try my new approach. I will tell Peppy the truth.

Roger's in the family room, snoring, the news blaring from the television set. Peppy is in the kitchen, listening to some stupid love song from the '80s. I must get Peppy out of earshot of the drizzly monster in the Barcalounger.

I tiptoe into the kitchen and stop short. Peppy is standing at the sink with her eyes closed, humming. A shaft of light is streaming in from the back door, softening her face, and for a moment she looks as young as her high school photo. I wonder what she is dreaming about. Or who. I feel a little guilty watching her, the moment seems so private.

I back out silently, into the living room. "Mom?" I call, warning her I am coming. I give her a second, then act like I am entering the kitchen for the first time. Peppy has grabbed a sponge and pretends to wash a pot. She opens her mouth to speak. I put my finger to my lips so she doesn't wake Roger, and pull her out of the kitchen into the living room.

"Harley, what on earth are you doing now?" Peppy looks almost frightened. Like, what kind of revelation am I going to dump on her this time?

I take a breath and lower my voice. "Mom, this boy asked me out to dinner tonight. His name is Evan and he's really cute and I really like him a lot. He's picking me up at seven and I really want to go. I've been grounded forever. Please, please, please, can I go? I'll be home by ten o'clock, I swear. I cleaned my room and everything. *Please*?"

Peppy looks relieved. She probably thought I was going to drag out Sean Shanahan again. I am thrilled that I have this new weapon in my artillery. I must be careful not to abuse my power. "I don't know, Harley. Your father…"

"*Please*, Mom. I never go anywhere. He's so sloshed he won't even notice that I'm gone."

"Don't talk about him that way." Peppy hesitates. She glances toward the family room. Roger mutters and stirs in his chair. "If he says it's okay."

I trudge into the family room and watch Roger's chest move up and down. His head is slumped to the side. I'm glad he's not my real father. Then I get sad. I guess he's glad he's not my real father, too. I reach over and touch his shoulder. "Dad?" Nothing. I shake him harder. "Dad?"

Roger mumbles and opens one red eye. "Mom said I could go out tonight if it's okay with you. Okay?" Roger stares at me as if he's trying to figure out who I am. Then he closes his eye and turns on his side. "Okay?" I ask again. Roger mumbles, "Okay, okay." Good. "He said okay, Mom!" I call to Peppy in the kitchen. Peppy shakes her head, but says nothing. I am out the door.

✱✱✱

My butt is cold. Seven-thirty and no Evan. Every couple of minutes I see the curtains move and Peppy peer out the living room window. Yeah, Mom, still here. I hate boys.

Maybe he forgot. Maybe he got caught in traffic. Maybe he changed his mind. Maybe…

Then I hear it. In the distance, the rumble of Evan's Camaro. He peels down the street and screeches to a halt in front of my house.

Peppy opens the front door. She is so predictable. "Harley…"

Evan jumps out of the car and runs up to the front porch. He hands me a bouquet of daisies. My first flowers. I put them under my nose and inhale; then I'm embarrassed because, of course, they have no smell. "They're beautiful."

"Sorry, I'm late," he says. "Traffic." He winks at Peppy in the doorway. "You must be Mrs. Columba." He grins and offers her his hand. Peppy's face turns from frowns to smiles. The boy has a natural charm.

"Mom, this is Evan." I swear, she's positively blushing.

"All that hair!"

"Mom—" I warn her.

She gets the message. "Nice to meet you, Evan."

I see the curtain pull back and Lily and Bean's faces peek out the window. I swear, I have the nosiest family. Bean squishes his face against the glass and makes a pig nose. What a jerk.

Evan turns to me. "Ready?"

"Ready." I am so excited, I can hardly breathe.

"Don't be late." Peppy morphs back into a mother.

Evan takes my hand. "How's eleven?" He tugs me toward the car.

Peppy hesitates. I let go of Evan's hand and dash back up the steps. I hand Peppy the daisies. "Can you put these in water, Mom?"

"Okay…eleven. Don't be late."

I am so happy, I reach up and give her a hug. Peppy is startled, then hugs me back. I fly down the steps to the car. Evan opens the passenger door for me. I slide onto the white leather seat and make a big show of buckling my seat belt. He closes my door and waves good-bye to Peppy. He jumps in the front seat and kicks over the engine. It roars.

"Be careful!" Peppy calls.

Evan beeps the horn and steers the Camaro off into the night.

✳✳✳

We are tucked into a wooden booth in Gilgard's over in Wynokie, this restaurant-dance kind of place. Rock music blasts from the jukebox and a bunch of couples are moving on the dance floor. Evan orders a beer and the waitress doesn't even proof him. I order a Diet Coke. I cannot eat, it is such a thrill to sit in a restaurant across from this boy.

"Aren't you hungry?" Evan has devoured his burger and is on his second beer.

"I'm…I'm just glad to be here," I say, like I do this every

Friday night, but inside I am Jello. I take tiny squirrel bites of my burger, hoarding the moment like a nut to crack open and dream over later.

Evan reaches across the table and touches my hand. "I'm glad you're here too, babe." Babe. He called me "babe." I cannot swallow. I am stuck with a mouthful of fries. I gulp my Coke. The music on the jukebox changes to a slow love song. Girls wrap their arms around their guys' necks and sway.

"Wanna dance?" Evan drains his mug.

"Sure." Please, God, do not let me stomp on Evan's feet. Evan tugs me out of the booth and leads me to the center of the floor. I watch what the other girls are doing. I wrap my arms around Evan's neck. He holds me tight, as if he is afraid I will float up off the floor. Maybe I will; I am nothing but air.

"You feel good, Harley." Evan buries my head under his chin. He is taller than I thought he was. I am tense, then I relax and lay my head against his chest. We fall into each other's rhythm: back and forth, back and forth. I close my eyes and think, I can die right now and I will die happy.

Evan pulls back. I look up into his deep gray eyes. He leans over me and touches his lips to mine. It is only the two of us here on earth; everyone else has left the planet.

Then the music stops and a loud bass cranks in. Evan kisses my forehead and leads me back to the booth. "What do ya say we skip the movies? Some friends are having a couple of people over. Wanna go?"

"Okay." I'd go anywhere with this boy.

Evan throws some money on the table and helps me with my jacket. "I'm having a really good time," he whispers in my ear.

"Me, too." Talk about understatements.

"Evan, hey!" I hear a girl's voice behind us. I turn and almost bump into this tall red-haired girl who looks like a model. She has big gold hoop earrings and long graceful arms. I go on alert.

"Hey, Tori." Evan's voice is cautious. "You know Harley?" The redheaded Tori checks me out.

"Hey, Harley." Her voice is dainty, like china.

"Hi." I sound like a fog horn. Now, go away, I think. I am not ready for the coach to turn into a pumpkin.

"We're going over to Oliver's." Evan is uncomfortable.

"Yeah?" Tori smiles. Of course, she has perfect teeth. The better to eat you with, my dear. "Maybe I'll catch you later." She winks at me like she's sharing a secret and swoops back into the crowd. I see a group of people surround her and turn to look at me. I feel my face turn red. I hope it's dark enough that Evan doesn't notice.

"I used to go with her," Evan says. "She's a good kid. Spacey, though."

"She seems nice," I say, and step out into the night.

chapter 16

"Oliver's folks went to Bermuda." Evan has parked a few blocks away, since the whole neighborhood is lined with cars. I can hear the thud, thud, thud of a bass guitar as we walk up to a gate. Oliver lives in Sunrise Estates. I guess his parents are rich.

People are sitting on the lawn and spilling out the door, which is wide open. Music blasts into the neighborhood. Beer bottles and cigarette butts litter the ground. We walk into the living room. Smoke curls through the air. Bodies are slumped in every chair, every sofa, on the floor. Microphones and a drum set are crammed into a corner of the living room. Roger has this old song, "Mama Told Me Not to Come," that he used to play on the stereo, and now that song spins inside my head.

"Wanna beer?" Evan shouts.

I hesitate. "Okay." I grip his hand and we walk into the kitchen where a keg sits in the sink. Some tall guy with long curly hair and a goatee is drinking beer from a pitcher instead of a glass. "Harley, this is Oliver." Evan lets go of my hand and pours some beer into a plastic cup and hands it to me. I take a big gulp.

Oliver checks me out. "Yum, yum. Hey, bud, not bad. Not bad at all." I feel like a piece of steak.

"Watch yourself, Oliver." Evan laughs, but I can tell that underneath he is serious. "Don't get any ideas."

"You from Lenape?" Oliver asks me.

"Yes." I try to smile a Tori smile. It feels fake.

"Lenape sucks." Oliver gulps down more beer and burps.

I nod. "It truly does."

Oliver grins at me. "I like this girl." He turns to Evan. "Wanna play a tune, bro? Everybody's been waiting."

Evan chugs his cup of beer. "Sure."

I follow them into the living room. Evan gets behind the drums and takes off his jacket. His arms are toned and bulge out of his t-shirt. Oliver picks up a guitar and starts playing riffs. An amplifier squeals. A guy with a shaved head and tattoos gets behind the keyboard. Another guy with spiked black hair picks up the bass. Oliver nods his head and together the four of them explode into song. Nothing like Johnny Bruno's snoozy folk tunes.

I watch Evan behind the drums, his blond hair flying. He is really good, and I am thrilled that I am here with him. People stare at me, and I know they wonder who I am, but no one comes over to talk. Fine. I am too shy to talk to strangers anyway. I wonder if everyone here is rich.

Then this girl with long black hair and white, white skin slinks over, puffing on a joint. "Wanna hit?" Her lips are deep red, and her eyes match her black hair. She looks like Morticia in the Addams Family. She holds the marijuana out to me. She has a silver ring on every finger, even her thumbs. I hesitate, then take the joint.

"Thanks." I'm not sure what to do with it.

She watches me. "It's really good."

My heart is racing, but I am curious. I raise the joint to my lips and take a puff. I am an expert inhaler now; I've been practicing with the Marlboro Lights. I concentrate on not coughing. "Nice," I say, blowing out a cloud of smoke. I wait to see if my brain starts frying, but I don't feel a bit different. Maybe I'm one of those weirdos who can't get high. Morticia nods to me to take another hit. I inhale again, this time a little longer, then pass the joint back to her.

"I'm Jessie," says Morticia. "Oliver's girlfriend. Are you Harley?"

I'm surprised she knows my name. "Yes."

"Evan's told me tons about you. You're an artist, right? I've never seen him so gone for somebody."

This bit of news gives me a boost. Evan's been talking about me! Jessie puts the joint to her lips. I watch her moves. She does not exhale right away, but holds it in for a long time. She passes the joint back to me. I mimic her and take a deep, deep breath. The smoke smells sweet and exotic. It stings my lungs. My ears buzz. I start to hand her back the joint. "Take another hit," she coaxes. "It's *really* good."

I place the joint against my mouth again and inhale. I hold it in for a long time, then breathe out slowly. I perfect my technique. Hardly any smoke comes out. I pass the joint back to Jessie. She takes a quick puff and hands it back to me. I inhale. No coughing, no choking. I think I've got it down now; I am gulping in smoke like an expert.

"You're not Evan's usual type." Jessie has a scratchy voice, like she smokes a lot of cigarettes. "Usually he ends up with these vacant blonds. I think he gets that from his old man, Q.C."

"Really?" My turn. I take another hit. My head is starting to spin. "Well, I usually end up with these dark Italians." I toss the words out like a pro, as if Evan is my first blond in a long line of brown-haired men.

Jessie laughs and laughs, like I have said the most amazingly witty thing. I start giggling too, although there's really nothing funny at all. "I know what you mean!" she says. "I go for those dark broody types myself!" She is cracking up.

Her laughter is making me laugh. "Right!" I giggle. "The broodier, the better!" We are smoking and laughing up a storm.

harley
like a person

151

"Feelin' bummed?" Jessie shrieks. "Call Jessie, she'll talk you off the ledge!"

Now we are absolutely roaring, we laugh so hard. The last time I laughed like this was with Carla in the old days. I decide I really like Jessie a lot. I decide that I really like being here a lot. The band is sounding better and better. In fact, everything seems fascinating, suddenly. Then I realize: I have crossed the border into Wonderland. Go ask Alice. I am stoned.

The music has stopped and Evan is now at my side. I wonder how long he has been standing there. I collapse, giggling, into his arms.

"I like your girlfriend," Jessie informs Evan, passing him the joint. Girlfriend. Girl. Friend. I am Evan's *girlfriend*. It's a wonderful word. Friend who is a girl. No, it's something more than that. I am Evan's friend. Means nothing. I am Evan's *girl*friend. I analyze the word over and over. My mind has turned into a dictionary. I start laughing again.

"Yeah, I like her, too." Evan takes a quick puff. He glances over at me standing there cackling at nothing. He grabs my hand. "It's loud down here. Let's go upstairs." He winks at Jessie. "Catch ya later, Jess." She smiles back, but her eyes are far away.

I am still chuckling as he leads me through the smoky haze, stepping over a jungle of bodies and empty bottles and up the carpeted steps where the bedrooms are. I imagine we are on an African safari, wandering through the wild brush, looking for an empty tent to spend the night. Oh, wow. I am *really* stoned.

It's quiet upstairs, like a church. Evan opens a door. He mumbles, "sorry," and closes it quickly. He opens another door and peers inside. He tugs my hand and whispers, "Come in." I hear Evan click the lock on the door behind me. He turns on a little light. The shade is made out of colorful fragments of glass. "That's a real Tiffany lamp," he says. I nod like I know what he is talking about. I am standing in a huge white bedroom with an enormous white king-size bed. The walls are white. The carpet is white. The furniture is white. There is a huge framed painting over the bed, all white.

I stare at the lamp, and the colors start to move. I pick up the lamp. "Hey, Tiffany," I say to the lamp. I hold the lamp up to my eyes and peer through the colorful shade. Now I am inside one of my paintings, looking at the room through a kaleidoscope. I move the lamp around and watch the colors change. I will paint this later, I remind myself. Don't forget.

Evan lies down on the bed and pats the space beside him. "Come over here, you." I set down the lamp and float over to the bed. I sink into the huge, fluffy mattress. I have never been on such a soft bed. Ah, ha. This is the-princess-and-the-pea test. There is a panel of experts downstairs, waiting for the result.

I lie down next to Evan. Hmmm. I cannot feel the pea. I cannot feel anything. I am a princess with a blank face, awkward and stiff. He strokes my hair, and I start to melt. Yes, now I can feel the pea underneath the twenty-third mattress. Evan leans over and kisses my lips. I put my arms around his neck. He feels strong. He moves on top of me. His fingers start to unbutton my shirt. His hands are feathers on my neck, my belly; my body tingles. He reaches behind my back to unhook my bra. He hesitates. I think I am supposed to stop him, but I don't want to. He releases the hook in one expert move, then kisses my neck, my throat. We are both trembling. He reaches down and fiddles with the button on my pants. This, I am not ready for. I stop his fingers with my hand. "Not yet," I murmur. "Okay," he whispers, and his lips once again touch mine. I kiss him for hours and hours, it seems. I cannot get enough of those lips, that tongue. Finally, he lies back and just holds me in his arms. "I better take you home."

✖✖✖

The blue Camaro slides up to the front of my house. Two minutes to eleven. Cinderella is back from the ball with both glass slippers on her feet. I see Peppy sneak a peek from behind the iron curtain. I swear, that woman hasn't moved since we left.

Evan turns off the engine and sweeps me under his arm. I kiss him back, but my heart's not in it. All I can think of is my mother with her binocular eyes. I slip out of Evan's embrace.

"My mother is spying on us."

"Let's give her a show." Evan kisses me again. I can feel Peppy's eyes burn through the window, right into my brain.

"I can't."

Evan sits up. "That's okay." He is compassionate, as I now understand the word. I straighten my clothes and run a brush through my hair. I get logical. There's really no way Peppy can see inside the car. I hope I'm not going to be one of those paranoid people.

"I had a really great time tonight, Evan," I say as I open the car door. "Thanks."

"I'll call you."

I stand there with the door open, looking back at him. I feel daring. I put my knee on the passenger seat and lean into him. I smack a big fat kiss right on his lips. Have a gander at *that*, Peppy-poo.

Evan laughs. "You devil."

I run up the stairs to the porch. Peppy opens the door as I reach the top. Evan's Camaro starts up and roars away. I step into the house.

"Did you have a good time?"

"Wonderful."

"He seems like a nice boy. If he got a haircut."

I give Peppy a hug. "Oh, Mom. I'm in love!"

Peppy smiles. "Sshh! Don't wake your father."

"Good-night, Mom." I peck her on the cheek.

"Good-night, Harley." Peppy clicks off the front porch light. I tiptoe upstairs, too excited to sleep. If she only knew.

harley
like a person

It's lunchtime. I could not concentrate all morning, just thinking about Evan. I am truly, madly, passionately in love. I drop *The Complete Illustrated Works of Compassion* by Harley Columba off at Ms. Minelli's office, but she is not there. I leave the paper on her desk, then head toward the Pond Hole. I see Evan talking to a bunch of rowdies.

"Hey, babe. Where've ya been?" Evan throws his arm around me. Here I am, standing on the Pond Hole steps, immersed in the center of the elite. Last week I was just passing through and today I am the nucleus. I wish that Carla would walk by. If they could see me now...

"Oh, I had to write this poem so Minelli wouldn't give me a detention." I toss this off over my shoulder. Detention is a status thing with this group.

"A poem? Cool." Evan lights a cigarette and hands it to me. I take a drag. With each puff I feel myself drift further away from the person I used to be. Sometimes I miss that girl, the old me. Even though I sit on one of the high stone steps, smoking like an expert, a piece of me is outside of them all, watching. People make their way back from lunch. The rah-rahs clamber up the long driveway so they don't have to walk through the center of this crowd. A punk or two approaches and abruptly changes direction. Indies march straight up the middle as if to say, I don't care who you people are. Sometimes the elite snicker behind their backs. I wonder if they ever made fun of me and Carla in the old days. It seems so long ago.

"…you wanna go?" I realize Evan has been talking to me.

"I…I didn't hear you."

"I said, you wanna go to the Spring Ball? I know it's weird and all, but a couple of people are going—"

"YES!" I shout. Everybody looks at me. I lower my voice. "I would *love* to." Is this boy perfect or what? I never thought Evan would be the type to go to some stupid high school dance.

"Get excited, Harley, why don't you?" Evan grins at me like I'm five years old and he just handed me a lollipop.

I squeeze his hand. I, Harley Columba, am actually going to the Spring Ball. Wait until Carla hears about *this*.

✳✳✳

I must move quickly. There are important things, like a new dress to consider. The good ones were snatched off the racks weeks ago.

"Mom?" Peppy is ironing Roger's handkerchiefs. I swear, she's an indentured servant, the things she does for that man. "Mom, Evan's asked me to the Spring Ball, and I need a dress."

"When is it?" Peppy doesn't even look up. The iron spits steam from its nostrils.

"Saturday."

"Why don't I make you a dress? We'll get some nice material…."

"Oh, Mom. A *homemade* dress? I'd be humiliated."

"Do you have the money for a dress?"

"Twenty bucks. Enough to buy a zipper."

Peppy sighs. "You *are* supposed to be grounded, young lady."

If anybody ever said, "Oh, I'm so happy for you, dear," I would drop dead, I swear. I will strike a deal. "What if I promise to do the ironing for an entire month?"

Hiss. Thump. Hiss. Thump. The iron flattens the handkerchiefs into perfect white squares. "I'll split it with you."

"YES!" I jump in the air. "Let's go to the mall right this second." The mall is a half hour away; too far for me to go alone.

"Tomorrow."

I do not push it. Tomorrow is better than never.

✳✳✳

I am in the library. Miss Wrigley is humming behind the counter, scribbling student's names on yellow post-its and sticking them on books like she is preparing birthday presents.

"Hey, Miss Wrigley."

"What can I do for you today, Harley?" she asks, as if I wanted a first edition of *Tom Sawyer*, she'd pull it out of her carpetbag.

"Could I please see the New York City telephone book again?"

Miss Wrigley scratches the back of her hair with her pen. "Oh, dear. I think I might have returned it...."

"Really?" It took over a week to get it the last time, and I don't have any time to lose. "I need to see it again. It's sort of important. I should have told you...."

Mrs. Wrigley frowns. "Actually, it could still be here. Maybe I just *thought* about bringing it back. Wait a second." She zips off into the depths of the back room and appears immediately with the fat Manhattan White Pages held high over her head like a trophy. "Got it!"

"Thanks." I smile at her and carry the book over to a table. I flip to the section where it says "Manhattan—Residence." I run my finger down the "S's," lose my place and start again. Between

"Shamir" and "Sharkey" I find it: "Shanahan." I stare at the name. Shanahan in black and white. I skim the column. No Sean, but three "Shanahan, S." I scribble down all three names, addresses and phone numbers on an index card and stick it in my pocket, close to my heart.

✳✳✳

We are in the mall. Packs of girls roam the corridors, searching for boys and accessories. I am the only one here with a mother. I walk a little in front of her so it is not so obvious we are together. But I really don't mind; Peppy took off work early to bring me, and for that I am grateful.

We pass by a jewelry store. In the window is a pair of delicate earrings, hand-painted roses entwined in gold. "Oh, Mom, look. Aren't they beautiful?"

Peppy glances at the earrings and keeps walking. "Too expensive."

"Yes, but aren't they *pretty*?" I swear, Peppy is so suburban. If it's not on sale at Sears, it means nothing to her.

"Come on, Harley. It's getting late."

I know exactly what I want: a little black dress. This will be tough. If it were up to Peppy, she'd have me in ribbons and floral prints. She is so far out of the loop, it's embarrassing.

We walk into my favorite store. Videos play overhead on monitors. Dance music blasts. I love this place. There is a whole rack of little black dresses. I grab three and head for the dressing room. Peppy sits outside the door in an overstuffed chair like an armed guard, ready to veto my selections. This is a woman who wouldn't let me shave my legs until last year.

I try on the first dress. I don't really want it, but it is so risqué that by the time I get to the last one, Peppy will be ground down. I emerge from the dressing room and strike a pose.

"Absolutely not, Harley Marie."

"But, Mom—"

"No."

That's okay. I try on the second one. Same response. I slip the third dress over my head. I step up to the mirror and smile, no teeth, only lips, like a sphinx. "Ooo, girl." I wink at myself in the mirror. "You are *hot*." I turn sideways and press my palms against my stomach. I thrust out my chest. *Yes*. It looks better than I dreamed it would. I twirl and leap out of the dressing room. "Ta da!"

Carla, not Peppy, sits in the overstuffed chair.

I blink. She is real, not an illusion, and does not disappear. Peppy and Ronnie stand on either side of her. No one speaks. For a second I am off-balance. Then I realize: Carla has wandered into my den.

"Why, hello, Carla," I purr, growling underneath. "Hello, Ronnie. Long time no see." The music pounds in the background to the rhythm of the tension in the air. I wonder if Carla asked Ronnie about our mutual father. I doubt it. Here we are, four women with the same secret. I imagine, many years ago, Sean Shanahan delivering the harlequin to his little blue-eyed daughter. Ring! The doorbell chimes. Ronnie sobs on the front lawn, holding baby Carla in her arms, begging Sean to come back. Roger answers the door. In a drunken stupor, he punches Sean in the face and tells him never to set foot in Lenape again. Peppy grabs the harlequin doll and hides it away in the storage area to give to her love child when she is old enough to understand.

"I hear you're going to the Spring Ball with Evan." Well, well.

Carla is actually speaking to me. She is green, she is so envious.

"You heard right." I delight in rubbing it in.

"That dress is cute on you, Harley." Ronnie looks uncomfortable.

"What do you think, Mom?" I am clever. I see an opening and make my move. I must have this dress. Peppy will not want to be shown up by Ronnie.

Peppy frowns. For a second I think she is going to disappoint me. She sighs one of her famous sighs. "I suppose so, Harley. Though it still seems too old for you."

"Thank you, Mom!" I give Peppy a big hug. It is like hugging an ironing board.

"They grow up so fast, don't they, Patricia?" I see Ronnie's hand tug on Carla's blouse, a signal that she wants to make a quick exit.

"Some faster than others." Peppy gets in a dig. Columbas two points, Van Owens nothing. Now I know why Peppy hates Ronnie. Scandalous. Carla is four months older than me. If Sean Shanahan is my father, that means Peppy had an affair with him while Ronnie was pregnant. Juicy, juicy, juicy.

"Well, we'd better get going, Mom." Carla flips her hair, and I swear, lifts her nose in the air. She turns to me and rips out a zinger. "They say I'm up for Princess of the Ball. We're trying to find me a pair of shoes to match my outfit. You should see my dress, Harley. It is *so* incredible. You can't *believe* how much it cost. We got it at Frangelica's."

Three points! Carla scores. Everything at Frangelica's costs a fortune. I hear they serve tea while you shop. My own sad little price tag dangles from my sleeve for all to see. What a bitch.

My tongue has talons. "Just because something costs more

doesn't make it better, Carla." Carla, Princess of the Ball! I hate her guts. I can't believe she was ever my best friend.

"Of course it doesn't." Even Ronnie seems embarrassed that she gave birth to such a greedy monster. "Come on, Miss Vanderbilt. The mall is closing in an hour." Ronnie yanks Carla toward the front of the store. I stand next to Peppy in my little black dress and watch them go.

"Are you sure that's the dress you want, Harley?" Peppy's voice is quiet. "We can go to another store…."

I feel so bad for her, I want to cry. I put my arm around my mother's shoulders. "It's perfect, Mom. I love it. It's the best dress I ever had. I don't care how much it costs. I really don't."

"That Carla is spoiled. Veronica gives her everything she wants."

"Maybe she feels guilty."

"Guilty about what?"

"About Sean Shanahan running off and abandoning them."

Peppy's mouth turns into a straight white line. "Don't push it, Harley."

I know when I have gone too far. "Okay." I duck into the dressing room and slip my new dress back onto the hanger. Revenge. I want revenge. Carla Van Owen will be Princess of the Ball over my dead body.

chapter 18

Homeroom. Johnny Bruno's voice blasts over the P.A. system and into the auditorium. He sounds like one of those boppy top-forty radio jocks. I swear, I don't know what I ever saw in him.

Carla has been lobbying hard for Princess of the Ball. Today we write down our nominations. Whoever gets the most votes from each grade gets to be in the finals. Then tomorrow the whole school picks one of the top four. The winner is the Princess and the others are her Duchesses. Usually a senior wins Princess because nobody knows who the underclassmen are.

They hand me a slip of paper. On it I write: Harley Columba. I nominate myself. Maybe Evan will nominate me, too. I turn around to look at him. His class sits all the way over in the third section of the auditorium. Evan is having an intense conversation with the guy sitting next to him. He doesn't see me watching.

Then, suddenly, everything changes. Evan stands up and fiddles with the front of his pants, then sits back down in a hurry. At the same time, Mr. Petranski runs up the aisle and yanks Evan out of his seat. Evan shouts, "Hey!"

I stand up, amazed at what I am watching. So does everybody else. The hardwood auditorium chairs squeak as everyone vies for a peek. Evan and Mr. Petranski are struggling. The seats squeal and flap, squeal and flap as hundreds of people try to see what's going on. Mr. Petranski grabs Evan's arm and drags him out of the auditorium. I try to make eye contact with Evan as he is whisked away, but there are too many people blocking my view.

Everyone whispers, "What happened? What happened?" A

game of telephone begins over in Evan's section and spreads throughout the auditorium. Buzz, buzz, buzz. Ms. Auberjois clambers up on the stage and starts yelling, *"Asseyez-vous! Asseyez-vous!"* which means "sit down" but no one pays any attention.

Finally the whispers reach me. Marijuana. Selling. Busted. Evan has been busted for selling pot. Oh, *no*. My stomach drops right out of me. *Busted*. It sounds tough, like a gangster word. Will he go to jail? I will visit him behind bars, and sob, oh, yes, I will wait for you, my love. Will they cut off all his hair and make him wear blue jump suits? I will bake him nail file cakes and mastermind the escape. I am an accomplice in spirit. Will they arrest me too? Yeah, Lieutenant, she's the girlfriend. Cuff her.

I hear police sirens in the distance. Closer. Closer. I watch myself run to the long auditorium windows, even though I'm not allowed out of my seat. I press my cheek against the glass. The red light on top of the police car flashes across my face, like I am in a movie. I stare as they handcuff Evan, shove him in the car and drive away.

✳✳✳

I drift through my classes in a dream. Teachers teach, but I don't hear them. Every so often someone touches me and says, "Hang in there, Harley," or asks me about Evan like I have some secret source within the police department. Strangers and upperclassmen, people who never talk to me, come up and offer a word or two. People whisper and point at me when I walk through the hall. I have become an instant celebrity because of Evan. I stop by my locker to put on some lipstick. I might as well look good.

"Looks like you're not going to make it to the Spring Ball, huh,

Harley?" I turn around and Carla is standing there with Nancy Peterman, a nasty smile on her face.

"What…what do you mean?" She has caught me off guard.

"You don't think they're going to let a druggie into a school dance, do you? Evan'll be lucky if he doesn't get expelled."

I didn't even think of that. Of course she's right. It's hard to have your best friend as an enemy; they spot all the weaknesses in your armor.

Carla knows she got me. "Too bad you're going to miss my coronation." She hikes her books onto her hip and swivels away. Nancy Peterman follows right behind her like a lap dog. "In your dreams," I yell to her back. I lean against my locker. What am I going to tell Peppy?

✳✳✳

I hang out on the Pond Hole steps at lunch. All the elite engulf me. Lisa Kowalski and Debbie Nagle give me a cigarette.

"Can you believe that narc Petranski?" Lisa says, puffing on her Marlboro. It dangles out of her mouth like an old billboard ad.

"Evan got a raw break," sniffs Debbie. "Everybody deals pot."

"Really?" I am so naïve, I swear. "Do you think he'll go to jail?"

"Nah." A senior guy spits on the ground. "He's not old enough. Maybe Juvie Hall or something. Does he have a record?"

"I don't think he's ever been in trouble before," I say. "Nothing that I know about, anyway."

"He'll just get a slap on the wrist," says the guy. "Marijuana is nothing. Just be glad it wasn't junk."

I nod and puff on my cigarette, and wonder what I am doing here, chatting about junk and pot. I look around at all these people who seem to be so cool. I am separate from them like an island, even though I am in the center of the group. In the back of my mind this little voice whispers that I am in over my head.

✳✳✳

I let myself in the front door. "I'm home!" Peppy is in the kitchen. Roger isn't home yet. I have decided to tell them nothing.

"How was school?" Peppy calls out to me. Oh, great. The one day I don't want to talk, and Peppy is feeling chatty. I brace myself and walk into the kitchen. She is cooking lemon chicken, my favorite.

"Same old thing." I grab one of Bean's apples and bite it.

"I left something on your bed. Go see." Peppy pours the sauce over the chicken and shoves it in the oven. Terrific. Today of all days she decides to break down and turn into a mother.

I climb up the stairs and go into my room. There on my bed, next to my freshly ironed black dress, is a red jewelry box. I pop open the lid. Ooooh. Inside is the pair of hand-painted rose earrings we saw in the mall. I feel so guilty, tears fill my eyes.

"They *are* beautiful, aren't they?" Peppy has silently appeared in the doorway behind me.

I sniffle. "They're incredible, Mom. But you shouldn't have spent the money." There is no way I can tell her I'm not going to the ball.

"I remember how exciting my first Spring Ball was. All the decorations, the flowers—it's so romantic. Everything should be perfect. See how good they look with your dress."

I cannot take it. I burst into sobs. I throw my arms around my mother's neck and cry. It's been so many years since I've held her, she feels funny. Peppy strokes my hair. "What's the matter, Harley?"

I want to tell her about Evan, but she will never understand.

"I…they're…they're just so wonderful, Mom. I love them." I have to get a grip. I straighten up and wipe my nose with my sleeve.

"Use a tissue," Peppy says automatically. Then she goes into the bathroom and brings out a box. "Here."

Her kindness is making everything worse. I take a tissue out of the box and blow. She squeezes my arm like we are a female alliance, then turns to leave. "I've got to go down and finish supper, honey. I'm glad you like the earrings." Her feet pad down the stairs. I lay down on my bed, exhausted by the weight of it all. God is laughing at me, I think. I am his little joke.

✳✳✳

The phone rings. Peppy answers it. She hollers, "Harley! It's Evan!" I jump off my bed and race down the stairs. Roger has come home and is watching the news. I pull the telephone cord as far as I can into the living room so no one can hear me.

"Evan! How are you?" My voice is full of panic.

"Q.C. is threatening to kill me. Otherwise I'm all right." He doesn't sound too upset.

"What's going to happen?" I can't believe he is so calm.

"Oh, I'll have to go to court, but Q.C. has a pretty good lawyer. They'll try to get me released into Q.C.'s custody. I'll get probation or something. No big deal."

Maybe I've been making this worse than it is. Everyone seems to think it's nothing. Except Carla. And if I'm honest, except me. Then Evan says: "But it doesn't look like we'll be going to the ball. They suspended me from school for a couple of weeks."

My worse fear has come true. I cannot talk. "Harley? Harley, are you there?" Evan's voice echoes in my ear. "Harley, answer me."

"I'm…I'm here, Evan." I swallow. The romantic jailbreak has disappeared; reality hits me cold in the face. I lower my voice so that I am almost whispering. "What am I going to tell my mother? She just bought me new earrings."

"Look, babe, we'll figure something out. I'll pick you up after school tomorrow. Meet me at the steps, okay?"

I feel the tears sting my eyes, wrap around my throat and squeeze. "Okay. I've got to see the director of the play first."

"I'll wait. Hang in there, Harley. Bye."

I hang up the phone and keep my face away from the kitchen so Peppy can't see my tears. There goes Old Faithful. I must have a geyser so deep inside it will never run dry.

"Set the table, Harley," calls my mother.

"Okay, Mom." I put on a phony face and get the silverware from the drawer. I take the silver princess spoon out for myself from the potholder drawer. I hesitate, then grab the best steak knife, too.

✲✲✲

In homeroom, I can feel the empty space where Evan once sat behind me. Everyone is still buzzing about yesterday's big bust. I catch a whisper or two about me: the poor girl with the new little black party dress, the only one not going to the ball. The hot redness starts at my ears and spreads to my face. I open my French book and read the same paragraph over and over.

Mr. Petranski begins handing out stacks of paper to the first person in each row. Out of the corner of my eye, I watch as everybody takes one and passes the rest on. Finally the pile gets to me. It is the four nominations for Princess of the Ball. I stare at the paper trembling in my hand.

Freshman: Carla Van Owen
Sophomore: Melody McCormick
Junior: Prudence Clark
Senior: Betsy Hamilton

She did it. Carla actually did it. I glance over at her, sitting among the other end-of-the-alphabet people. Everyone is hugging and congratulating her and she is grinning like she's the new mayor. And then there's my other good buddy, Prudence Clarke. This is too much. I put a big red "X" next to the senior girl's name, even though I don't know who she is. I'll be damned if I'll vote for the Gorgon Sisters.

Well, this is it, then, the way life goes. The way wars start. Maybe I'll sneak into the ball and drop a bucket of thumb tacks from the ceiling. Or put liquid shoe polish in the ladies' room soap.

✷✷✷

I dip my brush into the yellow oil paint, then dab it onto the palette and soften it with a little white. Miss Posey stands at my side, nodding. "Good. Good. Nice choice of color."

The painting for the first act is done, the princess with no face. I tried to paint the body standing as if she is uncertain, hesitant, since this is when Anastasia first meets the Empress. She wears a ragged shawl over her shoulders, and her long brown hair is limp and tangled. The second portrait is almost done. This time I've drawn a vague outline of her features, but purposely left the details off so there is just a hint of a nose, a suggestion of a smile. In this painting Anastasia stands taller, a little more sure of herself.

The painting for the third act, the oil, will be a life-sized portrait after the Empress is convinced she is the real Anastasia. It is my *pièce de résistance*, although I am still working on the background and haven't even started on the actual face. It takes longer because I have to wait for the oil to dry.

Bud Roman comes striding into the room. "I'm late. Sorry."

Miss Posey and I move to the side and wait as Bud Roman paces up and down in front of my three portraits. He strokes his goatee. Backs up. Squints. Moves forward. Miss Posey looks at me and shrugs. I shrug. We wait. I have performed my trick. I am a dog waiting for my master's approval.

Finally Bud Roman speaks. "They're perfect. Keep going, Motorcycle Mama. Keep it going." I smile. This is what keeps me sane, I think. These paintings. I am so starved for a compliment, I lap it right up. He turns to Miss Posey. "You ready, Emma?"

Miss Posey glances at her watch. "We've gotta run, Harley. Stay as long as you like. Good work."

I stand alone in the art room facing the three princesses. I dip my brush into the oil and start to paint.

✳✳✳

When I finally get to the Pond Hole steps, Evan is there, mobbed by a crowd. He's down in the parking lot since he's not allowed on school property. Everybody is moshing against him like he's a rock star or something. He's got a cigarette in one hand and a bottle in a brown paper bag in the other. He sees me and waves. "Hey, Harley!"

I smile in spite of everything, I am so happy to see him. I waltz down the steps like a princess at a ball. Except my court is a bunch of smokers and stoners, not dukes and duchesses. I try to squeeze my way into the mob. "Let her through!" yells Evan. Someone in the crowd moves aside. People turn to look at me as I push my way into the center, next to Evan. It's a Pond Hole party, and we are the main attraction.

Evan wraps his arms around me and gives me a big, long kiss. A couple of people whistle and hoot, and I feel great. Let Carla and Prudence have their stupid nominations. We are the vanguard stars on campus, the musician and the painter.

Evan grabs my hand and leads me through the crowd to his car. He opens my door, helps me in, revs up the engine and squeals out of the parking lot. He zooms to the top of Lover's Peak and parks. Finally he turns to look at me. "I missed you, babe."

I throw my arms around him. He kisses me. We are all lips and tongues. He takes my jacket off and runs his hands over my body. I press against him and kiss him until I think I will never breathe again.

This is what we decide to do: I will get ready to go to the ball in my new dress and earrings. Evan will pick me up. We will pretend we are going to the ball, but we'll really go to the drive-in movies or something with Oliver and Jessie.

Evan pulls me to him. He strokes my cheek. "Don't worry, Harley." He puts his arm around me and squeezes. "I'll make it up to you. I promise." There is a tiny part of me that hesitates, worried if we can pull this off. Then he kisses me and I bury that part away.

✳✳✳

For the first time in a long while, me and Lily are alone in the house. My heart is pounding. I'm in the kitchen. I have my Shanahan list in front of me. These calls are too complicated to make from a pay phone. I will deal with the consequences when the phone bill comes.

I dial the first S. Shanahan on West Seventy-first Street. I am so nervous, I am breathing heavy; they're probably going to think I'm an obscene caller. The phone rings. And rings. A click. An answering machine picks up. There is a child's voice babbling in the background. A man says: "You have reached the Shanahans'. If you have a message for Steven, Annie or Parker, please leave a message at the beep. Thanks." I hang up. Hmmm. Steven Shanahan, I presume. He sounded like an accountant, not at all like a man who would be my father. I cross his name off the index card.

I dial the next number. It has no address. One ring. Two rings. "Hello?" It is a female voice. Maybe this is his wife. I am such a wimp, I can't speak. Come on, Harley, I tell myself. It's now or never. "Hello?" The woman on the other end sounds a little testy. "HELLO? Is someone there?" Talk, Harley, talk!

"...Hello?" I say. "Hello, I'm trying to reach Sean Shanahan."

There is a pause at the other end of the line. At that moment, Lily runs into the room. "Harley! Harley! Come quick! Riley's got my doll!"

I glare at her. I cover the mouthpiece. "Quiet!" I hiss. "Leave me alone!" Lily's eyes get wide. Her lip trembles. I pray she doesn't start to cry.

"I'm Susan Shanahan, but there's no Sean," says the voice. "What number did you dial?"

Lily's face is scrunching up and she is moments away from

tears. I talk fast. "Oh, I'm sorry." I try to cup the receiver. "I must have the wrong number. Bye." I hang up. I turn to Lily. I count to ten. "Come on, Lily, knock it off. This is important. Just let me make one more phone call and then I'll come, okay?"

"But Riley's eating her NOW!"

There is no reasoning with Lily when she is in this mood. I run into the other room and grab Barbie's head out of Riley's mouth. I twist it back onto her body. A big chunk of hair is missing and her nose is gone. "Okay, I fixed it. Now leave me *alone*! Watch TV."

I go back into the kitchen. I take a deep breath. I cross Susan Shanahan off the list. I dial the last number on West Eleventh Street. It rings. And rings. And rings. No answer. No answering machine. After the tenth ring, I start to hang up. Then I hear a man's voice. It sounds sleepy, like I woke him up at four o'clock in the afternoon. "Yeah?"

I rush the phone back up to my ear. I try to make my voice sound calm. "Hello," I say. "Hello. I'm looking for Sean Shanahan."

"Speaking," says the voice.

Speaking. I am stunned. Speaking! There is a real person named Sean Shanahan on the other end of the line. I don't know what to do, so I hang up. I take a deep breath. Then I do something crazy: I start laughing. I laugh and laugh, which is really strange because inside I feel like crying. Maybe this is enough, I think. Just to know he's out there.

chapter 19

Tonight is the night of the Spring Ball. Peppy is curling my hair. She has gotten Spring Ball madness. I feel like a real live Barbie doll she is dressing up. She is letting me wear lipstick, eye shadow—the works. Lily's eyes are wide as she watches every detail.

"I wanna go, Mommy."

"When you're older." Peppy rolls a lock of my hair into the curling iron. "Hold still, Harley. This curl won't curl." Steam hisses. She holds the wand against my head until I think my scalp will fall off.

"Ouch! Mom, you're burning me!"

"Just a second more. There." Peppy unrolls my hair, and the curl bounces. "You're going to be the most beautiful girl at the ball. Much better than Carla and her silly Frangelica dress."

I am living the worst lie of my life. If I could, I'd start all over again and tell Peppy the truth. But I am in too deep and Peppy is too excited. I want to be excited too. I want to be getting ready for the ball instead of some drive-in movie sham.

Peppy brushes me out. My long brown hair bounces and shines. I spin around. I think I really might look good.

"A little more lipstick. Sit." Peppy pushes me on the bed and applies a lovely red to my lips. I watch her face as she concentrates. She has tiny wrinkles around her dark brown eyes and her mouth droops. I imagine she is as old as me, going to her first ball and Granny is painting her lips bright red with one of those old gold lipstick holders.

"What did you wear to your Spring Ball, Mom?"

Peppy hesitates. Something flickers across her face. "Actually, I didn't go to my first ball until I was a senior."

"Really? Who did you go with? Dad?"

Peppy stops painting my lips. She spins the lipstick closed with a click. "Come on, now. Let's put on your dress."

I stand up, and she scoops the dress over my head. It tumbles around my shoulders. "Did you go with Dad?"

Peppy turns me around and zips up the back. "Your father and I had broken up at the time." Peppy straightens my hem. She backs me up and examines me. "You look fantastic, Harley."

I move over to the mirror and gaze at my reflection. My blue eyes are two brilliant opals. My cheeks are rosy. My lips are red. "Who, Mom? Who took you to the ball?"

For a moment, Peppy looks dreamy, like she is remembering a time long ago. Then she says, "I went to the Spring Ball with Sean Shanahan."

***

At exactly seven o'clock, the doorbell rings. Somehow Peppy scraped Roger out of his Barcalounger and planted him on the living-room sofa so he could play his part in the Daughter-Goes-to-the-Ball ceremony. I hear Peppy open the front door. Riley barks.

"Hello, Mrs. Columba." Evan's voice floats up the stairs and into my ears. How I love that boy.

I take one last glance in the mirror and race down the stairs. I cannot leave Evan alone in the monster's lair for too long.

"Hey, Evan!" My feet barely touch the floor as I swoop into the living room. Evan turns to look at me. He whistles. "Wow." He hands me a corsage of daisies and roses. He has his hair pulled back in a pony tail and is wearing a suit and tie like a model in a Calvin Klein ad.

"Wow yourself." I smile at him. I am so nervous, my head is throbbing. I don't know if we're going to pull this off, but we sure get an A-plus for effort. Peppy takes the corsage from me and sticks the pins in her mouth. "Come here, Harley. Let me pin this on you."

Roger stands up and extends his hand to Evan. "Roger Columba." This is his introduction. He teeters a little, and I am embarrassed. Evan is taller than Roger. He shakes Roger's hand and smiles as if he is running for president.

"Very nice to meet you, sir." Boy, can Evan play the part. I see that even Roger the Dragon-Hearted is impressed.

Bean bounces through the room all dressed in black. "See ya." He opens the front door.

"Where are you going?" Roger asks like he really doesn't want to know.

"Manhunt tonight. I'm late."

Peppy mumbles through the pins. "Say hello to Evan, Bean."

Bean rolls his eyes like it's this huge effort for him to be polite. "Hello, Evan."

Evan grins. "Hey."

"Bye, Evan." Bean slams the door on the way out.

"That kid." Peppy sticks me with a pin.

"Ow! Mom!"

Lily carries her headless Barbie doll into the room. She has dressed her in a fancy evening gown. "Barbie is going to the ball tonight, too," she informs Evan.

"What happened to her head?"

"Riley ate it. He chewed it, then he buried it, and I can't find it."

"She looks pretty good even without a head." Evan winks.

"There!" Peppy fastens the corsage over my heart. "They match the roses on your earrings."

"Thanks, Mom." I pick up my big black pocketbook and swing it over my shoulder. "We probably should get going."

Peppy frowns. "Wait a second. You can't bring that ugly purse. Go in my top drawer and get Granny Harley's little white pearl bag."

"Really?" I am surprised. Granny's bag is a real treasure, with tiny hand-sewn beads and sequins.

"Yes, Harley. I can't bear to think of you at the ball with that giant suitcase." Peppy smiles at Evan. Tonight she is going so far above the call of duty, it's almost embarrassing.

I scoot off down the hall and into my parent's room. I tug open the top drawer of my mother's dresser. It's stuck. I pull and yank. It opens a crack. I stick my hand inside and feel around to see what is blocking the drawer. A crumpled piece of paper is wedged way in the back. I grab an edge and gently tug. The drawer opens, but all I can see is the crinkled document I hold in my hand. It is black with white letters. It is a birth certificate.

It says:

> Name: Baby Girl Harley
> Mother's Maiden Name: Patricia Harley
> Father's Name: Unknown
> Mother's Occupation: Secretary
> Father's Occupation: N/A

The wave is sudden; it knocks me off my feet. I am trembling and almost drop the paper. Baby Girl Harley. This must be my real birth certificate. It almost seems too easy, finding it this way. Peppy must have stuck it in the drawer when she saw me snooping around, then forgot about it. *Baby Girl Harley*. The words hit me like a slap. It is the name of a doll, not a child. Hi, I'm Baby Girl, who are you? Yes, Baby Girl Harley. Do you know my father, Mr. Unknown? I have no name. I have no father. I am the Baby Girl Harley doll. I cry real tears.

"Harley?" My mother calls from the other room. "Did you find it?"

I jump like a jewel thief caught with my hand in a safe. "Got it!" I take a deep breath. The Baby Girl Harley doll can do anything. Just wind her up and watch her go. I shove the paper back inside the drawer. I grab Granny's little white purse and dump some stuff from my pocketbook into it. I run back down the hall, clutching the beaded bag, and try to hold onto my sanity.

"That's better, Harley," Peppy says. "You look like a real lady."

I try to act normal. I smile and do a pirouette. My black dress flares. "Thanks, Mom," I tell her. "You sure are being nice."

"That dress is awfully short, Harley," Roger says.

I spin the other way. My dress collapses, then swirls in the opposite direction. I force a laugh. "It's the style, Dad."

"Did anyone ask *me* if you could wear that dress?"

Oh, no. Roger is going to be a jerk. "Dad…"

"I pay for the roof over your head and the clothes on your back. I say that dress is too short." I bite the inside of my cheek. My stomach knots up.

Peppy throws him a warning. "It's what they're wearing, honey."

"Well, you should know, Patricia," says Roger, slurring his words a little. "You're the prom expert. You're the Queen o' the Ball." Peppy opens her mouth to say something, then decides against it. I realize Roger has been knocking back the vodka. I have to get Evan out of here before we all wind up dead on the floor.

Roger doesn't stop. "I've never been to the ball, not like my wife here. Or the prom. Or even the eighth-grade dance. I don't dance. My wife loves to dance. She'll dance with anyone who asks her." Warning. Warning. Roger on the warpath.

"Roger..." Peppy takes Roger by the arm. He yanks it away and turns to Evan.

"Do you dance, Ethan?"

"His name is Evan, Dad. And we'd better run before we're late." I grab Evan's hand and pull him toward the door. Escape. Escape.

Evan's chin rises slightly, and he looks straight at Roger, his gray eyes gazing into Roger's brown ones. Like a snake charmer he hypnotizes the cobra. I remember his father, Q.C., on the phone and think, ah, well, he knows what *this* is about, he knows how to handle this. Maybe Evan is a doll, too. Maybe we are both toys for grownups to play with. Hey, folks, you've got the Baby Girl Harley doll, now get her boyfriend, Evan.

Evan says, "I like to dance to the slow stuff as long as the girl isn't wearing spikes. Dangerous weapons, spikes."

Roger considers this for a moment. Then he bursts out laughing as though Evan has just cracked the funniest joke. "Spikes! Spikes! I know what you mean. Spikes!" Roger moves away and collapses back on the sofa. Peppy snatches the opening and practically shoves us out the door. "Run along, you two. Have a good time. Don't be late."

Baby Girl Harley and her boyfriend Evan fly out of the house and into their shiny blue Camaro accessory. Peppy, Roger, and Lily watch through the front window. Evan makes a big show of holding my door open as I scoot inside. He slams it shut and tosses a wave back at the House of Columba.

✸✸✸

Father, UNKNOWN. Father, UNKNOWN. Father, UNKNOWN. The loop plays inside my head as we rumble into Sunrise Estates. I really am adopted. I wasn't imagining the whole thing. I'm not crazy. Breathe, Baby Girl, breathe. I am getting dizzy.

Evan reaches across the stick shift and touches my hand as we pull up in front of Oliver's gate. "You okay?" I nod. I am afraid to speak. If I say one word I will dissolve into a puddle. I am spinning, spinning, spinning out of control. I wonder if I should tell Evan the whole, sordid story. It's too much for me to deal with. It's just too much. I close my eyes. I can feel pieces of myself shutting down. Clank, clank. Shut down the heart, shut down the brain, this kid's going into overload. Maybe this is what happens when the pain is too great, I think. You become plastic and feel nothing at all.

I hear Evan shut off the ignition. I can feel him watching me. I swallow. I am far away; I can almost feel his touch. I blink. He cups my chin in his hands. He gray eyes look deep into mine. Lights on, nobody home. "You'd really like to go to the ball, wouldn't you, babe?"

My eyelids flutter as the first wave of salt water hits. Yeah, I want to go to the ball, but as the real thing, not an imitation. I want my real father and my real mother to send their darling daughter off to the real ball. I turn my face away from Evan so he can't see my tears. I nod. "It's okay, though." I think I say these words out loud.

Evan runs his fingers down the back of my neck. "Is there anything else bothering you, babe? You seem… I don't know."

harley
like a person

Earth to Harley. Earth to Harley. Come in, Harley. I try to answer, but it's hard to speak when your lips don't move. "Harley?" Evan's voice is far away. "Harley, are you okay?"

Call me Baby Girl Harley, I want to say. My name is Baby Girl Harley, and you are my boyfriend Evan with arms and legs that bend. He strokes my hair. I start to cry. "What?" he whispers. "What, babe, what?" I feel Evan scoop me into his arms. He is so strong. Stronger than G.I. Joe. I could tell him, I think. I could tell him and he would understand. I start to answer....

"Hey! You guys! Stop making out in there!" I look up. Jessie and Oliver stand on the stoop, waving. They're dressed like some freaky bride and groom. Oliver wears a black top hat and tails. Jessie has on a black crushed velvet gown that makes her look even more like Morticia. They are ready to party. I blink and remember why we're here.

"Will you get a look at those two," says Evan. I wipe my eyes. My cheeks are made out of flesh, not plastic. Flesh, streaked with tears.

"Come *on*!" yells Jessie. "Get your butts in here!"

Evan fishes a tissue out of the glove compartment and hands it to me. "Blow," he instructs.

I obey. "I'm sorry, Evan," I sniffle. My voice is hoarse. "I just—"

Evan hushes me with a kiss. "It's okay, Harley. It's my fault. If I hadn't gotten busted—"

"No." I don't want Evan to get all guilty on me. "It's not that—"

"COME ON, YOU GUYS!" Jessie is jumping up and down on the porch.

"Jessie, shut up!" Evan shouts out the window. He turns back to me. "Come on, babe." He kisses me again. "Smile." He tickles the edges of my mouth.

God, I am such a drag. I don't want to ruin the night for everybody. I give Evan a little smile. "I'm okay." I try to convince myself. "I'm fine." I wrap my arms around his neck. I slip the elastic off his ponytail. He shakes his head and his blond hair tumbles around his shoulders. He kisses my nose. "We'd better go inside."

I take a compact out of Granny's purse and repair my face. It actually doesn't look too bad. I dab some powder over my red nose. Evan pulls me out of the car and tugs me up to the porch. Oliver and Jessie applaud our entrance.

"Greetings, friends." Oliver tips his top hat. "Welcome to my humble abode."

"Geez, it's about time, you love birds." Jessie twirls and shows off her Morticia gown and makes me smile. "We wanted to get fancy, too!" she giggles. "Come in, come in. Oliver's folks went to Maui." I swear, Oliver has the best life with parents who are never home.

Jessie grabs my hand and pulls me inside the house. She is awfully excited for a trip to the movies, I think. Then I see why. I step into the hallway and gasp.

"*Voilà!*" Jessie curtsies with a sweep of her hand.

The house looks completely different than it did on the night of the party. The living room has been transformed into a crazy version of a medieval castle. A red carpet runs down the center. Candles flicker. Logs burn in the fireplace. Vases spill over with daisies and baby breath. A waltz plays on the stereo. Whoa, I think. Oliver's parents must be *really* rich.

Jessie places a rhinestone tiara on top of my head. "Princess Harley, welcome to the Ball of the Misbegotten!"

"It's beautiful." I am amazed. I step into the room and sink into the carpet. For a second, I do not think my knees will hold me up. Evan grabs my shoulders. "Surprise!" he laughs. "Your own private ball."

Oh, wow. The three of them went through all this trouble so I wouldn't be disappointed. Against the far wall is a long banquet table covered with a white linen cloth. On the table are plates of food and hors d'oeuvres. Stacked at the end are china dishes and real silver, every teaspoon a princess. "It's too much," I say.

Oliver shrugs. "Just some crap my parents keep stashed in a closet. Jessie went nuts. She's been at it all day."

Evan pulls me into the center of the room. He bows. "May I have this dance, Your Highness?" Clarinets and flutes tug at my feet. One, two, three. One two three. The waltz is so happy, it's hard to stay sad. Oh, I don't want to think tonight, I just want to have fun. I want to play Medieval Ball with Evan and Oliver and Jessie and dance and dance and dance. I adjust the tiara on top of my head. Yes. Tonight I will be wild. Tonight I will be free. Tonight Baby Girl Harley goes to the Ball. I nod at Evan. "I'd love to dance with you, Sir Lennon." He sweeps me into his arms and spins me around the floor.

Oliver tips his hat to Jessie and she tumbles into his arms. Together they move to the music. The crystal chandelier above our heads throws tiny stars across the walls. One, two, three. One, two, three. My hair flies out as Evan twirls me around the room. French horns and violins lift us off our feet. Round and round we spin until the room is just a blur.

The music builds to a crescendo, then fades to a finish. We all collapse onto the sofa, breathless and giggly. A bouncy little minuet starts playing, and Oliver reaches for a bottle that is chilling in a silver ice bucket. "Tonight we drink champagne," he declares as he twists off the cork. The bottle explodes with a pop, and golden suds spill over the rim. He fills four tall, delicate glasses and hands one to each of us. He raises his glass. "To the Princess of the Ball of the Misbegotten, Harley Columba!"

We click our glasses together and drink. I've never had champagne before. The bubbles burst inside my mouth and down my throat. It tastes bittersweet. I take another sip. The bubbles tickle my nose. "Thank you, thank you, my Royal Misbegotten Court," I declare.

Oliver reaches for a crystal bowl that is on the coffee table. I see it is filled with rolled joints. Hmmm. He takes one and passes the bowl to Jessie. She takes one and passes it to Evan. Evan offers the bowl to me. I hesitate. Go ahead, I think. Go ahead, orphan child. I take one out of the bowl.

Oliver strikes a long fireplace match and holds it over his head like the Statue of Liberty. "And now, in honor of our daring misbegotten prince, Evan Lennon, who has just this fortnight escaped from the evil dungeons of Lenape, we do hereby smoke this ceremonious weed." Oliver lights each of our joints with the match and winks. "This stuff is potent, kids."

We all inhale together. I feel the smoke tumble around my lungs. I exhale a big white puff and blow myself right down the rabbit hole. "The Ball of the Misbegotten is most enchanting." I issue a royal proclamation from my lips.

Jessie laughs. "It's the best ball in town." She is smoking her joint as if it were a cigarette. I take another puff and set mine down. I already feel a little buzzed, and I don't want to get too whacked. Evan tucks me under his arm and then his lips cover mine. "Happy?" he asks.

"Very," I say, and, at that moment, full of golden bubbles and white smoke, I mean it.

Oliver stands up and bows in front of me. "Let us partake of some nourishment from the royal banquet table, Your Highness. I'm starving."

I float to my feet. I drift over to the table crammed with food. I pick up a white china plate, a linen napkin, a knife, a fork, and a shiny silver teaspoon. "You don't need a spoon right now, Harley," Evan says.

"But I want her!" I titter. "I want her just to have her!" Evan smiles and shakes his head. He fills my plate with mutton and pheasant and Yorkshire pudding. Or maybe it's steak and chicken in disguise.

We sit on a sheepskin rug in front of the fire. I nibble my food. Viking food. I chew slowly and watch the flames leap and sway. I am fascinated by the fire. A piano and harp start playing, and I think the fire is dancing to the music. I recognize the tune from Mrs. Tuttle's house. "Ooo," I say. "I love Schumann."

Oliver snorts. "*The World's Most Beloved Melodies*. Belongs to my parents."

"I don't care." I wonder if Oliver is making fun of me. "It's romantic."

I turn to Evan. The firelight flickers across his face. "Nice tune," he assures me. I smile at him. We touch without touching, using only our eyes. Jessie motions to Oliver, then tugs him out of the room. Evan reaches out for me. His hand glides over my shoulder, my neck, my arm. I move next to him. Gently he pushes me back on the sheepskin rug. Evan is over me, his blond hair spilling across my face. I wrap my arms around his neck and pull him closer. I feel the heat of the fire and the warmth of Evan's kisses. I close my eyes and let him take me where he wants to go.

***

Me and Jessie are in the bathroom, putting on fresh lipstick. Jessie's lips are so red, they look almost purple.

"I think you guys fell asleep," she says. "Let me zip you up."

I yawn. "I think we did, too. Where'd you go?"

"Upstairs." Jessie grins. "You looked like you were having fun."

I catch her eye in the mirror. "I was having a *very* nice time." I turn my back to her so she can reach my zipper.

"Oliver wants to ask you something."

"What?" I am curious. "What does he want to ask me?"

"Wait and see." Jessie smiles mysteriously, and her teeth are, brilliant white pearls inside her big purple lips. "It's something good." She takes my hand and pulls me into the living room.

Oliver and Evan sit on the sofa, drinking beer. "You girls finish off the champagne," says Oliver. "We men will drink the big beer bubbles."

Jessie perches on Oliver's lap. She pours me a glass of champagne. "Here you are, M'Lady."

I take a sip. The champagne is ice cold from sitting in the bucket. It tastes even better. "Mmm. I could get to really like this stuff."

"Ask her, Ollie, ask her." Jessie wiggles on Oliver's lap, almost spilling his beer. "Ask her right this second."

Evan takes an envelope out of his suit jacket. He tosses it on the coffee table. "Inside this simple white envelope are two tickets to the Spring Ball, bought and paid for. Oliver has volunteered to escort you, our dear Princess, if you would like to go."

My mouth nearly falls right off my face, I am so surprised. Go to the Spring Ball with Oliver? I say nothing. Evan grins. "Well?"

"I…I don't know what to say," I stammer. In a way I want to go, but in a lot of ways I don't. I barely know Oliver. I don't want to leave Evan. I am having too much fun at the Ball of the Misbegotten.

"This way you won't have to lie to your parents when they start the interrogation," says Evan. "You don't have to stay long, just a dance or two. Me and Jessie can drive around or something, then come back and get you. I mean, I paid for the tickets. There's no reason why you shouldn't go just because I can't."

He has a point. I know Peppy's going to cross-examine me. Plus, I'm dying to see if Carla gets Princess of the Ball.

Oliver burps. "We'll get there around ten and they don't crown the damn princess 'till around midnight anyway. I took some babe from Lenape last year." Jessie pouts. Oliver ignores her. "It's worth a laugh. We'll get a good buzz on the way over."

I smile. "Okay." Not exactly the way I planned on going to the Spring Ball, but what have I got to lose?

chapter 20

Evan does a skid in front of the Elks Lodge, which is this drab concrete building they rent out for banquets and dances. The rah-rahs have decorated the place with red and yellow balloons. The theme of this year's ball is "Spring Fever," so there is a huge fake thermometer on the door. Tacky.

Evan kisses me good-bye. I'm a little tipsy and really anxious, and for a second I want to tell him that Baby Girl Harley can't go through with this. Instead I climb out of the car and shiver in the parking lot. Oliver staggers out of the back seat wearing his top hat and tails, still smoking a joint. He has brought along a black cane with a white tip. He looks like a deranged ballroom dancer.

Jessie scoots up into the front seat. "Have fun, guys!"

Oliver hands her what's left of his joint and leans over to kiss her. He nearly falls onto her lap. He straightens up and grins at me. "Ready?" He offers me his arm. I don't want to take it, but I don't know what else to do. I grab on. He puts his left foot out and does a little hop like a drunken scarecrow in the Wizard of Oz.

Evan peels out of the parking lot as Jessie waves good-bye. I turn to watch them go and part of me wants to chase after the blue Camaro and hide in the trunk. I sigh. Oh, well. I will try to make the best of this. We hum as we skip and stumble up to the door.

Hairy Mr. Petranski guards the entrance like he is protecting Buckingham Palace. Just my luck that old Mr. Detention-Giver is the faculty chaperone. Oliver saunters up to him, his long dark hair flapping underneath his top hat. He taps his cane. He whisks the two tickets from the pocket of his long black jacket and speaks

harley like a person

191

with a phony British accent. "Entrance for two to the Spring Ball, please, my dear sir." He hands the tickets to Mr. Petranski and clicks his heels.

Mr. Petranski's mouth falls open like he can't believe what he is seeing. "That's some get-up, son." He takes the tickets from Oliver and puts them in a huge fishbowl. "For the raffle," he says. He peers at me. "Harley Columba, is that you?"

I am a nervous wreck. "It's me!" I titter.

"You're a little late. I don't know how much food is left, but find a table and help yourself."

Oliver takes my arm and pushes past him. "We've already dined, sir." He leads me into the room, leaving Mr. Petranski behind us with his eyebrows raised in one furry arch.

They have decorated the hall with construction paper flames and crinkly red cellophane. Orange and red balloons drip yellow ribbons from the ceiling. Spring Fever. It looks like we stepped into hell.

The band is called The Magpies, a bunch of boppie seniors who play disco music. Couples are boogeying on the dance floor. I spot Mr. Donovan, wearing a red bow-tie, moving to the beat. He looks like he's at the wrong party. I'll bet he hired the band. Across the front of the room is a long table where all the nominated princesses sit with their boyfriends. I see Carla draped all over Troy. What a floozy. Scattered around the hall are round tables, big enough to seat eight.

"Where you do wanna sit?" Oliver asks.

Hmmm. Good question. I look around the hall at all the laughing faces and see no place where I belong. It is then I realize I do not have a single friend anymore. "I…I don't know." I never even thought of this. The only open chairs I see are at a table full of geeks. This is such a mistake, coming here. I want to run right out the door.

Then, from behind me, someone puts their hands over my eyes. "Guess who?" It is a girl, but I have no idea which one. I turn around. It's Debbie Nagle.

"Debbie! Hi!" I am so glad to see anyone, even if it's the class nympho.

"Where's Evan?"

"He's banned from the ball." I giggle as if everything is fine and dandy, but inside I am wilting fast. "This is his friend, Oliver. Oliver, this is Debbie." Oliver tips his top hat and kisses her hand. I cringe.

Debbie laughs. "Cool. Come sit at our table. We're over in the corner." We follow her through the crowd. Roger would die if he saw how short Debbie's dress was. You can see right up her butt. Everyone points at Oliver's outfit, whispering and snickering. I try not to walk next to him, but it is obvious he is with me. Evan, Evan, where are you?

Lisa Kowalski is the only other person I know at the table. Her hair is stringy and her eyes are wild. "Harley, hey. Ya jus' get here?" She sounds like she's whacked.

"Yeah. This is Oliver."

"You didn't miss nothin'. Have some punch. We spiked it." Lisa pours me a plastic cup full of orange liquid and spills half of it on the table. "It tastes like crap, but it does the job." I stare at the cup. No way am I going to drink spiked punch at a school dance. Just having it in front of me makes me nervous.

Debbie plops down next to us. "This dance is so boring, I'd leave, but I gotta see which one of those bitches wins."

Oliver chugs a couple of glasses of punch and yawns. I'll bet he's sorry he ever volunteered to bring me. I'm sorry, too. Without Evan here, I really have nothing to say to him. He turns to me. "You wanna dance?"

Before I can answer, the music stops. Ms. Minelli walks up to the microphone. She is wearing a lime green dress covered with sequins, so she twinkles as she talks. "May I have your attention, ladies and gentlemen?" The microphone screeches feedback.

"Step back!" bellows Oliver, drunk on punch. He is a donkey braying in someone else's field. The entire hall turns to see who dares to challenge Ms. Minelli.

"Sshh!" I kick him under the table. If anyone missed him before, they sure won't now.

"I hate it when people eat the mike," mutters Oliver, tossing down another glass of punch.

Ms. Minelli edges back a baby step and leans into the mike, tentative. "Is this better?" No feedback. "Good. And now, the moment you've been waiting for: the tally of the votes for Princess of the Ball!"

"It's only a littl' after 'leven," says Lisa, taking a swig of punch.

"They figured we'd all leave if they waited any longer," says Debbie. "Pass that pitcher, will ya?"

All the girls who are nominated step up on the stage. I have to admit, Carla looks great. She stands there, beaming in her Frangelica dress, and there is a little part of me that wishes it was me up there.

"First, we will announce the Duchesses of the Court." Ms. Minelli runs down her list, reading off names. Each girl steps up and is handed a rose by some preppie senior guy. Ms. Minelli calls out, "Carla Van Owen." Everyone claps politely. Good. She didn't win Princess. Carla looks disappointed, but she smiles when the senior guy hands her a rose. Next Ms. Minelli calls out Melody McCornick's name, the sophomore, and Melody does a corny little curtsy when the senior guy hands her a rose.

"And now, our last Duchess, Besty Hamilton." Prudence Clarke squeals like a pig. That means she won Princess. I can't believe it. She practically shoves Betsy Hamilton off the stage. Ms. Minelli says, "May I present this year's Princess of the Ball, Prudence Clarke!" She places a sparkling tiara on top of Prudence's head. The senior guy hands her a huge bouquet of roses. The Magpies break into "There She Is, Miss America," as Prudence prances around the stage. Johnny Bruno appears from behind a curtain and escorts Prudence to the dance floor. They move together as the band plays a slow song I never heard before. They look like the perfect All-American couple. I am a little sad. That could have been me.

"Just think. That coulda been you, Harley." Lisa Kowalski punches me in the arm. "You and Johnny Bruno!" She laughs like that is the funniest thing she can imagine. Me and Johnny Bruno. Yeah. Instead it's me and Oliver the Scarecrow.

"And now, the rest of the Court will join their Princess," announces Ms. Minelli. The Duchesses descend to the dance floor. Troy sweeps Carla into his arms. She rests her head against his shoulder. I watch Prudence and Johnny and Carla and Troy twirl around the dance floor. There is scarcely anything left of the person I was a short time ago, all straight A's and proper. Now I am sitting at a table full of druggies, escorted to the Spring Ball by a guy in a clown suit that I barely know. I am miserable.

"Everybody dance!" Ms. Minelli shouts, and all over the room guys tug their girlfriends onto their feet. Oliver chugs some more punch and looks over at me. He burps. "Wanna dance, Harley?"

I am getting really depressed, but I nod. I wish this ball was over. I wish I'd never come. But what I really wish is that I was the Princess of the Ball and Evan was by my side. Oliver struggles to his feet. He picks up his cane, hesitates, then sets it back down. Good. I didn't feel like getting impaled.

We wade out into the crowd of dancers. I put my hands on his shoulder and try not to get too close. He leans against me. I am afraid that if I let go he will fall on the floor, he's so drunk. We shuffle around the dance floor and I can hear everyone whispering. Oliver in his top hat towers over the crowd. I want to shrink down to a whisper and disappear.

Oliver stumbles and stomps on my feet. "Ouch!" I yelp.

"Sorry," mumbles Oliver. His breath smells like stale whiskey. I turn my head away. Finally the music stops and I am relieved. I turn to head back to my table and come face to face with Carla the Duchess and Troy the Magnificent.

"Harley!" Carla pretends to be surprised to see me. "What are you doing here?"

Troy seems uncomfortable. "Hello, Harley."

I don't have the strength to deal with these two. "Hey." I force myself to smile. I wish Oliver would vanish back to the table, but he is glued to my side. "This is Oliver. Oliver, this is Carla, Troy…" My voice trails off. Carla and Troy stare at Oliver like he is some bizarre new life form.

Oliver tips his hat and nearly falls over. "Please ta meetcha."

"Oliver's… a friend of Evan's." I am so lame, I swear.

Carla flips her hair. "Nice hat," she says to Oliver, all sarcastic. She rolls her eyes at Troy and snickers.

Oliver's eyes narrow. Something dark crosses over his face. I've seen that look before: on Roger right before the thunder breaks. "Whaddaya mean, 'nice hat'?" Oliver mimics Carla's voice.

Oh, no. Disaster ahead. I grab Oliver's arm and try to push him toward our table. "Congratulations, Carla," I say over my shoulder. Oliver jerks his arm away from me. He strides back to Carla and looms over her. "Whaddaya mean, 'nice hat'?" His anger has boiled up from nowhere, and Carla looks frightened.

Troy steps in between Carla and Oliver. "Hey, pal. Take it easy."

"Your girlfriend's a bitch," Oliver informs Troy. "A snobby little bitch."

Troy pushes Oliver in the chest. "Watch it, bud."

"Hey!" Oliver trips backwards and falls to the floor. His top hat tumbles off his head and wobbles in a circle, then comes to a stop. Oliver sits there, stunned. A couple of girls scream.

The dance floor clears a circle around Oliver. Oliver shakes his head and jumps up, then smashes Troy right in the face.

Troy roars and rushes at Oliver. I try to get between them, but I am shoved out of the way. "Stop! Stop!" I hear a voice cry and then realize it is my own. Oliver and Troy are two pit bulls, going for each other's throats.

The music stops. I see Mr. Petranski and Mr. Donovan run toward us from the side of the hall. Mr. Petranski yanks Oliver off Troy. Oliver swings around and punches Mr. Petranski in his hairy belly. Mr. Petranski doubles over. Mr. Donovan jumps in the middle of the chaos and puts his arms up. "KNOCK IT OFF!" he orders. Somehow his voice makes everyone freeze. Troy and Oliver move away from each other and pant, blood dripping from their noses.

I feel fingernails rip deep into my arm. I turn and look at

harley
like a person

Carla's twisted face. "You've ruined everything!" says the Duchess to the leper. No, no, I want to say. Everything will be fine, you'll see. You're my best friend. This is just a stupid dance. Instead I whisper, "Sorry."

✳✳✳

I am numb. I sit in exile at the faculty table waiting for my parents to arrive. Mr. Petranski called them to come and pick me up. Around me, the ball is winding down. The music has stopped, the lights are turned up bright, and the rah-rahs on the clean-up committee are sweeping the floor. Oliver left with Evan after a big discussion of what the school policy was for students from another district. Lucky for him, his parents are in Maui. They wouldn't let me go with them. They wouldn't even let me see Evan.

I look up and see Roger and Peppy in the doorway talking to Mr. Petranski. Peppy's mouth is a tight white line and droops almost past her chin. Roger's fists are clenched. He sees me watching him and slaps me with his eyes. He is going to kill me. I don't care.

Roger and Peppy approach the table. "You disgust me." Roger talks to me as if I were a dog. "Let's go." I stand up. I shuffle between them out the door, a mutineer walking off the plank.

I climb in the back of the minivan. Peppy starts right in.

"You lied to us. We trusted you. Your teacher told us you didn't get there until after ten o'clock. Where were you? Who was that boy? Your teacher said Evan was suspended from school for selling drugs. There was alcohol in the punch at the table where you were sitting. You lied to us. We trusted you...." Peppy's voice hammers at me. I stare out the window. I am trapped. I am suffocating. I am alone. There is no way out of this. There is no way out.

I sit on the sofa in the living room. I stare at the floor. Peppy's blue K-Mart specials shuffle back and forth. Roger's cowboy boots trample the carpet. I am fascinated by the movement of their feet.

"What are we going to do with you?" Peppy is shrieking. She has turned into a banshee, and her voice is hurting my ears. I stop listening. "I just don't know what to do!"

I say nothing. I stare at the floor. Roger's boots need a polish, I think. And maybe some spurs. Roger removes his belt. "Answer your mother, Harley. Answer your mother if you know what's good for you."

I cannot *hear* my mother, I want to explain, I can only hear static. I have turned into a plastic Baby Girl Harley doll whose battery is dead. I cannot answer. I cannot move my mouth. All I can do is sit in my little black party dress and watch their shoes dance.

"Look at me, Harley Marie. LOOK AT ME!" Roger is roaring. I look up and see Bean and Lily crouched on the stairs, cowering against the railing. They are both sobbing. I want to wrap my arms around them and tell them it's all right, but I cannot move.

"What's wrong with you? Are you on drugs? Are you on drugs right now?" Peppy's voice pierces through the static in my brain. I shake my head no.

"Answer your mother, goddamn it!" Roger clenches the big silver Texas buckle in his hand. I open my mouth but no sounds come out. "ANSWER HER!" Roger raises the belt above his head. He has mistaken me for a piece of furniture, I think. He swings the belt down. I feel the side of my head go numb and realize he has whipped me across my face. I think it hurts, but my body is too far away.

harley
like a person

I start to raise my hand to my cheek, then stop. I will not give them the satisfaction. My vision turns to ice. I lower my arm. I stand up. Icicle eyes. I glare at Peppy and Roger with my eyes of ice. Their mouths move, but I cannot hear what they say. I walk to the stairs. Step by step, I climb up to my room. As I pass Bean and Lily, I pat them on the head. Bean takes my hand and squeezes it; I squeeze his back. I walk into my room and lie down on my bed. I close my eyes and drift up to the crystal blue lake in Strawberry Fields.

chapter 21

All morning on Sunday I lie in bed with my door closed. I get up to use the bathroom, then lie back down. My body is too heavy.

No one enters my room. I am in a dark cocoon. I am a caterpillar that will never turn into a butterfly. I drift in and out of sleep. I dream I am in a strange room in a strange bed. I am dying. Peppy is with me. Doom. I feel doom. It's only a dream, I tell myself, and then: How can you know it's only a dream if you're dreaming? I am dying, I tell Peppy. Please don't leave me here alone. She asks me, are you frightened? No, I say. Just don't let me die alone. I am here, she tells me. You are not alone. In my dream, I fall asleep. When I wake up in the strange room, Peppy has left and I am alone.

Time passes. I open my eyes, and I am alone in my own room. It is dark. I hear the phone ring a thousand miles away and Peppy's voice say, "I'm sorry, Evan." I weigh too much to do something about it.

I see the bedroom door open. I hear tiny footsteps patter into the room. I blink and Lily is standing over me.

"Harley," she whispers. "Harley, I snuck you a cookie." She places the cookie on the pillow next to my mouth.

"Thank you," I whisper back. I sit up. "Lily, come here."

Lily looks scared. She backs up. "It's okay, Lily," I say. "I just want to give you a hug."

She comes to the edge of the bed. I wrap my arms around her tiny body. I hold her forever and she lets me. I cry and cry and she pats my head with her little hand. Her hand is the wing of a butterfly. "It's okay, Harley," she says. "It's okay."

On Monday morning, Peppy is an army tank plowing through my bedroom. "Get up. I'm driving you to school."

I don't look at her. "I'm not going to school."

Peppy rips the covers off me. "Oh, yes, you are. I'm driving you there and picking you up. I've already made arrangements with my boss. If you're going to act like a child, I'm going to treat you like one. Now get dressed."

I pull the covers back over my body. "No." I am not getting out of bed for the rest of my life.

Peppy grabs my arm and yanks me onto the floor. "Now you listen to me, young lady. When I tell you to do something, you do it. Get dressed before I call your father up here." She turns and walks out of the room. "And leave that door open."

I stand up. I pull on a pair of dirty jeans and a tee shirt from a heap on the floor. I don't brush my hair. I don't care what I look like. I am a slob. So what.

I look at myself in the mirror. The person reflected back is no one I know. There is a red welt on the side of my face from the slap of the belt. I do not know how I will make it through the day. I hate my life.

My eyes drift to the edge of my easel. There is the postcard of the Imagine mosaic in Strawberry Fields. *Imagine*…imagine no Lenape. I slip the postcard off the board. I grab my backpack. I open my night table drawer. I flip through my artwork and find the bus schedule. I toss it into the backpack. I reach under my bed for my harlequin. I stuff him in my backpack, too, and zip it up.

I take off the jeans and pull on some tights. I tug a dress over my head. I step again in front of the mirror. I run a comb through my long brown hair. I cover the red welt with makeup. I put on some lipstick and mascara. I smile. Now I recognize myself. I am Harley. Like a person.

✱✱✱

I stand on the steps of the Pond Hole, smoking, hoping for a glimpse of Evan in his blue Camaro.

Debbie Nagle slithers over to me, a cigarette dangling from her lips. "You got Lisa busted, Harley." She blows a puff of smoke into my face.

I am astounded. "Me? What did I do?"

Debbie spits on the ground. "'Cause of the spiked punch."

I can't believe she is nailing me too. "I didn't spike the punch. You guys had it before I ever got there."

"Yeah, but if you didn't bring that loser, Oliver, nobody woulda found out. Think about it."

Debbie turns away and stands with the rest of the group, far away from me. I hold my head high and act like I don't care, even though it takes all my willpower to keep my feet planted. My head is throbbing. I am an outcast among the outcasts.

I hear the roar of Evan's Camaro and see his car whip through the parking lot. Thank you, God. I start down the stairs. I stop. Flying outside the passenger's window is a banner of red hair. Tori, his old girlfriend. My knight in shining armor has got Tinkerbell riding shotgun. I think I hear Evan yell, "Harley, wait!" but I do not obey. I dash back up the stairs and hide in the bushes outside the gym and cry.

✱✱✱

I am standing in homeroom not saying the Pledge of Allegiance. We sit down. Miss Auberjois hands me a note and says, "Mees Meenelli weeshes to see you right away."

I stand up and listen to the whispers bounce off my back. I have scabs on my feelings; nothing can penetrate. I walk down the hall. I go into Ms. Minelli's office. She stands behind her desk with her arms crossed. Her face is an iron mask. I wait. Finally she speaks.

"Harley, I'm taking you off the drama department project."

Boom. Her words are cannonballs. I am blown off my feet. I sit without her telling me to. I look down at my hands and bite my lip. I chew it hard to keep from crying. I summon up the last drop of my strength.

"Why?" My voice is feeble. "What did I do? I didn't do anything! That's not fair!"

Ms. Minelli slaps her hands on the desk and leans over me. I have never seen her angry before. "You ruined the Spring Ball for everyone, that's what you did. If it weren't for your parents, you'd be suspended."

"How did I ruin it?"

"You brought a strange boy from another town. You drank spiked punch. You caused a fight. You're dating Evan Lennon who was suspended for selling drugs."

"I didn't drink that punch! I didn't know Oliver would get into a fight! I'm not selling drugs!" This is totally unfair; I cannot believe it.

Miss Posey and Bud Roman appear in the doorway. I am so happy to see them, I almost jump into their arms. "Miss Posey, *do* something!"

"Bernice, can we talk to you?" I never thought of Ms. Minelli having a first name. Miss Posey's eyes are big and round beneath her bangs. She does not look like she is a match for the fury of Ms. Minelli. "We really need Harley to finish the project."

Bud Roman winks at Ms. Minelli as if he does not take the whole thing seriously. Maybe there is hope. If anyone can save me, he can. "Come on, Bernice. Give the kid a break."

Ms. Minelli is not amused. "Harley, wait in the hall and close the door."

I am five years old. I am a bad girl. I stand up and walk outside. I throw Miss Posey and Bud Roman a desperate look on the way out. "Please," I whisper.

I stand in the hallway and listen through the door. I catch bits and pieces. "She's the best…I'm sure there are other talented…not enough time…all kids go through it…her benefactor…I'm sorry…" Finally the door opens. "Come in, Harley," calls Ms. Minelli.

I step inside. Miss Posey stares at the floor. Bud Roman stares at the wall. Ms. Minelli stares at me. She does not hesitate. "Harley, I'm afraid you'll have to turn over the art department key." Boom. I take another bullet, this time in the heart.

I reach into the pocket of my dress and pull out the heavy brass key on the red shoelace. Crack. Something snaps inside my head. I think it is my sanity. I throw the key on the floor.

"Pick up that key and hand it to me," orders Ms. Minelli. I do not move. "Pick it up, I said."

I bend down and pick up the key. I do not give it to Ms. Minelli, I give it to Miss Posey. She looks like she is about to cry, but I feel nothing at all. Miss Posey takes the key and gently squeezes my fingers. I do not squeeze back.

"Return to homeroom now, Harley," commands General Minelli. I want to salute, but I do not. I turn and walk out the door.

Behind me I hear Bud Roman say, "This is asinine, Bernice. No wonder the poor kid is a mess."

I march down the lonely corridor. I am cold. I am deadly. Stomp. Stomp. Stomp. My shoes are combat boots on the tile floor. I head to my locker. I open it. I take out my backpack. I pull it over my shoulders. This is war. This is life. I close the locker. Clank. I march. Stomp. Stomp. Stomp. I am a soldier and this is war. I head toward the side door of Lenape High. Clank. I push down on the steel bar. I walk out the door. Thud. It slams behind me. Stomp. Stomp. Stomp. I do not look back.

chapter 22

I am at the bus stop. The bus with the "NEW YORK CITY" sign idles in the parking lot, doors closed, ready to roll. Escape. That's all I can think: I want to escape. My heart is pumping so hard I can feel the blood pounding in my temples. I stand on my tiptoes and knock on the bus's door. It swings open. A pudgy man in a gray uniform looks bored. "Is this the bus to New York City?" I call up to him.

The driver yawns. "That's what the sign says, kid."

"How long before you leave?"

The bus driver rolls his eyes as if he cannot answer this question once more in his life. He checks his watch. "Five minutes."

I think I should call Mrs. Tuttle and tell her I won't be there after school. Sometimes I am so conscientious it's ridiculous. Or maybe…maybe a part of me wants her to talk me out of this little adventure. "Don't go without me," I instruct the driver, who yawns again and looks like the only place he wants to go is to bed.

I run over to the pay phone outside the luncheonette. I put a coin in the slot and dial. "Hello?" Mrs. Tuttle is all cheery, and I want to dash right over there and curl up in her rocking chair voice.

"Hello, Gran—" Whoa. I almost called Mrs. Tuttle, "Granny." What is *that* about? "Mrs. Tuttle, it's Harley." I talk fast so I won't chicken out. "I'm…I'm not feeling well, so I won't be over after school. Sorry."

The bus driver revs his engine. I pretend to cough and cover the receiver so she won't hear the noise. "Oh, okay, honey." Mrs. Tuttle sounds disappointed. "Too bad. I wanted your opinion on my sunflowers. I've gone Van Gogh."

Yeah, well, no more artwork for this kid. She is still talking, "…the canvas for your play."

"I'm—I'm sorry. I didn't hear you."

"The canvas for your play. The last time I saw you, you hadn't started it yet. How's it working out?"

Well, that is the worst possible question anyone could ask me right now. "It's…fine."

"I hope it's the right size."

I know she means well, but now is not the time. "Mrs. Tuttle—"

"They didn't tell you?"

I am confused. "Tell me what?" Either I'm completely out of it, or Mrs. Tuttle is talking in code.

"I've always wanted to be an anonymous donor, but it's not in my nature. I've just got to blab!" The bus driver taps his horn. I hold up a finger, one minute. Mrs. Tuttle is rambling on about generosity of spirit and giving back to the community. I am getting a little impatient with her. I try to interrupt. "Listen, Mrs. Tuttle, I've really got—" Then suddenly I understand what she is trying to tell me. "*You* donated the canvas!"

Mrs. Tuttle laughs, pleased with her little surprise. "I did, I did."

I want to drop the telephone and leave it swinging like a spy movie and jump on the bus. I have done everything wrong with her. Everything. First the *New York City* book, now this. It's completely over, my life, this town. I've got to get off the phone before I start bawling. "The canvas is perfect, Mrs. Tuttle, but you shouldn't have, you really shouldn't…" My voice is trembling. She is talking at the same time, about encouraging creativity and planting seeds in the youth of the country and how she can't wait to see me bloom. "I really don't feel good, Mrs. Tuttle. I've got to go." I am straight-out crying now. She is still talking when I hang up the phone.

There it is, another dream, gone. Snatched away. Me and Mrs. Tuttle side by side, with our smocks and palettes, dabbing on the oils with Beethoven in the air. I inhale my tears. I wipe my eyes on my sleeve. I walk back to the bus. My knees are wobbly as I climb up the steep steps. I have never been on a regular bus before, only those clunky yellow school ones. I stand on the platform next to the bus driver. "I'm back!" I force myself to sound normal.

The driver doesn't even look at me. "One way or round trip?"

"One way." I don't ever want to come back.

"Five dollars, thirty cents." I fumble in my backpack. I give the man a ten dollar bill. He punches a machine. It whirs and spits out a receipt. He hands it to me along with my change. He looks at me like he sees me for the first time. "Hey, kid. How come you're not in school?"

My heart is pounding so hard, I think he can see it thump through my jacket. "I…I'm going to visit my dad." I'm getting really good at thinking up lies on the spot. "He's sick."

The driver seems to buy it. I make my way to the third seat and scoot over to the window. I want to see where I'm going, but I don't want the driver staring at me. There are only five other people on the bus. I don't recognize any of them. Lenape Lakes is in the middle of the line, so I guess they came from towns further north.

The driver checks his watch again. He closes the door. He grinds into gear. The bus grunts, hesitates, then moves forward.

The driver swings the bus out onto Main Street. We pass the bank, the Deli and Tony's Pizza, everything that is familiar and safe. What I am doing suddenly hits me: I am leaving Lenape. At the corner, the bus makes a left and heads toward the edge of town. The driver shifts into high gear. The trees whizzing by on either side of the road are just starting to bloom. The bus groans and snorts and speeds faster. I press my face against the window and watch Lenape fade away.

✱✱✱

The schedule says it takes an hour and two minutes to get to Port Authority, the bus station. We have made several stops along the way and now the bus is almost full. I wanted both seats to myself, so I tried to beam everybody away with my force-field, but an old man in a funny hat and big thick glasses is sitting next to me. He stares straight ahead and is silent. He smells like stale cigars. I watch the scenery change from trees to industrial complexes as we race up the highway, passing places I have never seen before.

After about forty-five minutes, I see a dark silhouette far off in the distance, hovering above the horizon like a city in the clouds. I recognize it from a thousand different photographs. Oh, wow. It is the New York City skyline glimmering right in front of my eyes. It looks like the Emerald City, and I feel like Dorothy going to Oz.

"Look!" I say to the old man. I cannot contain myself. "Look!"

The old man peers through his thick glasses. His eyes are giant eight balls. "What?" He bends his neck. "What? The skyline? Is that what you're all worked up about?"

"I've never seen it before! Which one is the Empire State Building?"

The old man smiles, and I can see his teeth are yellow. His tough white whiskers sprout like little needles from his chin. "The one in the middle there. The biggest one."

"Wow." I sit back in my seat and watch as the skyline grows larger. "Wow."

"Where you headed, young lady?" The old man's voice is sandpaper. He coughs.

"I'm going to visit my dad," I say. "He lives on West Eleventh Street."

"Down in the Village, eh? Is he meeting you?"

I hesitate. I don't want to get too elaborate with this lie. "Actually, no. I'm surprising him."

The old man coughs again, all phlegmy and gross. "Alone? Be careful. How you getting there? Taxi?"

"Are they expensive?"

"Rip off. Used to be, cabbies knew where they were going. Now you even gotta tell them how to get to the Garden. They don't speak English anymore. Me, I take the subway."

I am silent. The subway sounds too frightening for this girl. I never really thought about what I'd do once I got to New York City. "Is West Eleventh Street far from Port Authority?"

The old man coughs and takes out a handkerchief. He spits into it. Disgusting. "Far enough."

The skyline is almost in front of us now. The bus slows. It winds down a long circular stretch of road and stops at a toll booth. Up ahead is a long white tunnel.

"Lincoln Tunnel," reports the old man. "We're going under the Hudson River now. I always look for cracks in the wall."

Oh, great. We zoom into one of the shoots of the tunnel. Cars and busses merge together and speed under the water. I imagine the Hudson River above us. One crack in the wall and the water will gush in, drowning us. This old man is starting to get to me.

After forever, we pop into the light and streak up a ramp and back into darkness. Everyone fidgets and stands. The bus flies into an enormous building and screeches to a stop inside a gigantic bus garage.

The old man wobbles to his feet. "Follow me, young lady. I'll point you in the right direction."

I don't want to follow the old thing, but I really have no choice. He tips his hat to the bus driver and grabs the handrail. I think he's going to tumble right down the steps, but he makes it. He leads me to an escalator. I step onto the moving stairs and glide slowly down to Oz.

Inside the terminal, there are about five million people scurrying around like ants who just had their hill stepped on. My mouth falls open. I have never seen so many people, even in the mall. Newspaper stands and florists, ticket sellers and restaurants—people, people everywhere, shouting, running, wheeling suitcases, getting shoe shines, pushing and stampeding past each other. The footsteps of a million soles trample the floor. Bus arrivals and departures blast over the loudspeakers. Waves of languages crash against my ears. The old man is running himself now, scurrying down escalators, dashing down the stairs. I try to keep up with him.

"Come on, young lady. I'm late. Faster, faster!" I run alongside him. He is the White Rabbit and I am Alice racing to I do not know where.

Finally he stops. The crowd surges around us. He points straight ahead. "Go out that door. That's Eighth Avenue. Make a right and keep going for thirty blocks or so till you get to West Eleventh. Or just hail a cab and tell him where you want to go. I gotta run." The old man takes a step and gets swept into a whirlpool of people. I watch the top of his funny old hat bob along the surface until I can see it no longer. "Come back!" I want to yell. I stand there alone in Port Authority. I take a deep breath and let the current carry me out the revolving door.

✳✳✳

On the street, there are even *more* people. Ladies in bright long dresses, squinty-eyed bald men in white togas, women in business suits wearing sneakers, little girls in fiesta dresses, all bustling along like some kind of crazy costume ball. Everyone is moving, moving, moving. Except for the traffic. That is not moving at all. Cars and trucks and yellow taxis and a bride and groom riding in a horse and buggy are bumper to bumper. People are yelling at each other through their car windows. Everyone is blowing their horns like an out-of-tune orchestra gone mad. A businesswoman knocks me with her briefcase and mumbles, "Sorry."

I look up. The buildings stretch so high I cannot see their tops. Across the street, a grimy building says: "LIVE NUDE REVUE OPEN 24 HOURS." On one corner, a construction worker is chopping up the sidewalk with a jackhammer. On another, a man is selling big soft pretzels out of a cart. A guy with a beard sticks a dirty hand in front of passersby, asking for spare change. I have to admit, this is a lot scarier than I thought it would be. This town is so enormous. I feel so small. I take a breath and force myself to start walking.

From the corner of a building, a fat man with elephant jowls steps right in front of me. "Got a match, kid?" His voice is a gravel pit.

"N-n-n-o." I look up at this wall of a man who is blocking

my way. His black hair is an oil slick. Tattooed on his wrist is a green devil with red eyes. An unlit cigarette drips from the side of his mouth.

The fat man squints. "Where ya goin', kid? You running away from home?"

I am speechless. Do I have "runaway" stamped on my forehead or something? "No," I manage to say.

The fat man sneezes and wipes his nose on the back of his sleeve. "Lotsa kids from Jersey get off the bus, runnin' away, is why I ask. You sure look like you're AWOL. Whatcha got in the backpack?"

I try to act calm. I shrug. "Nothing much."

"'Nothin' much?' Well, let's have a little look-see." Before I know what is happening, the fat man tries to yank the backpack off my back.

"Hey!" I holler, scared. "Leave it alone!" I spin around and hold tight to the straps.

"You tormenting kids again, Harry?" I turn. Behind us, dressed in blue with a gun and a nightstick hanging from his belt, is a policeman, chewing gum.

"Nah." The fat man named Harry spits on the ground. "Just tryin' to keep her occupied. You know these runaways from Jersey."

The policeman looks down at me. "That true, kid? You running away?"

My head is spinning so fast, part of me wants to confess and just go home. Then I remember: home to what? My parents hate me, Carla hates me, Evan's dumped me, I have no friends. They have even taken away the last thing I love, the portrait for the play. I try to think of how all this happened, what I did wrong, but I don't have a clue. Fat Harry is right. I am a typical Jersey runaway. There is only one thing left: to get to Sean Shanahan. "I'm going to visit my father," I say.

The policeman makes a face like he doesn't believe me. "Oh, yeah? Where does your father live?" This question I can answer. I take an index card out of my backpack. On it I have neatly printed Sean Shanahan's address and phone number. I hand it to the officer.

The police reads. "In the Village, huh? I think you should take a cab, kid. What's your name?"

"Harley. Harley Columba."

"If your name is Harley Columba, how come your father's name is Sean Shanahan?"

I want to say, why, that's what I'm here to find out, Officer. Instead I say, "Divorce."

The policeman frowns. "You know, I've got a daughter about your age, and I wouldn't like to see her walking around here all alone." The policeman moves to the edge of the street. He puts his arm up and yells, "Taxi!" Immediately a yellow cab zooms out of the river of cars and pulls to the side of the road. The policeman opens the door. "Take this kid down to the Village, will you?" He gives the driver the address and almost shoves me inside the cab. "Be careful, kid." He slams the door.

The driver has dark skin and a big turban on his head. He takes one look at me, sighs, then steps on the gas so hard I am thrown back against the seat.

The taxi careens back and forth across the street, beeping and honking. I clutch the back of the seat, hanging on for dear life. As we speed down the avenue, I see there are yellow cabs on either side of us, accelerating fast. My driver floors it. We are in a crazy race with the other yellow cabs, darting and weaving through the traffic. At a red light, we all line up at the starting gate, five yellow cabs across. My driver revs the gas pedal, a wicked grin on his face. The light turns green. It is a starting pistol. Vroom. We're off.

A strange language crackles over the radio, and for a moment I think I am in a foreign country. The buildings grow smaller the further down we go. I press my face against the window. Skyscrapers shrink into apartment buildings and restaurants. The road narrows into two lanes and cobblestones and my driver is forced to slow down. Mothers with babies sit in a park. People stroll instead of run. Fruit and flowers are stuffed into bins outside the storefronts. Everything is clean and cozy. Down here it is quieter, almost peaceful, like a small village. Uh, duh, Harley. You must be in Greenwich Village.

We turn right and pass an old corner building that looks like horses should be tethered out front. The White Horse Tavern. Children play in the road. I'm starting to feel better.

The taxi slides to a halt in front of a red brick building. "West Eleventh Street," the driver says. At least I think that's what he said. I can barely understand him. He presses a button on the meter. "Five dollars and twenty-five cents." He says those words loud and clear.

I hand him my other ten dollar bill. He hands me four singles over his shoulder, without looking back. I wait for my seventy-five cents. He jingles some coins, but doesn't give me my change.

"What about my seventy-five cents?" I ask.

"YOU WANT YOU SEVENTY-FIVE CENTS? I GIVE YOU YOU SEVENTY-FIVE CENTS!" The driver practically throws the coins at me.

Geez. Maybe I was supposed to give him a tip. I hand him back the seventy-five cents. "Thank you."

He takes the money and says nothing. He shakes his head. I wonder what is under his turban, if he has long hair or a bald head. I open the door of the cab and get out. The taxi peels away, leaving me alone in front of Sean Shanahan's doorstep in Greenwich Village, New York City.

chapter 23

I stare at the row of stoops and shops in front of me, amazed. I have never seen a setup like this. A laundromat is on the ground floor of the next building, a pastry shop on the other side. Next is a hair salon. Imagine, pastries and a haircut right downstairs! I inhale baking bread and dryer lint. It's impossible to believe that this morning I was in homeroom in Lenape Lakes, New Jersey.

Well, I could live *here*, I think. I could start a new life. I could hail cabs and go to art school and come home and prepare dinner for Sean Shanahan. Or we could eat at that restaurant across the street, The Black Sheep; it looks all cozy and inviting. He'd say, "Let's eat out tonight, Harleykins, you're doing too much." And I'd say, "Oh, we don't have to," but secretly I'd be thrilled to waltz into a restaurant on the arm of my father.

I walk up the stairs, excited now. Sean Shanahan will make everything all right, I'm sure. I open the heavy glass-and-wood door and step inside a cubicle. Here, another glass door leads into the building. It's locked. I peer inside and look down a long white tile corridor. On either side of me are mailboxes. My eyes skim the names. I see the words, "SHANAHAN — 5W" and take a quick breath. He's *real*. This is real. That name makes the whole thing real. I rub my fingers over the letters like I am summoning up a genie out of a lamp.

Next to the door is a panel with rows of buttons. After each button is an apartment number. 5W. That is all I see. Press 5W and you will get Sean Shanahan. My heart is thumping. My finger is shaking. I cannot do it. Pull it together, Harley. I close my eyes and jab the button, one quick press. My finger is electric; I feel the energy flow right out the tip and into the button. Moments later, I hear a buzzing sound. I push the inner door. It clicks open. I step inside.

I walk down the long white corridor, silent, in a dream. I come to marble stairs worn down in the center from years of footsteps. Next to the banister is the tiniest elevator I have ever seen, big enough to fit one person. I decide on the stairs. I add my imprint to the marble as I grip the banister and walk up. On each floor, I pass four closed doors with numbers on them. Apartments. There is only one apartment building in Lenape; everyone lives in houses. I've never been in an apartment building before. I hear muffled conversations going on behind closed doors. I want to stop right here in the hallway and listen to their lives.

At the third floor I stop and catch my breath. Sean Shanahan must be in pretty good shape to climb up this mountain every day. Maybe I should have taken the elevator.

Finally I reach the fifth floor. There are only two doors on this level, 5E and 5W. I walk up to 5W. I stare at the deadbolt. My heart is pumping the blood through my body so fast, I think my veins will explode. I raise my hand to knock. It stops in midair. Oh, come on, Harley. I am ridiculous. I have turned to stone. Come *on*, Harley. I make a fist. I knock. Rap, rap, rap. I hold onto the doorjamb so I don't collapse.

I hear footsteps. A man's voice yells, "Coming." On the other side of the door, someone fiddles with the deadbolt. Click. Whoosh. Light from the apartment streams into the hallway. The door opens halfway and there stands Sean Shanahan. "Yeah—?"

He is beautiful. His hair is brown, just down to the top of

his shoulders. He has a beard and an earring. He looks surprised, as if I am not what he is expecting to see. He smiles, and I see that his eyes are blue, brilliant blue. He is beyond gorgeous. He is perfection.

"Well, hello." He talks fast, like he wants to get back to doing something. "Are you selling candy bars? I'm trying to cut back on the chocolate."

I open my mouth to speak, but nothing comes out. All I can do is stare. It seems impossible, but this time, life has delivered better than what I could imagine. He cocks his head. "I don't want to be rude, but I've got a deadline...."

Still I say nothing. I just stand there with my mouth open.

He gives me a curious look. "Cat got your tongue? What's up?"

"I'm...I'm...Harley Columba." I drop the bomb.

It does not explode. I watch his face. It is blank. "I'm sorry," he says. "Do I know you?"

This is not going the way I expected. All this time, I imagined he would grab me in his arms at the mere mention of my name and shout, "Harley Columba? My long-lost daughter!" I clear my throat. I try again. "Patricia Columba's daughter?" I am one inch tall. "From Lenape?"

He frowns, trying to remember. "Why is that familiar?" Then his face lights up as if suddenly all the connections have been plugged into the right outlets. *Peppy Harley's daughter?* " He sounds stunned. He backs up, and for a second I think he is going to slam the door right in my face. "This is some shock, I've got to tell you." I watch him gather himself together. "This is some surprise. You're...gigantic. The last time I saw you, you must have been two years old. You're like a person."

"I *am* a person."

"How old are you?"

"Fourteen."

"Fourteen years…" Now he is acting as nervous as I am. I wait for him to invite me in, but he doesn't. Instead he says, "Honestly, Harley, you've caught me at a very bad time. I'm really busy. I've got a deadline—"

He is almost being rude. He is throwing me off balance. "I'll only stay for a little while, I promise." People never act the way you want them to, I swear. I'm not sure what to do, so I stand, expectantly, waiting for him to let me in.

He hesitates, then steps aside and opens the door all the way. "Come on in, then. But I'm warning you, I've only got a minute."

"That's okay." He isn't exactly making me feel at home. I step inside his apartment. It's wild. There is a dark burgundy sofa and a tech center. All over the walls are theatrical posters like Bud Roman has, only in frames. Off to the right is a kitchen. Off to the left is a bathroom.

"How did Peppy know where to find me?" Sean asks, as if he has been in hiding for all these years and now I've blown his cover. He leads me down the hall to the back of the apartment, a huge open space with bare hardwood floors. It looks like the high school art room, only with furniture.

"I found you myself." Against one wall is a long slanting table. Miniature cardboard models of living rooms, bedrooms, kitchens, are scattered around the floor and the desk. They look like doll house rooms with no walls. Drawings and sketches are tacked onto a big bulletin board. I point. "What's all this?"

"I'm a set designer," he explains. "Those are different sets for the play I'm working on."

"I'm working on a play, too!" I tell him. This is too eerie. Like father, like daughter. I want to impress him. "I'm painting a portrait for *Anastasia*, the drama club play. I want to go to art school. I'm really good at drawing and stuff, you know. I must have gotten that from you."

He raises an eyebrow. "From me? What are you talking about?"

Shut up, Harley. Don't go so fast. "Oh, nothing." I walk around the space. "Where do you sleep?"

Sean grins, like it is a relief to change the subject. "You walked right under it. Up there." He points to a platform with four long legs. "A loft bed."

"Aren't you afraid of falling out?" I am asking ridiculous questions. I'd better watch it or he'll think he spawned some kind of moron.

"I am, actually, I am. But I need the room." There is a long pause. He looks at me as if he doesn't know what to do with me. "Do you want a drink or something? I think I have a can of Coke...."

"That's okay. I'm not thirsty."

"Some lunch?"

"No, thank you."

"Well, sit down. You know, I haven't been back to Lenape in years." I sit on this weird-looking black leather chair. He sits across from me on a lumpy red sofa. There is a miniature cardboard meadow on the glass coffee table between us. A small cardboard wolf is in the middle of a herd of cardboard sheep.

Sean examines me as if I am a bug and his blue eyes are a microscope. I squirm, his stare is so intense. I remember the welt on my face and hope my makeup is holding up. I shift my position and smooth my hair so it covers the mark. He doesn't say anything for a long time, then: "So. What brings you to New York?"

"Oh…" I glance around the room. "Actually…" I have rehearsed this a million times, but now that the moment is here, I don't know what to say. Instead I say the first thing that pops into my mind. "Actually, I want to see the Imagine mosaic. You know, in Strawberry Fields?"

Sean nods. "Yeah. It's a great spot. Tranquil. I used to sketch up there, but I don't get past midtown much these days."

"Really? Is it far from here?"

"Nah. Not if you catch the subway. The uptown C train drops you right there on Seventy-second Street."

I nod. We sit in silence, all awkward and stiff. He smiles. I smile. Talk, Harley, talk. Sean says, "You know, I've got another…" His voice trails off. He coughs into his fist. "I was going to say, I've got a daughter about your age…. It's hard to believe."

"Carla," I say. "She's my… *was* my best friend."

"Really?" Sean contemplates this for a moment. He wipes his hands on his jeans. "What a small world."

Well, this is about as far away from what I thought would happen as it can get. We are both acting like the executioner is sitting next to us, ready to throw the switch. I have never been so nervous in my life. I cannot focus. I try to grab onto one of my thoughts, but they are wispy, like smoke. Finally Sean asks, "Is that why you came? To see the Imagine mosaic?"

"No…" I shift in my chair. I take a breath. I may as well come right out and ask him. I unzip my backpack. I take out the harlequin. I can tell by the look on Sean's face that he recognizes it immediately. I hold it out to him. My hand is shaking so much, I drop it.

Slowly Sean leans over and picks the harlequin up off the floor.

He stares at the doll for a long, long time and doesn't look at me. Then he examines the card around the doll's collar. He reads out loud: "Happy Birthday Two Year Old." He turns the doll over, fiddling with its clothes, straightening its baton. He murmurs, "He jests at scars that never felt a wound...." He talks to the doll, not me. He is quoting Shakespeare. He is quoting from *Romeo & Juliet*. In a moment he will tell me he's my father. I am so dizzy, I can hardly breathe.

"Read the inside." My voice cracks.

He flips open the card. He reads: "A harlequin for my Harleykins. Papa loves you forever and a day." His voice is low. He has no problem reading the scribbled handwriting. Then he is quiet. His head is down so I can't tell what he's thinking. When he finally speaks, he says, "I don't get it."

"*What*?" The word bursts out of me. This is not what I was expecting to hear.

He coughs and shrugs. "I said, 'I don't get it.'"

My heart has tumbled somewhere around my feet. He is not making this easy on me. "I found this hidden in my storage area. Don't you recognize it?"

He shakes his head. Now he looks at me. "No...should I?"

I think he is lying straight to my face. My voice trembles. "Isn't this your handwriting?"

"Not even close." He is still shaking his head, no, no, no. "What do you think, Harley? Do you think I'm your *father*? Is that what Peppy told you?"

"My mother doesn't even know I'm here." This is horrible. This is not at all the way I planned. I never thought he'd deny being my father. "But it's got to be you!" Do not break. Do not break. I feel my face getting ready to cry. A tear escapes from my eye and travels down my cheek. "I'm sorry," I sniff. "I don't mean to start bawling all over the place."

"It's okay." Sean reaches across the miniature cardboard meadow and touches my arm. Now the silence falls in his corner. He taps his fingers on the table. He looks over at me and manages sort of a half grin. "This is pretty much freaking me out. How about you?"

I nod, afraid to speak.

Sean stands up. "Are you sure you don't want a Coke? I'm gonna have a beer."

"Okay." My voice is a peep. I watch him disappear and concentrate on not crying. He has left the room to get himself together, I think. Now he will come back in here and tell me the truth.

Sean returns with the drinks. He does not sit down. He pops open the beer can. I open the soda but do not drink. He leans against the wall. "There goes my deadline." He laughs, but not like something is funny. "Seriously, Harley. I've got to get to work...." His voice trails off, as if he is hoping I will get up out of the chair and disappear from his life.

I am getting desperate. I try again. "What about the stuff you wrote my mother in the yearbook, about the wild times you had?" I plant myself in the chair like I am going nowhere.

Sean is startled. "Harley, that was a long time ago. Lenape Lakes is like another planet." He is looking everywhere around the room but at me.

"But did you...did you go out with my mother?"

Sean is uncomfortable. "Your mother and I were very good...friends."

"Friends? What does that mean, 'friends?'" Now I am the lawyer, and he is the accused. I force him to listen. I tell him about finding the harlequin, the birth certificate, the marriage certificate, the blue eyes—the whole bit. I outline my adoption theory carefully, step by step, somehow hoping that I can convince him that he is my father by the overwhelming evidence. When I get done, he asks, "What has Peppy told you?"

"She tells me nothing. Now you're telling me nothing. I'm not stupid, you know. I know something's going on."

"Look, Harley." He coughs again and takes a swig of beer. I think he has a nervous cough. "There are answers to everything you've just told me. Did you ever think that maybe Peppy and Roger weren't married when you were born? And they changed the birth certificate later, after Roger had another job? Things were different back then. Having a kid when you weren't married wasn't the coolest thing to do. It still isn't. Especially in a town like Lenape."

Can it be as simple as that? That they weren't married? His words are like water thrown in my face. I never thought of this. Have I made a total fool of myself? It is getting hard for me to think, I am so confused.

"What about my blue eyes?" I am trying hard not to cry.

"Your grandparents could have had blue eyes, it skipped a generation, then went to you."

I am listening through a tunnel. I swear, he has an answer for everything. "Are you saying I came all this way for nothing?" My voice sounds far away.

Sean's grin is lopsided. "Well, I wouldn't say for nothing. You look so much like Peppy, it's like I stepped back twenty years. I'm glad I got the chance to meet you." His words tell me this conversation is over.

My ears are ringing, like I just sat through an entire concert, right in front of the amplifier. What an idiot I've been, wanting a father so bad that I stole Carla's. Maybe there really is something wrong with me. I created a fantasy world and moved right in. The tears that sting my eyes are hot.

I lean over to pick up my harlequin and his glass eyes stop me. "A harlequin for my Harleykins…" The faded card around his neck is a flag, waving. Wait a minute… I straighten up and turn to Sean, the harlequin evidence in my hand. "I saw your face when I handed you this doll. I think you recognized it."

Sean looks away. He is thinking fast. "Harley, I've always liked harlequins. It's from the commedia dell'arte, you know, the Italian theatre—"

He is rambling. I do not let up. "Why aren't you answering me?" Here come the tears.

"I'm trying, Harley. I'm trying to tell you there are other explanations for everything you've said."

I am so upset, my words are cracking all over the place. "Really? Well, explain *this*: Somebody wrote this note. *Someone* is my father. Someone loved me when I was two years old enough to give me this doll!" The sob in my voice scares me. "Where is that man now? Or are you trying to tell me he doesn't exist?"

Sean doesn't answer. He stands there surprised.

I keep going. "Look in my eyes." This is the end of it, all my hopes splattered on the floor. "Look in my eyes and tell me you didn't write this note!"

Sean opens his mouth, but says nothing. After a long trembly moment, I know he is not going to answer me. I hear a high-pitched sound and realize it is coming from inside my head. The ground below my feet is crumbling. I've got to get out of here. I've got to get away. I do not think. I just run. My feet separate from my body and dash off down the hallway. I hear Sean call after me, "Harley! Harley, wait!"

I trip up to the front door. I fumble with the dead bolt. It sticks from years and layers of paint. I yank hard. I hear Sean's footsteps follow after me. I finally get the door open when he appears behind me. He catches the door with the top of his hand. "Harley, wait." He gently pushes it shut. "Wait." I try again to pull it open, but his hand is hard against it, blocking my exit. I stand, my back stiffening, facing the closed door.

"Let me out, Sean." My hand is tight on the doorknob. "Please."

I wait for him to open the door, but he doesn't make a move. Instead I hear these words, hesitant, behind me: "I can't let you go like this." I can feel his breath, hot on my hair. Now it is Sean's voice that is shaking; he is having a hard time getting the words out of his mouth. He speaks to my back. "Harley, I was with your mother the night of the John Lennon concert, not Roger. I went with your mother to the hospital." Sean takes a breath. I am very still, waiting to hear what will come next. "I was there the night you were born."

The world is shifting in front of me. My knees are weak and trembling, like I just got off a roller coaster and left my heart up in the air. I want to tell him to knock it off, I can't take any more disappointments. Sean takes my hand and forces my blue eyes to look into his own. I see a tiny mirror of my face reflected in his pupils. He says, "The man who wrote the note exists, Harley." Then he closes his eyes; my face disappears and all I see are tired crevices around his eyelids, splashed with tears. In that moment, I realize why I have been painting blue-eyed ponds: for him. He takes a deep breath like he is saying a prayer, and confirms: "For what it's worth, that man is me."

My other hand drops off the door handle. "What are you saying?"

Sean's face is different now, older and worn. He breathes out and leans against the wall, as if his body is too heavy for his legs. Then he straightens up and reaches for his jacket hanging on a post by the door. "Come on, Harley. Let's get some air. We have a lot of catching up to do."

chapter 24

We have been walking and crying and talking on the cobblestone streets until we wound up at Fourteenth Street. Now we are inside the subway train to Strawberry Fields, jammed together on the seats, rubbing up against complete strangers. A man reading *The Wall Street Journal* sits next to me, his legs spread far apart. He reeks of cologne, and I will probably smell like him before this ride is over.

Sean is telling me pieces of the past, starting back when he and Peppy and Roger and Ronnie were all in high school. I am listening to the story like I'm watching old reruns on television; it doesn't seem quite real. He says, "I had been going out with Ronnie for a couple of years, and Peppy had been with Roger forever. But in our senior year, I wound up in art class with Peppy. We worked on a collage together, and well…that was that. I knew right away it was a big one." My mouth is practically falling off my face, I can't believe what I am hearing. "Peppy was so sweet and shy…."

"Peppy?" He is talking about another woman, not my mother.

"She was always blushing. Like you."

I feel my face turn red. This is the second time I've heard about Peppy being shy. From shy to shouting. I wonder if people can change so much with time. I try to imagine the woman who is my mother kissing this man sitting next to me in the subway, and I'm sorry, it's impossible.

"After high school, things got messy with the four of us breaking up and getting back together. You know, stuff you do when you're seventeen, eighteen. Ronnie was still in school." As he says this, I realize he is talking about people not much older than me. I can't even think about it, it is too strange. "After a while, things settled down, Peppy got a job as a secretary at the chemical plant, and I started art school here in the city. We were together all the time. Even though Roger worked with Peppy, he backed off. Everything was great."

The train stops at Forty-second Street and most people tumble out, but another load piles right back in. Sean takes a breath. "This is the hard part." He looks away from me, then continues. "One night I ran into Ronnie over at Gilgard's in Wynokie. You know it?" I nod, anxious now, waiting to hear what I already suspect. Sean coughs. "Well, anyway, that night…we…we…how should I put this?"

"You slept together?" I lower my voice, suddenly the adult.

"Yeah." Sean shakes his head. "It was just that once. I refused to take her calls after that. I would hang up on her, I felt so rotten." There is guilt in his eyes, but I am thinking: Here is a man who is used to getting away with things. Charming, like a snake.

Sean coughs his nervous cough. "I never told Peppy what happened. Not then, anyway. Things were too good. I was getting a few art gigs. Me and Peppy were in the city all the time. Everything was fine until one day Peppy found out she was pregnant. We didn't know what to do. We didn't tell a soul. I wanted to be an artist and get out of Lenape. I wasn't ready to be a father. But we talked about it and decided to go ahead and have the baby. We figured we were strong enough for anything…." Sean shakes his head. "God, we were stupid. Young and stupid."

I feel like he is telling a story of some other strange family, a family who lives in a make-believe city like Hollywood or New

York. I look around to see if anyone is listening. No one is paying attention to us; everyone is reading newspapers or staring into space. Sean's voice brings me back. "And then, one day the phone rings and it's Ronnie...who tells me *she* is pregnant. At first I thought she was playing some kind of sick joke. But it was true."

"*What*?" I am stunned. Sean has got my full attention now.

He speaks quietly. "Peppy broke down and told Roger what had happened. And Roger came up with the solution: If I would agree to leave town, he would marry Peppy and raise the baby as his own." Sean's face is grim. "It didn't surprise me. I knew he was still in love with her." He takes a breath. "Well, Roger had the job at the chemical plant, and I was this struggling art student. What was I supposed to do? Stay there with two kids from two different women?"

Clackety-clack. The steel wheels roll. I can feel my shock at Sean's words slowly burning into anger. The baby he is talking about is me. The two kids from two different women are Carla and *me*. Everything is suddenly clear, like I've been looking through blurry binoculars and just found the focus. "What about accepting your responsibilities, *Dad*?" The words jump out of my mouth.

Sean looks like I just slapped him across the face. "Roger made me swear never to tell anyone the truth, and I agreed. I thought I was doing what was best for you. But it was the hardest decision I've made in my life." His voice is full of apologies, but right now I have no room for forgiveness. All I am thinking is, these people are supposed to be grownups? To me, they are worse than anybody I know.

A black guy dressed all in white enters the car. "I AM HUNGRY AND HOMELESS," he shouts above the screeching brakes. "ANYTHING YOU CAN GIVE TO HELP WILL BE APPRECIATED.

THANK YOU AND GOD BLESS." He holds out a dirty Styrofoam cup and totters through the subway car. Nobody looks up from their newspapers. No one gives him a dime. As he passes by, his dark brown eyes look right into mine. Up close, he does not look much older than me.

"Peppy told me that Roger was at the John Lennon concert, not you. What is that, another lie?" My words are sharp, accusing.

Sean takes a deep breath. "The night you were born, Peppy came into the city so we could see each other one last time. You weren't due for a few more weeks. Peppy went into labor right in the middle of the concert. When we had to tell the hospital what name to put on the birth certificate, it was impossible for either of us to say Roger was the father. Holding you in my arms…seeing my *child*…I couldn't do it. But it forced Roger to change the birth certificate later. I don't think he ever got over it."

Sean looks at me, and I can see his eyes are wet, but I am having a hard time summoning up any sympathy. Now his voice is low. "The last time I saw you was when you were two years old. Roger was at work, and Peppy was home taking care of you. I bought you that harlequin down in the Village. It reminded me of you. I called you Harleykins. It was the only time I broke my promise, but I just had to see you. I had no idea that Peppy had kept it hidden all these years."

My feelings are so mixed up, I don't know whether I want to laugh or scream. It is anger that wins. "And Carla?"

"Carla and Ronnie still don't know the truth. They think I'm just some jerk who deserted the family to be an artist." He considers this. "Well, I guess I am."

This explains so much. So much. Why Peppy is so angry. Why

Roger is so mean. Finally, the train pulls up to Seventy-second Street and lurches to a stop. The reality of what these people have done slams me hard in the chest, and I am burning mad. I jump up and push my way through the crowd, Sean following behind me. I step off the train as soon as the doors slide open. "Why didn't you just tell me the truth?" I hammer the words back at Sean. People stop and stare at me, but I don't care. "You all made me feel like I was crazy. Do you know what it feels like to *know* something and have everyone around you tell you that you're wrong? I don't think it was the right thing to do!" I take off down the corridor that leads to the exit.

Sean chases after me and grabs my hand. He lets a few stragglers move past us. "We all thought we were doing what was best. You have to understand, Harley, how much I loved your mother. When I saw your face…you look so much like her, except for your eyes: Your eyes are mine."

We are the only ones in this part of the tunnel now. I yank my hand away from him. "You loved her so much you slept with another woman? You didn't do what was best, you did what was easiest! Look in my eyes now. What do you see?" I move right in front of Sean's face, but he looks away. "Yeah, these are your eyes, all right."

My voice is getting loud. Three people at the other end of the tunnel stare at us. Sean glances over at them, and they look away. "Harley, my life is not easy. I sleep in a loft. Sometimes there are months when I don't work. It's no kind of life for a kid. It's why I left you with Roger."

"What kind of life do you think *I've* been living?" I am really furious now. "Did you ever bother to check? Look!" I pull my hair back and show him the red welt. "I am walking around with a slap on my face. This is the kind of man you left me with. A drunk who beats me. And you worry about sleeping in a *loft*?"

"Harley, I'm sorry—"

"You're sorry? For which part, Sean? For lying? For leaving? For making me think I was crazy? Well, there's one thing I know, I'm not the crazy person here. I found out the truth without any help from you or Roger or Peppy or anyone else. I found out the truth by *myself*. None of you can face the truth, but I can. And the truth is that there is only one person I can depend on and that is *me*."

My words echo off the cold walls of the tunnel. I watch his face. He is a boy in man's clothing, and I am the mother, hollering. His jaw is stiff, like he is trying to hold everything inside, but the tears come spilling out of his eyes and onto the ground, all the fear and the guilt and the shame. As I watch him crumble, I realize: I am stronger than all of them. I, Baby Girl Harley, am stronger than the manufacturers. My dream of a white-knight father dissolves in a puddle of Sean's blue-eyed tears. I feel my anger leak out of me, leaving sadness in its place, like someone has just died.

After a long while, Sean straightens up and gains control. He slaps the tears from his cheeks like he has had it with himself, coughs, blows his nose. Then he looks at me with something new in his eyes, as if he finally recognizes who I am. When he speaks, his voice is quiet. He says simply: "Come on, Harleykins. Let's go to Strawberry Fields."

When I answer him, my voice is just as quiet. "I think I'd rather go alone."

✳✳✳

When I pop up from underground, I am surprised that the

236

sun is still shining. I feel like I've just been through a war. For the first time, I see kids my own age with backpacks and notebooks. They look chic and rich. School must have gotten out. I wonder if anyone back in Lenape has missed me yet. I doubt it. Sean gave me money for a cab back to Port Authority and said he would call Peppy and Roger. I can't even think about them right now.

I look around and try to get my bearings. I stand in front of a dark castle surrounded by wrought-iron gargoyles. I read the street sign, Seventy-second Street and Central Park West. Can it be…? Yes. I recognize the building from Mrs. Tuttle's picture book. It's the Dakota, the place where John Lennon lived and died. People are strolling past, like it's just an ordinary building. I want to stop and shake them. Don't you *see*? This is the Taj Mahal right in front of your eyes.

Across the street are trees and policemen on horseback and people on skates. That must be Central Park. I take a deep breath. I am on a pilgrimage. I know Strawberry Fields is around here somewhere.

I walk up to this preppy-looking kid with brown glasses waiting to cross the street. "Excuse me. Where's Strawberry Fields?"

The preppy is startled. "Cross over and stay to the left." He points. "Follow the signs."

I wait for the light to change and join the mob pouring into the park. Police barricades block the street. Bicyclists and skaters zip down the road, faster than cars. I swear, this city is so wide awake, not hibernating like Lenape.

I realize I am starving. Food. I need food. I see a cart parked on the corner and smell steaming hot dogs. A dark-skinned man stands behind the cart.

"I'll take a hot dog."

"Mustard?" He opens up a steamer and plops a hot dog into a bun.

"Ketchup, please." He squirts some ketchup onto the hot dog and hands it to me. I bite into it. Juice spurts out the other end. Mmmnnn. If I had my oils, I would paint this taste. I pay him and follow a stream of people pouring down an asphalt pathway and into the park.

The noise of the city is muffled in here. Quiet. Peaceful. Leaves crunch under my feet. The stream of people slows to a trickle. I am in the country in the city. A sign on a pole says, "Strawberry Fields." I finish my hot dog with two big bites. I come to a fork in the pathway. And then I see it.

There, in the center, flanked by park benches, is a large mosaic circle. Bits of black and white tile form spokes of a wheel. In the center of the wheel is the word, "IMAGINE." It is my painting come alive.

I step into the center of the mosaic and close my eyes. I almost expect a shaft of light to shoot down from the sky and beam me up to the heavens. I want to kneel. I want to pray. When I open my eyes, they are glistening. People are staring at me, but I don't care. I walk back to a park bench and collapse, gazing at the circle and blinking through my tears. These are good tears, happy tears, tears of relief.

I have done it. I am here.

Flowers are strewn all over the mosaic in memory of John Lennon. A drunken guy throws handfuls of birdseed across the word, "Imagine," then snarls, "Scram!" to the hungry pigeons. A man in a suit reads a newspaper. Sitting next to him is a cat on a leash, eyeing the pigeons, and licking his chops. Mothers picnic with their children on the grass. Joggers dodge tourists posing for pictures. Executives bicker on their way home from the office. Now the enormous world passing in front of me seems wondrous, not scary.

A group of East Indian tourists link arms and form a wheel around the Imagine mosaic, an exotic ring-around-the-rosy. Slowly they move, their colorful saris fluttering, while one of the men with a video camera captures the whole kaleidoscope on tape.

A guy with long brown hair stands off to the side, dabbing watercolors onto an easel, his back toward me. As I watch him paint, I get a stab of sadness right where my heart used to be. Part of me wants to live here among the rebels, but another part wants to be safe at home with the sheep. The sun is starting to go down, and the air is turning cool. Bean and Lily have been home from school for a while now. I wonder who is watching them. Maybe Bean called Peppy at work and said, Harley's not here. And Peppy said, damn that girl! Well, they are Peppy's children, not mine. After all, who is watching me? Myself. I am taking care of myself. *Oh, but I don't want to*, the thought creeps into my head. Not all the time, not like this. It is too much.

I watch a mother on the lawn kiss her baby on the forehead, and I am so lonely. Maybe Sean called Peppy by now and told her the jig is up. My...*parents*. Ha. I think I am homesick, but for what? I have been betrayed by the people I should have been able to trust. I am tired of it all. Exhausted. I watch a homeless man asleep on the grass. I wonder if one day he said, oh the hell with it, life's too hard, and just gave up. I want to curl up beside him. How easy that would be. Just lie down and go to sleep. Forever. It is a temptation, that thought, like a pillow softly calling me to rest my head. I close my eyes and lean against the back of the bench. I sigh, and there is a little sob at the end of it.

"This is the best part of the park, don't you think?" I sit up, startled. The long-haired guy painting the watercolors is talking to me. I blink. He is wearing little round glasses. He has an English accent. For a moment, I think I have fallen asleep and dreamed up John Lennon alive in my painting of Strawberry Fields. I glance around to see if anyone else notices this guy. Everybody seems intent on what they are doing, which is basically nothing. The guy winks at me behind his glasses. I feel my face turn red.

"It's peaceful, isn't it?" he says. "Perfect spot for painting." I smile at him and nod, but say nothing.

The guy dips his brush onto his palette and shades some grass under a tree. "I noticed you checking me out." He hums and peers at his painting, adding a little touch of gold. "Do you paint?"

"Yeah." My voice comes out sharper than I mean it to be. "Well, I used to." A small boy comes flying across the Imagine mosaic, holding a pinwheel, a little girl chasing behind him.

The John Lennon guy grins at the kids like he's part of the family and pushes his glasses back on his nose. He points to a group of foreign students a little older than me tossing daisies and roses onto the mosaic. "Look at that. Twenty years later, and the guy still draws a crowd." He turns back to his painting and frowns. "I can't get this tree right."

Without thinking, I am on my feet, walking toward the easel. I examine his painting of Strawberry Fields. It is strangely familiar, almost like the oil I painted myself in my bedroom in Lenape. "You know, if you mix a little yellow in with some green and brown…" I stop. I hope he doesn't think I'm being rude.

The guy grins and hands me his paintbrush. "Go ahead." I

hesitate, then take the brush out of his hand. I swirl the watercolors around on the palette. With a couple of strokes, I fix his tree and add a ray of sunlight beaming down on the Imagine mosaic.

The guy examines the painting. "Cool." I feel the paintbrush light in my hand, so much a part of me it's like another finger. This is what I love, I think. The paint and the brush and the canvas. I remember what Miss Posey told me a long time ago: Just getting behind an easel helps.

I hand the paintbrush back to the John Lennon guy, the tip facing my palm, like I'm handing him a sharp tiny sword. "Thanks," I say and he understands.

The guy winks at me, "Not bad for someone who *used* to paint." He turns again to the easel.

As I head toward the path leading from Strawberry Fields, I stop and look back at the John Lennon guy. He waves after me, paintbrush in hand, and calls, "See you around," and I think: yes.

chapter 25

When I get off the bus in Lenape, I feel like I've stepped into a greeting card, a quaint suburban scene complete with red caboose. I head up the cracked sidewalk toward the high school, not Willoby Court. It is another world here, full of gabled houses and two cars in the driveway. I wonder if there are as many secrets behind every curtain as there are in the House of Columba. Even though it is dark, I can see lights on up ahead in the gym. Good. This means a door will be open.

I hear a basketball and squeaking sneakers against the hardwood floor as I head toward the side entrance of the school. A whistle blows, and Mr. Anderson, the boy's coach, starts yelling at the team. There is no game tonight; they are only practicing. I push open the heavy door, closing it softly behind me.

As I walk down the hallway, I feel like I'm moving inside a distant memory, even though I was just here this morning. When I get to the art room, I hold my breath, then try the door. It's locked. This is what I was expecting, but I am still disappointed. I jiggle the handle, hoping it will magically open. It does not. I throw my shoulder against the door and turn the knob at the same time. Nothing. I am just about to start kicking the door, find a battering ram, anything, when I feel a hand on my shoulder. I spin around and look into the scraggly face of Mr. Wykoff, the janitor.

"What do you think you're doing?"

I am startled. "I forgot my key." I am surprised to hear that my voice is calm. "I'm doing the artwork for the drama club play, and I wanted to work for awhile."

Mr. Wykoff glances at his watch. "It's a little late, isn't it?"

I think fast. "I was walking around town and I got the urge. I'll just stay until the boys get done practicing, okay?"

Mr. Wykoff looks at me like this is not okay at all, but he opens the door. "Clean up after yourself. I already did this room."

I wait until I hear his footsteps shuffle off down the hallway, then I flip on the light and step into the middle of the room. It smells like years of turpentine and oils. The old wooden floor is speckled with paint drops and hardened chunks of plaster. A pile of rags are stacked neatly in the corner. *This* is my home, I think. Full of smudges and stains. The three portraits of Anastasia stand in the corner, just as I left them a lifetime ago.

I am a surgeon when I put on my smock. I lay out my brushes like scalpels. I turn on the scratchy record player, and the voice of another artist fills the room, singing extra colors. I take a clean rag from the pile in the corner and open my paints. I walk up to the final portrait, pick up my palette and plunge Granny Harley's sable brush deep into the oil.

Peppy and I are alone on the auditorium stage, except for the stagehands dressed in black, scurrying around adjusting furniture and props. The backstage lights are dim. We stand in front of the first portrait of Anastasia, the princess with a blank face. In my arms I hold a bouquet of roses, an opening night gift from Sean. I can hear the muffled buzz of the audience on the other side of the heavy curtain, accenting the silence between my mother and me.

"Do you think Dad will come, Mom?"

I am talking about Roger, not Sean, and Peppy understands. Her sigh is tired. We have been through a lot of tears these last three weeks. "I honestly don't know, Harley. It's hard for him."

Sean is reality, no longer a dream, and I am holding the roses that prove it. Everything and nothing has changed since my trip to New York. They tell me I am grounded for leaving home and cutting school. I stay at home to make them happy, but you can't ground someone for finding out the truth. Now we live in an unspoken truce. Peppy talked to Ms. Minelli, and I was allowed to finish *Anastasia*. And Roger has stopped yelling. He sips his drinks silently, as though he's waiting for something—I don't know what.

I try to pick the right words for the question I've been wanting to ask. "I understand why you married him…then…but *now*…"

Peppy's eyes warn me not to go any further. "You can see the kind of man Sean is. Roger…" She stops, uncertain for a moment. "Your father may be a lot of things, but he was there when we needed him. And he loves me." She looks at me with her dark brown eyes, and I see the life she has chosen reflected back at me. "It counts for a lot, Harley. You'll see."

But what about the rest? I want to ask. What about the fights and the secrets and the lies? But it is not the time for this conversation; old wounds are still bleeding in the House of Columba. Instead I turn to my portrait. "So, Mom, what do you think?"

I watch as she looks up at the princess; Peppy's face changes, then changes again. I wonder what she sees on the easel. "You're very good, Harley. At least Sean gave you that." She is still searching for answers, and I am still trying to forgive.

The buzz on the other side of the curtain is louder now, and I can hear the wooden auditorium seats squeal and flap as people file in and take their seats. Bud Roman strides from one side of the stage to the other. "Five minutes, people. People, people, five minutes."

My heart does a little flip. "You'd better go out and sit down, Mom. I'll be there in a minute."

Peppy reaches out and touches my arm. "Okay." She turns to leave through the side curtains, then stops. "I'm proud of you, Harley." I watch her walk into the shadows and disappear.

I move in the darkness now, fumbling to find the slit in the heavy curtains that opens to the wings. Finally my fingers feel the opening and I slide through. Back here is one naked bulb illuminating a senior guy who sits, holding a copy of the play, ready to prompt the actors if someone forgets a line. He is studying the page, whispering the words over and over to himself.

Next to him, mounted on a large easel, is my *pièce de résistance*, the oil painting of Anastasia, barely dry. She stands expectantly, as if waiting for the third act when she will appear on stage. A diamond tiara sparkles on top of her long, brown hair. A red robe cascades down her shoulders. I look up at the princess I created. Head tilted, she gazes right back at me. Everything I've been through is there on the canvas, I think. Everything, there in the paint.

The senior guy glances at his watch, one that lights up and has a stopwatch counting down the seconds. "Just a couple of minutes now," he whispers to me. He sounds nervous.

"Okay." I try to calm him with my smile. I take one last look at Anastasia in oil. "Break a leg," I whisper to my painting, but the senior guy thinks I'm talking to him, and whispers "Break a leg" back to me. I scoot down the steps leading to the corridor under the stage. I dodge my way past the actors, whispering, "Break a leg, break a leg," to everyone I meet. I race along the corridor until I reach the heavy fire door that leads into the main hallway of the school. I push the door open, careful not to let it slam behind me. There is no one in sight; everyone is already inside. I am practically running down the hallway now, out the front door of the school and into the courtyard.

I enter the auditorium just as the house lights are starting to fade. Up front, Mr. Michaels is conducting a string quartet. I notice Carla and Ronnie sitting in the back. I wave to Carla. I watch her hesitate, then slowly lift her hand and toss a flutter of fingers back to me. Sometimes I am dying to tell Carla the truth, that we really are half-sisters, but I get the feeling that there is something inside Carla that doesn't want to know.

I stop in the center of the aisle and search for my seat. I see Evan standing up in the third row, motioning to me. Peppy sits next to him. And next to her, in a seat that was empty five minutes ago, is Roger Columba. I slide into my seat just as the house lights go out. Evan smiles at me and an entire sentence passes between us, comrades in the trenches.

The string quartet finishes their sonata and falls silent. We sit in the blackness. The audience coughs and fidgets, then grows quiet. I hear Mr. Michaels tap his baton. Softly, the quartet starts to play as the curtain slides open on a dark stage. For a moment, we sit there staring at nothing. Then suddenly, dramatically, the stage bursts into light. The music swells. Together the audience breathes, "Ooo!"

Standing there in the center of the stage, is my first portrait, the princess with no face. Looking at her over the heads in the audience, she seems almost real, like she could walk right off her pedestal and into the crowd.

"Harley," I hear Roger whisper. I turn toward his silhouette, and brace myself for his review. He leans across Peppy and Evan and says, "Good work." His breath smells faintly of vodka. It is small, his offering, but it is a start. I smile sadly into the darkness and give his hand a squeeze. "Thanks," I whisper back to him.

I turn again toward the stage and gaze at my painting. I have captured Anastasia's hesitancy, I think, but also something else. Even though she is faceless, she stands noble, proud, as if waiting for the chance to prove she is royal, not an impostor. Now, the bright beam from the center spotlight swings across the stage and stops, illuminating the base of the portrait. If I squint, I can make out my signature at the bottom: "Harley S. Columba."

harley
like a person